LAST STAND

Libby laid her forehead against her arm and silently wept with defeat and frustration. She should have pushed on later into the night. Should have ground-staked Bob on the island or to her ankle or something! Instead, she'd left the gelding alone to graze along the riverbank, and the Indians had taken him as easily as if he'd been candy laid on a hitch rail for any child to grab.

She let her daughter sleep but checked her pistol and moved several yards away, keeping low and slithering through the freezing grass. The Indians were out there waiting and, if they wanted to attack, this was as good a place as any to defend. Libby took some comfort in remembering how the pepperbox had cut a big swath in the sage when it had misfired. Maybe she could even give a good account of herself before she joined Elias and her Matthew in heaven.

RIVERS
WEST

THE
HUMBOLDT RIVER

Gary McCarthy

BANTAM BOOKS
NEW YORK • TORONTO • LONDON • SYDNEY • AUCKLAND

THE HUMBOLDT RIVER
A Bantam Book / October 1996

ISBN 0-553-56796-9

Published simultaneously in the United States and Canada

Bantam Books are published by Bantam Books, a division of Bantam Doubleday Dell Publishing Group, Inc. Its trademark, consisting of the words "Bantam Books" and the portrayal of a rooster, is Registered in U.S. Patent and Trademark Office and in other countries. Marca Registrada. Bantam Books, 1540 Broadway, New York, New York 10036.

PRINTED IN THE UNITED STATES OF AMERICA

OPM   10 9 8 7 6 5 4 3 2 1

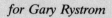

for Gary Rystrom

CHAPTER

ONE

"The Humboldt at last!" Elias Pike shouted as he reined in their team of weary horses and leaped down from their Conestoga wagon. "There she be, river to Caly-forn-ai-ay!"

His pale blue eyes were shining with happiness as he gazed up at his family. "I told you that we'd find her without losing a single horse. Didn't I tell you, Libby!"

Libby managed a smile although her lips were cracked and the salty desert dust made her eyes weep and sting. "Yes, you did, Elias."

"And all that worryin' you do was just for nothing," Elias said, jamming his big hands deep into his pockets and rocking back on his bootheels. "You all just worry too much."

Libby ignored her husband as she and her two children stared out at the vast desert and the crooked ribbon of silver that marked the infamous river.

But Elias wasn't quite through crowing. "And yep, there's Pilot's Peak!" he said, gesturing toward a prominence just to the west. "She's right where they said she'd be, markin' the start of the Humboldt River."

Libby helped herself down from the wagon and her

children were close behind. She *was* a worrier, but now
that they'd finally reached the Humboldt most of her
worries evaporated. "Thank you, Lord," she whispered,
blocking out the recent hardships of the Great Salt Lake
Desert they'd just crossed.

Elias yanked out his handkerchief and mopped his
perspiring face. "Libby, I knowed we had to find the
Humboldt real soon. And we crossed the Utah desert
without a guide and no bossy wagon master. And we
haven't seen a trace of a Paiute, now have we!"

"No, Elias, we have not."

"And we won't," he promised. "They've all gone
north to harvest pinion nuts."

Libby just nodded, refusing to spoil this happy and
long anticipated milestone. And perhaps Elias was right
this time. Maybe they really had been smart to start late
in the hopes that the grass would be rejuvenated after
the early crossings by large California-bound wagon
trains and that they could travel faster alone in the
cooler autumn season. One thing for certain, Elias had
always been a strong and independent man, definitely
not one to spend money on a guide or accept the rules
of a wagon boss.

As if reading her thoughts, Elias said, "Coming
across late and all by ourselves sure was the right thing
to do, Libby. Nobody to wait on 'cause their wagon
broke down and they don't know how to fix it, or their
horse got sick or some such foolishness."

He mopped his brow and shaded his eyes. It was
unusually warm for October and his lean, angular face
glistened with perspiration. "Nobody tellin' us when to
start, when to stop and rest, or when or where to make
camp every night. And the best part of it is, we saved
fifty dollars!"

"Pa, I knew you was right all along," fourteen-year-
old Matthew Pike said, looking up with his own blue
eyes radiating pride. "We may even catch that last
wagon train that left St. Louis nearly a month before
us!"

Elias affectionately mussed his son's hair. "You betcha we will, Matt!"

"Kin we go for a swim once we git to the river, Pa?"

"Sure," Elias said. "We'll *all* go for a swim."

"What about quicksand?" Libby blurted. "They said there was quicksand in places along . . ."

"Oh, Libby! I'll watch out for that!" Elias snapped. "It's time that our family enjoyed a day of rest and that water sure does look inviting."

"Mother, is it all right?" Fay asked, taking her mother's hand.

Libby glanced at Elias and then back to her twelve-year-old daughter. "Yes," she said, "it will be fine."

"We'll stick to the crossings," Elias said. "No need to add another worry to your mind, Libby."

She nodded, then climbed back into the wagon. Elias was too excited to sit and so eager to reach the river that he grabbed the lead horse and began to pull it ahead, urging the team to move faster. He wore a slouch hat once black but now stained white with alkali, salt, and powdery dust. A faded blue bandanna was looped loosely around his sun-burned neck. Elias was only five years older than Libby, but everyone they met thought he looked more like a father than a husband. Libby didn't mind. Elias seemed old because he had worked so long and hard on their farm supporting his family. But things would surely be much easier after they reached California.

And despite his annoying habits and stubborn ways, Libby felt blessed because Elias was a faithful husband, kind father, and devout Christian. Never mind that he was a poor farmer and had failed at raising crops. His frequent back troubles pained him often and besides, their Indiana farm was now almost two thousand miles behind them while California beckoned less than five hundred miles to the west.

Libby squared her shoulders. Nothing could be worse than the Salt Lake desert and now, with the Humboldt to follow, they would conquer this Nevada

desert and then make the final assault on the Sierra
Nevadas. Yes, Libby thought, California was so close
now that she could almost smell pines and wildflowers.
It was said that crops grew so fast in the California sun
that a farmer had to be careful that fast growing spring
wheat did not spear his legs.

"How soon can we see the California mountains?"
Matthew asked as he plodded alongside his father.

"Soon. Maybe a week, maybe even less."

Libby held her tongue but wondered at her husband's remark because everyone had told them the Nevada crossing was still three hundred miles away. And,
given their rate of travel, that would take them at least
twenty days, if they were lucky, the horses stayed strong,
and they had no wagon troubles.

But Elias was feeling good. "Son," he said, "we're
going to make it now for sure. We've already suffered
the worst of this journey. And now, there is just this
Humboldt River to follow the mountains, then over 'em
to California where even the poor folks live like royalty."

Libby wished her husband would not say things like
that. Yes, she also believed things would be far easier in
California, but not *that* easy. Life, even in California,
was always hard. The weak, the lazy, or the infirm never
prospered.

"Mother, will we be able to get another cow like
Emily?" her daughter asked.

"Yes," Libby said, "we'll get a cow."

"*Ten* cows!" Elias shouted up at them. "We'll have
a whole herd of 'em!"

"Elias, please."

"Well," he said, head thrown back and eyes dancing, "it's true. No more penny-pinching for the Pike
family!"

Libby's lips pulled tight and she stared ahead, bon-
net pulled low for protection. Tall, brunette, and once
considered especially pretty, Libby now felt old, tired,
and dry as sand. And although it was October, the tem-

perature was still suffocatingly hot and so arid that Libby's skin was as tough as boot leather. She had given up attempting to stay clean because the dust blew constantly and most of it was alkali and salty enough to get into skin creases and burn like nettles.

She had grown to hate the desert. As far as her hazel-brown eyes could track the Humboldt River, Libby could not find even one of the water-loving cottonwood trees which had flourished along the gentle Platte River. The only movement to be seen in this awful Nevada landscape were the graceful dust devils, willowy, solitary dancers swaying to the music of the wind as they waltzed around and around.

"We will make camp early," Elias informed his family. "Maybe rest the horses all day tomorrow even though it isn't the Sabbath."

He glanced up at Libby. "You'd like that, wouldn't you?"

From the corner of her eye, Libby saw a pair of buzzards circling the crown of a dead volcano. "I think we should push on."

Elias made no attempt to hide his disappointment. "We all want to push on, but we need rest. The horses are in bad shape and . . ."

Elias didn't get a chance to finish his argument because their team suddenly caught sight or scent of river. Almost in unison, their heads shot up and they became extremely excited.

"Whoa!" Elias shouted, grabbing ahold of the bay with both hands on their lines. "Easy!"

But the horses were nearly crazed for water. Where moments earlier they had been low-headed and dull-eyed suffering creatures, now they took on a new life and purpose. The front wheelhorse began to rear, throwing its head about while trying to drag the others along.

"Get down!" Elias shouted as he was being jerked completely off his feet. Matthew, who was trying to help, was nearly trampled. Libby grabbed Fay and jumped from the wagon. Pushing the child into the brush out of harm's way, she threw herself at the wheel-horse, grabbing its bit.

"Get back, Libby!" Elias ordered.

But she had no intention of getting back. Libby could feel herself being lifted and tossed about as all the horses became fractious, lunging, rearing, and bucking.

"We'll unhitch 'em down there on that flat and . . ." Elias's horse bolted forward, knocking him off his feet. "Whoa!"

Libby also was sent flying. She struck a bush and scraped her face, then twisted around just in time to see their wagon go thundering down the well-worn track toward the Humboldt. The Conestoga swayed wildly from side to side and Libby actually closed her eyes for an instant, heart in her throat. But somehow, the wagon reached the river upright as the thirst-crazed team plowed into a shallow crossing.

"Damnation!" Elias cried, picking himself up and running after the horses and wagon. "If they've jumped into quicksand, we're sunk!"

Libby rushed over to Matthew. The boy was shaken, but otherwise unharmed. "Can you get up?"

He nodded and climbed to his feet. A moment later, Libby had both children and began running after her husband. They had, she realized, been lucky. The shallows were hard-bottomed.

"It's all right," Elias said, finally managing to remove the harness and drag the animals out of the river one by one after they'd drank their fill. "It's going to be all right now."

"Mommy, your face!" Fay cried.

Her hand moved absently up to touch brush scratches. They weren't deep, her punished skin had become too tough. "I'll be fine," she said before kneeling in the river and cupping water to her face.

Libby choked and spat out her first mouthful of Humboldt water. Her children did the same. "It's pretty awful, isn't it?" Libby sputtered.

They nodded, but everyone managed to drink. At least the river *felt* cool and refreshing. Libby sat right down in it fully dressed. It was foolishness but she felt so battered and exhausted, there was no help for her actions. They were all physically drained by the desert and the disaster that they'd barely averted.

"Could we have gotten the wagon tipped back upright?" Matthew asked his father.

"Sure! Been a job, but we'd have done it."

Libby looked sharply at her husband because she knew that he was lying. Oh, they would have tried like the devil, but they would have failed just as sure as the crops had always failed on their Indiana farm. So they just sprawled out in the cool, greenish water, toes and fingers digging into the soft sand. After a while, the sun buried its face into the stark western hills.

"I wish you'd have let me handle the horses," Elias said, taking Libby's hand. "You and Matt both could have been hurt."

"We *all* could have been hurt," she said, washing her arms before climbing stiffly out of the water and feeling the first hint of an evening breeze.

Elias followed her around the wagon. "Are you really all right?" he whispered so that the children could not hear.

"Yes," she said, but also knowing she'd be very stiff tomorrow and the next day. "I'm fine."

"I didn't realize our horses were that thirsty."

"What is important now is that we follow this river and get out of this desert."

"Oh, that'll be easier," he said, slipping his arm around her waist.

Libby pulled away. "Elias, there's wood to be gathered, a meal to be cooked, and you need to get that wagon out of the river before the wheels swell and pop off the rims."

Elias scowled. "Yes, ma'am. But maybe it wouldn't hurt for the wheels to swell a little tighter."

"You know that we can't take the chance."

"*Life* is a chance, Libby."

She had started to go collect wood, but now Libby stopped and placed her hands on her hips. "Yes," she said, "life *is* a chance and nothing is certain, but we don't need to court disaster. Now that we've found this river, we should be fine unless we have Indian trouble."

Even in the dusky light, Libby saw annoyance cloud her husband's expression.

"Dammit," he argued, "everyone we met coming out swore that the Paiutes and the Shoshones move north this time of year to harvest pinion nuts. Ain't no pinion pines in this valley. Therefore, we ain't likely to see any Indians."

"I hope you're right," she said. "But now that we're in Indian country, I still wish that we'd come west with a wagon train."

"Had to sell the homestead first," he snapped. "Had to scrape a little money together to buy us a wagon and provisions. Didn't want to walk behind a wheelbarrow followin' a bunch of snooty folks in wagons, did we?"

"No," Libby agreed, "but we have to hurry along. If the Sierras are already covered with snow, we'll be forced out of California until next spring."

"I'm still thinking that we'll make it over them mountains this fall," he said. "We could sell the wagon and most everything, then . . ."

"Elias, we agreed that the wagon is going to be our home until we can get a cabin built next year. We need *something* to winter in. We can't have our children sleeping on cold, wet winter ground."

"The worst is over," he said, looking away. "It will turn cold any day now and maybe there'll be some rain. But I'm sure we can make it over them Sierra Nevadas before the deep snows."

"You always do expect things to work out for the best," Libby said. This was not the first time their basic differences in outlook had come up for discussion. Elias was forever the optimist while Libby knew she tended to see all the pitfalls.

"Elias, I don't mean to be a worrier. Really, I don't. But, if you prepare for the worst, it doesn't hurt so bad when it comes. Otherwise, your heart gets broken."

"Hearts heal!"

"Sometimes, but there is no reason for them to be broken in the first place," Libby argued.

Elias cracked his knobby knuckles. His hands were immense, always raw with cracks, sores, and cuts. "Libby," he began, "I'm sorta like my hands. They're rough . . . ain't nothing pretty about 'em. And I always beat 'em up when I do most anything. They're just a bunch of scars and scabs piled one on the next. But they get the work done, and they always heal. Hearts are like that . . . they always heal too."

Libby didn't think hearts and hands were at all alike, but Elias was so earnest and wanting of good things for his family that she nodded as if in agreement and made herself say, "You're probably right."

"Sure I am," he said, edging closer. "And tonight, after the little ones are asleep, maybe we can lay down together under the stars and listen to the river's song."

"You'd want to do a lot more than listen. You always do."

"That's because you're still pretty and you always will be to me. Stop worrying so much! The worst is past us now. We're going to have a good life in California. Better'n anything we could have hoped for back home."

Libby knew that he wanted a kiss but her lips were cracked and besides, the children were climbing out of the river, kicking water sparkles up against a pearly-pink sky. So Libby just told Elias to "shhhh" and then went to gather wood, turning her mind to supper.

But later that night, when Libby was sure that both Fay and Matthew were sound asleep in the wagon, she allowed herself to be led outside with a blanket wrapped around her nightgown and then she and Elias made love beside the river. It was their first time in weeks and afterward, Libby lay snuggled in her husband's arms and they listened to coyotes howl off somewhere in the desert while enjoying being serenaded by croaking frogs.

"I ought to cut us some sharp willow sticks so we could go froggin'," Elias said after a time. "It'd be mighty nice to have fresh frog legs for breakfast."

"It would," Libby agreed, "but we both need sleep and we've still a lot of salt pork that isn't improving with age in this desert heat. Besides, we ought to break camp at sunrise because we stopped early today."

He chuckled and pulled her closer. "A couple of hours ain't going to make any difference one way or the other."

"I guess not," she said, hoping to see a shooting star that might bring her family luck. But there were no shooting stars this night.

"Tell me again," he said after a long silence. "How much does the sun *really* shine in California?"

It was a little game they shared to keep up their spirits. "Most every day of the year, Elias. According to the almanac, it *never* freezes."

"No snow," he said, shaking his head. "And that means no blizzards, either. Just rivers of gold and skies warm and blue."

"Yes," Libby assured him. "And the California soil is so dark and rich you'd think it was chocolate."

"And the ocean," he said almost hungrily. "Tell me again about the ocean. I do yearn to see one."

Libby laced her fingers behind her head and admired the moon as she told her husband things they both wanted to believe. "The Pacific Ocean is very gentle, with warm, wide beaches. And in places like Monterey and near San Francisco, I have read that there are great harbors where ships come to drop anchor. And there used to be lots of sea otters, but the Russians hunted them all out."

"Damn Russians," he muttered. "Good thing they was bought out by Captain Sutter."

"As you know, Elias, I've never seen the ocean either. But I've seen pictures of sailing ships with their sails billowing in the wind, blue sky folding down to an indigo sea. Seagulls wheeling over the bow and waves white as cotton."

Elias sighed. "You sure can paint a pretty picture. You could even write a book. Maybe a book about this wagon journey."

"No," she said quietly, "because I'd want to write about beautiful things."

"You're enough beauty for this old farmer," he said, reaching for her again as the moon dodged into clouds.

Later that night, they did go frogging. After cutting willows and with her skirts tucked up into his belt, Libby helped Elias impale six big croakers. They had a grand time charging about in the warm river water and tromping through the tules. They laughed and even mocked the coyotes foolishly carrying on until almost morning. If they slept, it was only for an hour or two before the sun ballooned off the eastern Ruby Mountains, red and angry as a parent scolding a pair of misbehaving children.

"It was worth it," Libby confessed as she fried the frog legs over a smoky little fire. "Worth every minute of it. Now go ahead and wake the children so we can eat, then break camp."

"I love you," he said, drawing her close. "And we're finally going to be happy in California."

"I'm happy right now."

"I know, but *fat* and happy."

Libby considered fat and happy. Even that might not be so bad, just as long as the fat didn't add up to being pregnant again before she and Elias managed to get their new cabin built in California.

CHAPTER

TWO

They got a late start that morning but the wagon track that paralleled the Humboldt was hard so they made only six miles before Elias decided to let the horses rest and graze at noon.

"Best pasture appears to be across the river," he said after they'd passed a large tributary feeding into the Humboldt. "I'll tether the horses and take 'em across. The river ain't too deep here."

"But maybe there's quicksand," Libby said, unable to see the bottom.

"Nope. You can see how both riverbanks are marked where earlier teams have driven their animals across to graze. We won't have any problems."

"All right, but push the horses ahead of you."

Elias was unable to suppress a grin. "Trouble is, darlin', our horses are worth more'n I am."

Libby didn't appreciate the humor. "Don't even tease about that. You know what a fix we'd be in if anything happened to you."

His smile faded. "That's why I'm doing as you asked."

Elias fashioned a loose halter with a lead rope

around the head of their strawberry roan. He scooped up Matthew, placed him on the roan horse and warned, "Hang on, son."

"Yes, sir."

Elias hopped up behind the boy.

Libby didn't want to say anything, but the idea of her husband and son going across the river was fretful. "Maybe Matt ought to stay with me at the wagon."

"Naw," Elias called back over his shoulder, "he'd rather be with his father. Ain't that right?"

"Sure is," Matthew said, chin up and looking proud. He collected the lead rope as if it were a pair of reins.

Elias drummed the heels of his clodhopper boots against the roan's bony ribs and they began to drive the other horses into the Humboldt. Libby had heard it said that mules were too smart to get trapped in quicksand but that horses would do it every time. Libby wished that she and Elias had bought mules. Unfortunately, a good team of Indiana mules cost far more than this undersized and unmatched team.

"Is Daddy coming right back?" Fay asked, also looking worried.

"Yes," Libby said, "and don't go near that water."

Fay turned around, confusion in her eyes. "But we were playing in it yesterday."

"It was shallow where we camped last night," Libby explained, pulling her daughter away from the crumbling bank. "Here the riverbanks pinch in more and the water is deep and swift."

Fay sat down beside the river and watched her father and brother drive their horses across. "It is much greener over there on that side, Mama."

"The grass always looks greener on the other side."

When Elias and the horses had safely forded the river, Libby took her daughter's hand. "Come along and help me gather some sticks for a cooking fire."

As they gathered wood, Libby kept a watchful eye on Elias and Matthew, who had dismounted and hobbled all the horses. The animals were gaunt and famished because of their long, difficult trip across the Great Salt Lake desert, which was almost totally lacking in either feed or good water. Now, however, Libby had to smile because Elias and Matthew began to play catch with what Libby could only guess was a wad of river moss. Their laughter sounded strange; a rarity since they'd pulled up stakes in Indiana.

"Matthew always has more fun than me," Fay complained. "Mama, why don't *we* ever play catch?"

"Because," Libby said, tugging on a large, half-buried branch, "a women's work is never done."

"That doesn't seem fair," Fay said, brow furrowing.

"It isn't," Libby grunted as she tore the limb free, "but it's a fact of life that you'll have to learn to live with. Besides, we do have some advantages."

"Like what?"

"We are much better at making things nice and pretty," Libby told her daughter. "You never saw your father stitching a colorful quilt or picking wild roses for the table, did you?"

"No."

Libby pulled the heavy branch free and began to drag it back to their camp. She would cut enough firewood to cook over the next two days. "Give Mama a hand, honey."

They tugged and finally managed to drag the big limb back to the camp. Libby found their ax and whetstone, then began to sharpen the tool.

"You see, Fay," she said as she used the stone against the ax's dull and pitted blade, "most men just glance up at the sky only to figure out if it's going to bring rain or stay clear. Women watch the sky because it is beautiful and deserves to be watched. Men are always practical except when it comes to money. Women are dreamers, but more practical in matters of money."

Libby finished sharpening the blade, then regarded her frowning child with a hint of amusement. "Fay, does any of what I've just told you make sense?"

"No, but men go fishing and hunting," Fay said. "They think that must be fun."

"I suppose. But I've never understood why. I wouldn't want to hunt animals or go fishing."

Fay sat down on a box and rested her chin on her hands as she watched her father and brother play on the far side of the river. "I wish I was a boy. They have more fun than girls, that's for darned sure."

"We have our own special joys," Libby told her daughter as she chopped wood and then built a small fire to make coffee water and heat up beans and salt pork.

The swirling smoke caused Libby's eyes to water as she prepared their noon meal, then spread a blanket to lie down and rest until Elias drove the horses back across the river. Since the grass on the north side of the river was better, Libby expected her husband would allow the animals to graze until they had eaten their fill. Given the early stop they'd made yesterday and the long one at noon today, Libby figured that Elias would want to travel late tonight so a nap would serve her well come evening.

"Fay, stay away from the water," Libby called. "And don't go into the sage, either. Could be rattlesnakes in there, honey."

"Yes, Mama."

Libby laid down on the blanket. She was exhausted from the previous night's madness. She folded a forearm across her eyes to shield them from the sun. Libby willed an image of her imagined Pacific Ocean. Like the sagebrush sea surrounding her, it rolled on and on leading her into a pleasant reverie.

"Mama!"

Libby sat bolt upright in startled confusion. The sun had passed its zenith and she began to look wildly about for Fay even as she reeled unsteadily to her feet.

"Mama! *Indians* are coming!"

Cold sweat exploded through every pore of Libby's flesh and she shivered with dread. Like everyone else who had traveled this trail to California, she'd heard the warnings about the marauding Paiutes and Shoshones. During the last decade, they had killed many an unwary emigrant.

"Fay!"

The girl had wandered about a quarter of a mile upriver, probably collecting shiny river rocks, and had been the first to spot the four . . . perhaps even five Indians as they stalked the Pike camp with their short bows and spears.

"Libby!" Elias bellowed from across the Humboldt. "Fay!"

Elias grabbed Matthew's hand and began to drive their hobbled horses back toward the river. Libby heard her husband shout, "Get the weapons out of the wagon!"

Libby ignored his command as she raced forward to collect little Fay, who was running hard now toward the camp. It seemed to take forever to reach the child and then they whirled about and ran back toward the Conestoga. Libby didn't even dare look over her shoulder to see if the Indians were in pursuit. Once, Fay tripped in the sagebrush and fell. Libby carried her daughter the last twenty or thirty yards into their little camp before throwing Fay into the wagon.

"Stay down!" Libby gasped, fumbling to retrieve the family's clumsy six-shot pepperbox. She knew the pistol was completely inaccurate beyond twenty yards but it would thunder and smoke, perhaps scaring off the Indians.

Libby shoved the heavy pistol into her dress pocket then she pulled out Elias's big Hawken rifle. Before leaving their homestead, her husband had insisted that she learn how to fire the Hawken accurately. The weapon was loaded. Libby had no doubt that she could kill at least one of the Indians and possibly even two before they could reach her and Fay.

When the Indians saw her raise the Hawken, they skidded to a halt, heads turning to watch Elias as he chased their still hobbled team back into the Humboldt River. Suddenly, their best horse, a stout bay mare, lost her footing and tumbled headlong into the swiftest part of the river's narrow, twisting current. Elias drew his sheath knife, grabbed the mare's thrashing legs, and slashed the hobbles free. The bay rolled completely over in the water and then floundered for a moment before climbing to her feet, plunging up a steep riverbank and galloping into the sage. Elias could only watch as the Indians, deciding not to challenge the Hawken, chose to instead pursue the runaway mare.

Elias drove the other three horses into camp before he raced up to Libby and tore the Hawken from her grasp. Cussing and fuming, he threw the rifle to his shoulder and fired, no doubt missing the vanishing Indians by ten or twenty yards.

"Damnation!" Elias shouted. "Where's my pepperbox!"

"Here!" Libby said, yanking it out of her dress pocket but, in her excitement, dropping it to the dirt.

"Jaysus!" Elias bellowed, snatching up the pistol. "We almost shot ourselves!"

The Indians were way beyond pistol range but Elias pulled the trigger anyway and all six barrels accidentally discharged with a tremendous explosion. The crown of a tall sagebrush vanished. Everything was smoke and confusion. When the air cleared, the mare and the Indians had disappeared as surely as if the great basin had swallowed them whole.

"Where'd they go!" Elias cried. "Where'd they go, Libby!"

"I . . . I don't know!"

"Pa, look!" Matthew exclaimed, pointing off to the east. "They caught our bay mare!"

Libby could see now that the Indians and the bay mare had passed behind a low hill only to reappear a half mile farther away.

"Tarnation!" Elias swore. He quickly reloaded the Hawken, then ran over and began to remove the hob-

bles from the roan. "I guarantee they won't keep her.
Not when I get through with them they won't!"

"Please," Libby begged, "let them have that horse.
We still have three others!"

"Even the four were hardly strong enough to keep
pulling our wagon, Libby. I've *got* to get that mare
back!"

"We can dump some furniture!" she pleaded.
"That mare isn't worth risking your life!"

But Elias, once he made up his mind, was not a
man to change his plans. "I'll be back soon," he vowed,
fashioning an Indian bridle with a lead rope and then
swinging onto the bare back of the roan and banging its
rump with the butt of the Hawken. "Just reload that
pepperbox and stay close to the wagon!"

Matthew tried to run after his father but Libby
pounced on him. She ordered him into the wagon before she went to reload the empty pepperbox. Her
hands were shaking.

"Mama, you're spilling so much powder!" Fay
cried, looking pale and frightened.

"I know," Libby breathed, forcing herself to slow
down and gather her scattered wits. "I know."

As soon as the pistol was reloaded, Libby dropped
it back into her pocket and hurried to collect the pair of
loose but still hobbled horses. Both animals were nervous and Libby dared not unhobble them for fear they
would also run away, probably even to follow the bay
mare. Tethering them both securely to the wagon, Libby
ran to the edge of their camp with the pepperbox
clenched tightly in her fist. Her eyes scanned the empty
sage then followed the thin rooster tail of dust drifting
south. Other than that, there wasn't even a hint that any
living thing existed in that forever empty wilderness.

"Elias!" she called.

No answer.

Libby clutched the treacherous pepperbox so hard
that her knuckles turned white. A great stillness settled
over the basin and hot tears burned her eyes. "Elias!"

Her plea echoed against the hills and then was borne away by the dry desert wind. Libby collapsed to her knees, pistol limp in her fist.

"Please, dear God," she prayed, "bring him back. I don't care about the horse. Just *bring my husband back*!"

But despite the fervency of Libby's prayers, Elias did not come back. Libby waited and prayed, but God wasn't listening. And when the merciless sun speared the western hills and dark shadows shrouded their camp, Libby struggled back to her feet and returned to the wagon.

"Mama! What happened to Daddy?" Fay asked, cheeks stained with tears.

"He's coming back?" Matthew asked, chin quivering. "Mama, I *know* Pa is coming back!"

"Matt is right," Libby heard herself say. "Your father probably just wanted to chase those Indians so far away that they'll never dare to frighten us or try to steal our horses again. He'll be back soon, now that it's getting dark."

"But what if he *doesn't* come back?" Fay wanted to know.

Libby climbed into the wagon. She gathered both of her children into her arms. "Father *will* come back," she promised. "God wouldn't put us in such an awful fix without your father. He just wouldn't. And that's why we have to have faith. And pray lots."

Matthew drew away. "Maybe, instead of praying, I should go and look for him right now."

"No!"

Libby lowered her voice and tried to rid it of the terror she felt forming in her stomach. "Matthew, your father would want you to stay right here with us until he returns. Until then, you're the man of the family. And a man always stays to protect his family."

Her words rang hollow and the question resounded in Libby's mind that her own husband had not stayed with his family in this crisis. "Are you children hungry?"

"No," Fay said, struggling to be brave.

"I am," Matthew said. "I'm real hungry."

Libby was glad for something useful to do despite the scarcity of their provisions. "Then I'll cook . . . no, I'd better not feed the fire."

"But what if Pa is lost and needs a big fire to see us," Matthew argued. "Mama, it's so *big* out here."

"Maybe you're right."

"But what if the Indians see it and come to scalp us?" Fay whispered fearfully.

Libby had already weighed that possibility. She knew nothing about the desert Indians except that they were cunning and dangerous. She had read many accounts of California-bound emigrants being ambushed and scalped, their wagons looted, their horses taken away as a prize. Dammit, Libby raged inwardly, why hadn't she insisted that Elias wait until spring when they could join up with a big wagon train? Why had they both believed a disreputable old mountain man that the Paiute and Shoshone Indians would have all journeyed north by now to harvest their damned pinion nuts! Libby's head was spinning with a thousand regrets and recriminations. Steady, she told herself. Now is not the time to panic. You must think.

"If we light a fire," she began, thinking aloud, "then it *could* be seen by Indians as well as by your father. But the Indians must already know this country very well. I'm sure that they already realize our exact position. But your father might not. He *could* be lost."

"So we light the fire," Matthew said, jumping out of the wagon and hurrying toward the pile of wood that Libby had chopped.

"Yes," Libby said, praying that she was making the correct decision. "We'll burn what I've already cut. Then, we'll gather more driftwood along the riverbank and light a *huge* bonfire. And we'll . . . we'll act very brave and know that God and the firelight will guide your father back safely."

Libby was thankful that there was a three-quarter

moon to give them enough light to see as they began to feed their campfire and scavenge along the river for even more wood. Earlier that afternoon, she and Fay had stumbled upon a number of black, rock-ringed campfires where previous California-bound emigrants had camped in the spring and through the summer. In some instances, they had left half-burnt wood, which Libby and her children now collected and quickly hauled back to their camp. Each time she returned, Libby called out into the moonlight for Elias, praying that he would call back to her.

It seemed to Libby that she was locked into an unrelenting nightmare. She could not believe that, only last night, she and Elias had really laughed, made love, and played like children. And all of it under this same leering moon. Nothing seemed real anymore. Not without Elias.

The fire began to roar and Libby knew that it could be seen for miles. They kept feeding it, watching the orange flames lick at the darkness. Sometimes, they would walk out to the edge of the light and call again for Elias. Each time, Matthew and Fay's high-pitched, tremulous cries ripped Libby's heart like cats' claws. She bit her lower lip until she tasted blood to keep from betraying her own rampaging fear.

The children lapsed into an exhausted and fitful sleep. When Libby saw the first salmon-tinged fingers of dawn, she allowed their great bonfire to die. She carried her sleeping children back into the wagon, laying them on covers, and then returned to the dying ashes to sit and wonder what on God's earth she would do if Elias was actually dead.

She dozed as the morning grew warmer. Awakened, she hurried out into the sage and called until her voice grew raspy and hoarse, then faded to a tortured whisper. Libby finally collapsed beside the smoky fire and dozed through the long, still morning. When she awoke, it was with a cry and she looked wildly about, expecting Elias to kneel by her side and tell her she worried too much. But she was alone. The children still slept in the wagon. Weariness and despair smothered her mind like an oven lid until it was almost a relief not to be able to think clearly. She rested again.

"Mommy?"

She awakened with a tremendous start to discover her children standing beside her. The fire was dead. The sun was burning directly overhead and their camp was dead silent.

"Yes?" she asked.

"What are we going to do?" Matthew asked, fresh tears running down his cheeks. "I'm the man now and I don't know what to do!"

Libby took a deep breath. "We wait," she decided. "We wait and wait. Your father will return."

"But what if he's killed?" Fay was struggling not to cry.

"He's *not* killed," she said, trying to sound convincing. "He's gone away before, but he's always come back, hasn't he?"

They both nodded and Libby was ever so proud.

"And he'll come back this time too," she promised. "Now, let me tell you about California and the Pacific Ocean. Would you like that?"

Again, they bravely nodded.

Libby closed her eyes for a moment, struggling for the vision that had already carried her and her family so far on dreams and great expectations.

"Well," she began, "the Pacific Ocean is warm and so big that it covers most of the world. There are great whales and fish in the Pacific, and it has beautiful islands."

"How many?" Fay wanted to know.

"As many as the stars," Libby told her. "All with long white beaches and birds and wondrous animals, none of them unkind."

Libby knew she had a gift for storytelling. And she had never, ever needed it more desperately than now.

CHAPTER

THREE

As the cool, windy day wore into early afternoon, Libby found herself becoming more and more convinced that her husband was either dead or too badly injured to return to their wagon camp beside the Humboldt. Dark, foreboding storm clouds gathered on the western horizon and she could feel the temperature falling. If Elias was lying hurt somewhere out in that wilderness, he might freeze or catch pneumonia tonight if he was not found soon.

The thought of attacking Indians was constantly on Libby's mind and she kept the pepperbox close at hand but wished that she and Elias had sacrificed and bought another old rifle. Libby began to think that the Indians had deliberately lured Elias into a trap. But, if that had been the case, wouldn't Elias have at least gotten one shot off with the Hawken? Sound carried for miles out in this desert basin and Libby was sure that they would have heard a shot, unless it had happened later, when she had fallen asleep.

"With the weather turning foul, we need to try and find your father," she announced to her children. "Maybe he's hurt and needs us. We have to find out."

"I'll take a horse and go alone," Matthew volunteered.

"No," Libby said. "*I'll* go."

"We should *all* go, Mama," Fay said. "We only have that awful old pepperbox, don't we?"

"Yes," she admitted, struggling to think as clearly as her children. "All right. We've just two horses left. I'll ride the bay gelding, you two can ride double on the sorrel."

The children seemed relieved to finally be doing something other than waiting. Libby tore a nightshirt into strips for bandages and also stuffed a few pieces of bread, jerky, and dried apples into a sack that she tied with a cord around her narrow waist. Libby's most treasured possession was a tiny daguerreotype of her mother and father, which she now slipped into her pocket, just in case the thieving Indians came and looted the Conestoga while they were off searching for Elias. They had no saddles or bridles and only the team's harness, so Libby used a long boning knife to cut some of the harness into crude bridles and reins.

"We don't dare venture out too far from the river," she decided aloud. "We'll pitch the last of our wood on the fire and ride until it gets dark, then we'll have to return. I won't allow us to get lost out there tonight and risk facing a winter snowstorm or freezing rain without shelter."

Matthew protested. "We can't give up on Pa!"

"We'll have to if we don't find him by dark," Libby heard herself say. "If we got lost or the horses failed us, we could die in this wilderness."

Libby was encouraged because neither of the children became upset. Rather, they nodded with dull resignation. Maybe, Libby thought, we are all numb and in shock. Maybe we've gotten stoic and simply can't accept any more fear or disappointments.

Despite the threat of rain, Libby filled their only canteen, which had a very slow leak but would suffice for the short rescue mission she had planned. With the cooler weather and a storm rumbling in across the western horizon, the bay gelding acted cantankerous and didn't want to be ridden. Libby had no patience with the animal and gave it a couple of sharp whacks across the rump with a lead rope. It quickly submitted and allowed her to mount. The sorrel, thank heavens, was much more tractable and did not object to being ridden double by the children.

"Pa's trail is easy to see," Matthew said after they had left the camp in the direction that Elias had taken.

"It doesn't look all that clear to me," Libby said.

"Daddy showed me how to track things like raccoons and possum, so this is easy."

Libby accepted Matt's words although the tracks vanished for long stretches after they left the Humboldt River valley and crawled into the rugged, sage, pinion, and juniper dotted foothills. But Matthew wasn't bluffing and proved his tracking ability. Time and time again he excitedly pointed out the roan's shod hoofprints, often just faint smears across the rocky landscape.

They hurried on until they could no longer see the wagon. The farther into the barren foothills they went, the harsher the country. Other than an occasional jackrabbit or rattlesnake, they saw no living thing, not even a bird on the wing. Under the approaching mass of storm clouds, a thick wedge of gold on the far western horizon marked the approach of what promised to be a particularly spectacular sunset. Libby, despite her worries and doubts, chose to think of it as a favorable omen.

But after the sunset heightened, then slowly faded, she thought she had no choice but to return to the wagon. "We're going to have turn back," she announced to her children in the gathering gloom.

"Mama, the tracks lead straight up through those hills!" Matthew argued. "Father wasn't killed! He just had to go farther than he expected."

"But the light is dying and we can't follow his tracks any longer, Matthew. We have to go back to the river and wait for your father to find us."

"But he'll die if we turn back now!"

"Matthew, *we* could die if we get lost out here or are ambushed."

"I'd rather die than leave Daddy!"

"A little farther then," Libby said, surprising herself by the concession. "But I can't imagine how you can see the roan's tracks anymore. I sure can't."

Matthew threw his right leg over the sorrel's withers and slid to the ground. He was large for his age and trail tough. Crouching slightly, he began to trot deeper into the hills, reminding Libby of nothing so much as a bloodhound sniffing scent. Other than the distant rolling thunder, the only sound Libby heard was her son's labored breathing as he led them up a wash between a pair of huge, rocky outcroppings.

Libby knew that a surprise Indian attack could come from behind either outcropping, and they'd be helplessly trapped. She fumbled with the dangerous pepperbox, eyes straining in the fading light. She could see nothing but knew that the Indians would be skilled hunters, able to surprise and kill even wary things. Worse yet, when Libby looked back over her shoulder, she could not even see the Humboldt River, only its long, dark valley. She tried to assuage her fears by reminding herself that they could still locate the wagon, even if they could not recognize landmarks or see their own tracks in the deepening darkness.

"Do you think Pa is . . . is gone to heaven?" Fay asked softly.

Libby did not have the heart to tell her daughter the truth. "I don't know."

"If he is in heaven, I hope we'll all join him soon."

Libby reined her horse close and reached out to comfort her daughter. "We're staying right together on this earth for a good while longer. I don't think God is ready for us yet."

"Daddy said he wouldn't die and leave us alone."

"I know," Libby whispered. "But . . . but maybe God had other plans for your daddy."

Matthew must have heard that because he whirled around. "Pa *isn't* dead! He's just . . . just lost!"

"Of course he is," Libby said, knowing that she could not allow Matthew to become emotional out here in this unforgiving wilderness.

"And maybe," Matthew said, voice nearly breaking, "Pa is waiting for us right around this next hill."

"Yes, maybe," she agreed, forcing a note of hope that she did not feel.

But Elias was not around the next hill and when darkness fully cloaked them, Libby drew her horse up and said, "Matthew, we *must* go back to our wagon now. We can't search any longer."

"Mama, please!"

"No more arguments. Climb back on the horse and let's find our wagon."

"Mama," he begged, "I *know* he's just up ahead. Hurt and waiting."

Libby took a deep breath. She was afraid that her son would disobey her and race away into the night. "All right, I'll fire the pistol. One shot. And, if your father is alive, he'll call for help or fire the Hawken."

"But what if he's bad hurt so that he can't yell or shoot? I mean, what if he's laying stretched out cold just around the next hill?"

Libby didn't have an answer. The thought of stopping just short of rescuing her badly injured husband was something she could not deal with in her present fragile state of mind. So without a ready answer, Libby dismounted, giving Matthew the reins to both horses. She climbed high up onto one of the outcroppings of rock where she saw, far, far away the silvery thread of the Humboldt River.

"Hold on tight to those horses," she called down to her children. And then, she raised the pepperbox, stiffened her body, and pulled the trigger. The weapon fired correctly this time and a single, crisp shot overrode the nighttime thunder. They listened to the retort fade,

praying it would be answered by Elias's big Hawken.
Finally they lost hope.

Libby scrubbed hot tears from her eyes. "Dammit,
Elias, why did you do this to us," she choked as she
picked her way back down into the rocky wash they'd
been following for the last hour.

"Maybe he's already back at the wagon," Fay said
hopefully.

Both Matthew and Libby were so dejected they
couldn't even answer. Libby climbed up on a rock to
remount, then she reined back toward the river valley.
She would be surprised if their wagon had not already
been sacked and destroyed by the Indians. And soon,
very soon, she would have to decide whether to follow
the Humboldt River west, or turn back into the Great
Salt Lake Desert in one last desperate bid for survival.

They returned to the wagon long after midnight,
surprised that it had not been looted in their absence.
Their bonfire, so bright and protective when they'd ridden away in the afternoon, was now reduced to smoldering embers. The Humboldt River still gurgled as it
flowed westward. The storm was closer, the thunder
sounded like the approach of warring cannons. Libby
was so dejected and heartsick that it was all she could
do to heat up a little food for the children. After that,
they went to bed in the wagon, listening for Indians but
instead hearing the plaintive howl of coyotes.

When Libby awoke in the full light of morning, she
expected to find snow or at least rain, but found neither.
The wind was blowing hard, rippling and snapping the
canvas covering of their wagon. Fay was half buried in
blankets but Matthew had left, probably to water the
horses and maybe lead them to some fresh grass. Libby
didn't even think about Elias being there to greet them;
she supposed that meant that she had given him up for
dead.

Libby was very sore from the unaccustomed hours
she'd spent riding bareback and it was on her mind to

just stay in bed and rest until the storm finally blew itself out. And, dammit, if the cold wind and dust blew all day, she'd stay in bed hugging her children and telling them stories while trying to forget about . . . about everything.

It all sounded good except that Libby's stomach was growling and she was too nervous and worried to remain snug in bed, feeling the wagon rock to the gusty blasts. And there was always the possibility that Indians were coming to finish them off today, tomorrow, or sometime soon. Much as Libby yearned to mask ugly reality with fanciful stories, she knew that she had to make some hard, impossibly difficult decisions. Decisions that she yearned to avoid with every fiber of her being.

Libby slipped out from under the goosedown comforter that she usuually shared with Elias and pulled on her shoes. This past night had been the coldest yet. The wind still had a bite. Libby hated wind. She'd had more than her share of it on the northern Indiana plains after it curled like an icy claw off the freezing waters of Lake Michigan.

Elias's heavy leather coat was missing. Libby paused and then decided that Matthew had already arisen and used it for himself. It would droop nearly to his ankles but it would keep the boy warm and perhaps even give him hope and comfort. Libby reminded herself that if Elias was dead, it would be devastating to Matthew. The boy had worshiped his father.

Her own coat was made of dark blue wool. Shrugging it on, Libby parted the canvas and gazed out at the desert. Off to the west, she could see a trellis of dark storm clouds reaching down to the earth and knew that they were offering rain. She turned to study the Humboldt, noting how its normally glassy surface rippled under the hard, capricious wind. Off toward the Great Salt Lake, immense pale dust clouds covered the horizon.

Libby climbed out of the wagon, tying the canvas tight behind her and scanning their camp. The first thing she noticed was that the sorrel was gone. The second thing she noticed was that Matthew was gone too.

"Matthew!"

The wind snatched away her cry. Grainy sand and dust blasted her face. "Matthew!"

But he had vanished like Elias. Libby ran to the bay gelding and fumbled to untie it from the wagon. The animal was spooked, probably by the wind, but perhaps also from the nearness of Indians. Libby untied the horse, terrified that it would break away before she could climb onto its back and rush out to find Matthew.

She struggled with her crude bridle and reins. The horse attempted to break free. Libby fell and was dragged, clinging to the rope until she could scramble back to her feet. "Easy!" she cried into the animal's face, spooking it even worse. "Don't you dare leave us too!"

The horse tried to whirl. Libby lost her temper and booted it in the gut, just like she'd once seen Elias do when he'd finally lost his temper. The bay tossed its head and rolled its eyes, but it quivered into submission. She led the animal to a rock and climbed onto its back, then banged her heels into its ribs. The bay started to run and Libby gripped its barrel with her thighs and wound her hands into its coarse black mane. If she fell, their last horse would be gone like Elias and now Matthew.

She could *not* fall.

On and on they ran in the same direction they'd taken last night to find Elias. Only Elias was dead. Libby was sure of that now. The bay faltered within a mile of the river. It had not been watered or fed much since Elias had vanished. Libby felt the animal's stride degenerate into a choppy trot that punished her already sore body. She drew in the horse and it tried to buckle at the knees and collapse.

"Stop it!" Libby cried, jerking the bay's head up and driving her heels into its flanks.

But the bay was finished. If she tried to force it

another few miles, it would fall and be unable to regain its feet. And then . . . then they all would die.

Libby's head tipped forward and she wept bitterly as the bay reversed direction and began to weave back toward the Humboldt River. She could not stop weeping, not even when she felt the animal lurch down an embankment into the river and began to suck up great gulps of the foul-tasting water. As she sat there on the trembling horse in the middle of the dark river, Libby kept reminding herself that there was still hope for Fay, for Matthew, and even for herself. Not much hope, but a little.

She let the animal drink its fill and then reined it back up the riverbank to the wagon where she tied it with a double knot. She found grain and filled a feed bag. The bay gelding nickered with gratitude. Libby laid her face against its muscular shoulder and wound her arms around its neck. She loved the smell of a horse. It brought back a flood of happy memories of her own Pennsylvania childhood where her father had been a successful farmer and had even owned a fine surrey for Sundays.

Libby gained strength from the animal. She placed her hand on the horse's throat, feeling it swallow the life-giving grain. This horse was still hers and it would live. She and her children would also live. But she had to think. She *had* to be smart and brave and sensible.

Libby left the horse to finish its meager quota of grain and returned to the wagon. She climbed back under the goosedown comforter, closed her eyes, and let the wind rock her as if she were a babe in the cradle. Matthew would return soon, maybe even with his father. Libby kept telling herself that if she could still believe in God after all the tragedy that had befallen her family up to now, then surely she could believe that her husband and her son still lived.

It made sense. It made living bearable and, best of all, it offered her the merciful opiate of sleep.

CHAPTER

FOUR

Libby and Fay remained mostly inside the Conestoga until the storm passed three days later. By then, the hills were dusted with fresh snow and the air was pungent with wet sage. Runoff from the mountains fed the Humboldt River, which grew strong and fought to escape its banks.

"What are we going to do, Mama?" Fay asked.

"We'll keep waiting until we get very low on food," Libby said. "But by then, I'm sure that Matthew and your father will have returned."

"But what if the Indians return first?"

Libby took a deep breath and expelled it slowly. "Then we'll try to make friends with them."

"But they stole our horse!"

"Shhh! Worrying won't help."

"That's what Pa always said to you."

Libby allowed herself a thin smile. "Yes," she said, "it was. And it's still good advice."

The weather warmed into the upper fifties in the day, but the nights turned very cold. Despite her worries about the Indians, Libby grew extremely restless. She would pace back and forth along the riverbank, then whirl about and hurry to the eastern perimeter of their camp, peering into the empty gray distance, trying to will the return of her lost son and husband.

To keep her sanity, she and Fay became relentless wood gatherers. Ignoring the danger of being jumped by the Indians, they ventured farther and farther along the river, foraging for firewood. At night they burned great quantities of wood, huddling close to the fire, and listening in vain for the approach of their men or perhaps the arrival of Indians bent on taking their scalps. Most nights, Libby allowed Fay to sit up with her. Mornings found them pressed close together asleep beside the smoldering ashes of their fire.

By the end of the week and despite all her attempts to conserve food, Libby could see that her provisions were running low. They might not even be enough to deliver them to either Salt Lake City . . . or to California.

When she mentioned this concern to Fay, the child said, "We could fish or maybe even use the pepperbox to hunt."

"The pepperbox is useless," Libby said, wishing like mad that she still had the trusty Hawken that her husband had taken to scare away the Indians. "And even if I could hit a rabbit with that pistol, it would blow the poor thing to pieces. As for fishing, well, I don't think they bite in fall. But we can try to snare rabbits."

"Do you know how to make snares?"

"No," Libby admitted, "but they couldn't be that difficult. Let's try."

And so they spent an entire afternoon fashioning little nooses with slipknots and then scurrying around in the brush trying to decide where to place the snares.

"I don't even see any rabbit tracks in this sage," Libby complained.

"Perhaps they just go wherever they want," Fay suggested.

"Maybe," Libby said, rigging up another snare between a pair of low bushes, "but don't get your hopes up too high."

"I won't," Fay said. "I don't even like the idea of hanging little rabbits. Pa's shooting them was bad enough."

Libby finished setting out the last of their snares. She stood up, pressed both hands to the small of her back, and said, "Why don't we hunt up some line and fishing hooks and see if I'm wrong about the fish not biting?"

Fay liked that idea so they spent the better part of another day fishing without getting so much as a single nibble. "I guess," Libby said, "the fish just aren't hungry this time of year."

"If there ever were any in this foul-tasting Humboldt," Fay said. "I haven't so much as heard a frog croak since that storm."

It was true. No fish, no rabbits in their snares, and certainly no delicious frog legs to fill their hungry stomachs.

Each morning after awakening, the first thing that Libby did was to cut a notch in a willow branch. When she counted twelve, Libby drew her daughter close. "Honey, we're going to have to leave the wagon to try to reach help. There's no choice. If we wait much longer, we could starve."

Fay considered this for a moment, then looked up and said, "Mama, you've given up on them, haven't you? You think Pa and Matt have already gone to heaven."

Libby tried to hide her true feelings as she pulled her daughter close and said, "Fay, I just don't know what to think."

"But if you had to say, one way or the other?" Fay whispered, hugging her tight. "Be honest with me, Mama."

"All right." Libby drew a long, shuddering breath and expelled it slowly. "Your father might already be in heaven. However, I still believe with all my heart that your brother is alive."

"Why?"

Libby had considered the question a thousand times and so her answer came automatically. "Because, quite contrary to their cruel natures, Indians do value children. They will kill grown-up whites—but they spare *all* children, quite often taking them to raise as their own. Everyone knows that the Cheyenne, Sioux, and the Pawnee have raised white boys and girls. And our Matthew would want to live so that, someday, he could return to us."

Fay was on the verge of tears and, as Libby cradled her daughter, the child whispered, "What are we going to do?"

"We're leaving," Libby decided aloud. "But I still can't quite decide whether to follow this Humboldt River westward, or attempt to re-cross the Great Salt Lake Desert. What do you think we should do?"

Fay must have been thinking about it too for there was no hesitation in her reply. "Please, let's not go back. I want to hurry on to California. That's where Matthew and Pa would expect to find us."

"All right," Libby said with relief. "We'll follow this river all the way to the mountains, then push on to California. Just like we'd planned to from the start."

With that decision firmly made, they both felt much better and started to make preparations.

"Mama?"

"Yes?"

"Maybe we'll meet up with someone who can help us find Pa and Matt."

"It's certainly possible," she said. "But about as likely at this time of year as snaring rabbits or catching fish."

"But . . ."

Libby placed her hands on her daughter's shoulders. "Fay," she said, looking deep into the child's eyes. "If we do chance upon white hunters or trappers, we

can thank the Lord. But I think it's best if we just make
up our minds that we're pretty much going to have to
get out of this fix all by ourselves. Do you understand?"

"Yes," Fay whispered. "But I'm afraid of Indians!"

"So am I, darling, but I've got this," Libby said,
dragging out the clumsy pepperbox. "And I'll keep it
handy. Thank heavens that the Indians have no idea
how poorly it shoots."

Fay nodded.

"Now," Libby said, "let's go check our snares once
more. If they're empty, let's remove them so some poor
rabbit doesn't accidently hang itself long after we're
gone."

Fay turned and stared at their Conestoga. Libby
could read her daughter's thoughts and said, "It's just a
wagon, honey. Just wood, iron, and canvas."

"It's our home. It's everything we have."

"No," Libby countered, "we still have each other.
And the bay gelding and this pepperbox. We'll load the
horse with all kinds of food and a few precious things we
can't bear to leave behind."

"What about Grandma's rocker, or Grandpa's old
desk, and . . ."

Libby knew that her daughter also appreciated
these heirlooms that would have been passed on to her
someday. "Come on, Fay," she said, "let's check those
traps and then get our fire going. It'll be our last night
here and I can't say that I'll miss this place."

"Me, neither," Fay said, as they left the camp.

The traps were all empty, just as expected. Libby
and Fay collected the snares, then prepared to abandon
the wagon. Just the thought of doing it was enough to
bring fresh tears to their eyes. And no matter how often
Libby reminded herself that this was just a wagon, it was
much, much more. It was their link with the past as well
as their sturdy little sanctuary. Inside the Conestoga,
with their lamp glowing warm and cheery, they felt safe
and protected from the desert and all its dangers,
wrapped in a wood and canvas cocoon. The Conestoga

was a faithful friend. It had never failed them, not in all the miles it had bounced and jounced on the rough road from Indiana. They had nicknamed it "Rambler" and it had taken on an almost lifelike quality. In cold weather, it squeaked and rode stiffly, while in warm weather its axles and floorboards groaned. When it rained, Rambler's wheels swelled like an old woman's arthritic ankles.

Some days Rambler seemed happier than others, and it glided across the desert and the plains, free, loose, and easy. But there were other days when the wagon acted surly with axles whining a shrill protest. Libby and her family had come to know and love every splinter of wood, bolt, strap, and peg of their faithful Rambler. For these reasons, and many more, leaving Rambler alone, unprotected and at the complete mercy of the weather and the Indians, was like abandoning a family member. After traveling so long together, the wagon had even taken on their scent.

But now, without Rambler, Libby understood that things would immediately become much more desperate and that they would suffer from the elements. Still, what choice was there at this point?

They were both feeling so down about leaving the Conestoga behind that they didn't even notice the Indians until they were very close. Then they heard one of them shout from his horse.

Libby whirled. "Oh, dear Lord!" she whispered, hand reaching into her dress for the pepperbox. "Fay, get behind me!"

Libby raised the pistol and took aim.

"Mama, they're riding our sorrel and Papa's roan!"

"I know," she gritted, pulling the trigger.

The boom of the retort and the puff of smoke momentarily obscured the Indians but Libby fired another shot just for good measure. When she stepped aside from the smoke, she could see that the warrior had been knocked from his horse into the river and that their sorrel was trotting away. The Indian on the roan was already giving it chase.

"You got him!" Fay cried.

But the Indian who'd taken a tumble into the river suddenly jumped up and began to shout what could only have been angry obscenities. He unleashed an arrow that sailed over their heads. When Libby fired again, the Indian scrambled out of the water and dashed after his friend.

Libby grabbed Fay and hurried to the wagon. "Get inside and stay down!"

She reloaded the three empty cylinders and climbed into the wagon herself where they huddled for hours, expecting a full-scale attack as it grew darker. *They'll attack at dawn,* Libby told herself. *And they'll come in from all sides and finish us.*

It was a long, anxious night. Fay, despite all the excitement, soon fell asleep so Libby crept outside and hurriedly lit their bonfire. She piled on the last of their supply of wood, then even threw on her grandparents' desk and rocking chair. The flames shot into the sky and bathed the camp until Rambler's cover appeared as if it had contracted yellow jaundice.

When dawn finally arrived, the desert was very still and Libby, hand clenching the pepperbox, waited for the expected attack. But after two hours, when the sun was high and warm enough to make the sage steam, she decided that perhaps the Indians had actually gone away.

"Wake up," Libby urged after stuffing the last of their food and some extra heavy clothing into a pair of heavy burlap bags which she planned to drape over the bay gelding's withers, "we have to leave."

Fay started into wakefulness and scrubbed at her eyes. She looked pale and far too weary to endure the hardships that she must face in the days, maybe even weeks, ahead. But Libby knew her only daughter had pluck and was no quitter as she surveyed the sky, which was overcast. "Fay, pull on as many layers of your own as well as your brother's clothes as possible. Bring along extra socks and Matthew's blankets."

Libby had already followed her own instructions. Instead of a dress, she was wearing two pairs of Elias's pants and shirts as well as his old sweater, three pairs of woolen socks, his work boots, and torn jacket. She'd discarded her sunbonnet in favor of Elias's seal-brown slouch hat, which fit snugly after she'd crammed it full of her long brown hair.

"Mama, you look like a man," Fay said when she crawled out of the wagon a short time later wearing several layers of clothing.

"And you," Libby said as she finished tying their provisions and a few prized belongings on the bay, "look like a little fat boy. Are you ready?"

"Yes."

Libby saw the tears begin to slide down her daughter's cheeks and she could only imagine the terrible thoughts that were filling her child's mind as they were about to turn their back on Rambler and their past.

"Perhaps we can return with help and reclaim not only Rambler, but many of the things we're leaving behind," Libby said, trying to sound hopeful.

"Maybe Pa and Matt will come back with our horses."

Libby collected the bay's rope reins. She had bridled the animal and made sure that, if the Indians suddenly appeared, it would be possible to toss her daughter on horseback and send her racing for safety. Fay was an excellent rider and her light weight might even offset the bay's poor condition. Libby did not allow herself to think about the slim chance her daughter would have of surviving even if she did manage to evade capture by the Indians.

"There's room for you to ride," she offered.

But Fay shook her head, saying, "I really wish we knew how many days it will take to reach the mountains."

"So do I," Libby agreed, turning her back on Ram-

bler and leading both her daughter and the bay west.
"So do I."

They followed the river all morning. They often
came upon the decaying carcasses of dead oxen, mules,
cows, and horses. Sometimes too they also saw rough
wooden crosses marking shallow graves. Libby guessed
that she must have looked back over her shoulder a
thousand times that morning, always expecting to see a
swarm of Indians. But all she saw was the river, the
forbidding sky, and the oceans of sagebrush. She did
notice, however, that there were ranges of tall, verdant
mountains both to the north and south. They were quite
distant, hazy blue but with a tinge of green indicating
trees and other vegetation. Libby studied them with
more than a passing interest and, when she met a number of small feeder rivers that flowed into the Humboldt, she decided that there must be grassy valleys and
meadows hidden deep in those mountain ranges. That
seemed logical because, if there were not forests, pines,
and valleys, how else would these clear, cold streams be
formed?

"Are the Indians following us, Mama?" Fay asked
once when she caught Libby looking back up the river.

"I'm hoping that they'll settle for looting Rambler."

"But wouldn't they also want our last horse?"

"I . . . I suppose."

"I would if I were an Indian."

"I'm not letting them have him," Libby vowed. "We
need him far worse than they do."

"I don't think they care very much what we need,"
Fay said with the pure, uncomplicated wisdom of a
child.

Libby knew that Fay was right. And every frightened and weary fiber of her body told her to hurry, to
race westward, and to push their pace to the limit. Yet,
she knew that this would be exactly the wrong thing to
do. This desert was too immense, too unforgiving to
allow her to make even small mistakes. The only way

she and Fay could survive was to remain calm and logical, establishing a sensible pace with adequate rest stops for the weakened bay gelding.

So, it required an effort of will when the weak sun was at its zenith to halt for an hour beside the river and take their rest. When they nibbled dried apples, sourdough bread, and cheese, they watched distant black veils of clouds swirl downward, linking the earth and sky. To the west, mountains began to crowd in on the Humboldt River, narrowing this valley to less than ten miles. Libby observed layered rocky benches lifting toward huge broken red- and sand-colored bluffs sliced by deep canyons choked with juniper and pinion pines.

"If we were in trouble, we could hide in those canyons," she mused aloud. "They would protect us from blizzards and perhaps even hide us from the Indians."

"I don't want to leave this river," Fay said, looking frightened as she studied her mother's face. "Mama, we *have* to stay close to the river until we reach California."

"I know," Libby said. "And we will . . . unless we have to find somewhere safe to hide. There will be water in those canyons and they lead up into green mountains where our horse could fatten and grow strong again feeding in the meadows."

Fay said nothing and Libby dropped the subject. The Humboldt was their lifeline to civilization, but the idea of finally leaving the desert to enter pines and meadows was almost irresistible.

"Let's go," Libby said after an hour's rest.

"Can't we let Bob eat a little longer?" Fay asked. "He's so hungry and the grass is good here."

"Maybe it will be even better when we stop for the night," Libby said, beginning to unhobble their bay gelding.

They pushed on hard that afternoon and made good progress because Fay finally had to ride Bob. The poor child was staggering when Libby led their gelding up to a rock and Fay climbed onto its back. After that, Libby walked as fast as she could. She had always been a very good walker, blessed with strong legs and good, sound feet but this westward journey had really put them to the test.

It was late afternoon when they saw a band of mustangs. Libby would not have even seen the wild horses if Bob had not suddenly thrown up his head and nickered a greeting.

"Look!" Libby exclaimed.

Fay, who had been riding in kind of a stupor, raised her head and her eyes lit up when she saw the band. Their leader, a short but powerful chestnut stallion, came dancing forward, tail slightly raised, mane floating in the wind, blazed face held to the sun. He stopped, bugled a challenge to their weary bay gelding, and then pawed the earth. Bob responded with complete indifference.

"The chestnut is beautiful, Mama," Fay said, dismounting to watch the stallion put on a strutting show for the benefit of his mares.

"Yes," Libby agreed, "but other than the sunsets and sunrises, those wild horses are the *only* things of beauty I've seen so far in this terrible country."

The mustangs had been traveling off the higher benches to slake their thirst in the Humboldt River. The stallion soon grew weary of the human distraction and drove his band to intercept the river. But even as Libby watched, she saw the stallion and his band abruptly change directions to gallop back toward the hazy blue northern mountains.

"What happened?" Fay asked. "What scared them so?"

"Indians," Libby said, knowing there was no other possible explanation. "We'd better hurry on instead of making camp now."

Libby helped her daughter back onto their gelding and they pushed themselves until Libby could not walk another step and their poor gelding was staggering. The wind rose and blew sand and grit in their faces. Libby finally came upon what had once been a stand of cottonwoods, now all chopped to stumps by previous emigrants. In the rapidly dying light, she led Bob to a large patch of grass and helped Fay to dismount.

"Are we finally stopping here, Mama?"

Libby studied her surroundings with a practiced eye to select the best location for their camp. She spied a grassy island in the middle of the river, one of several dozen she had already passed that day.

"Let's hobble Bob," she said, "then we can carry everything over to the island and hide there tonight in the tall grass and reeds. If the Indians try to sneak up on us, maybe we can hear them crossing the water and drive them off with our gun."

They did not have much left in the way of possessions so it took Libby only three wading trips. They were so exhausted that, despite her fear of being caught unaware by the Indians, they both fell asleep almost the very moment they stretched out on the island grass.

Libby awoke quite late the next morning. The sun was up and the clouds had blown away, but it was cold enough that the grass around them was covered with frost. She scrubbed her face and rolled over to peer through the frosty grass. Libby didn't see any sign of Indians but then again, she didn't see any sign of Bob either, and it was all she could do not to jump up and run across the shallow water yelling and searching for their last horse.

Libby laid her forehead against her arm and silently wept with defeat and frustration. She should have pushed on later into the night. Should have ground-staked Bob on the island or to her ankle or something! Instead, she'd left the gelding alone to graze along the riverbank, and the Indians had taken him as easily as if he'd been candy laid on a hitch rail for any child to grab.

"Dammit, Libby!" she sobbed. "Now look at what you've gone and done to yourself and to Fay!"

Fay stirred but kept sleeping. Libby let her daughter sleep but checked her pistol and moved several yards away, keeping low and crawling through the freezing grass. The Indians were out there waiting and, if they wanted to attack, this was as good a place as any to defend. Libby took some comfort in remembering how the pepperbox had cut a big swath in the sage when it had misfired. Maybe she could even give a good account of herself before she joined Elias and her Matthew in heaven.

CHAPTER

FIVE

By noon, Libby was willing to concede that the Indians had her beat when it came to patience. She lay flat on her back, gazing up at the weak winter sun and wondering how she and her daughter were ever going to survive. Things, she decided, could hardly be more bleak.

"Tell me a story about California," Fay said, lying curled next to her mother. "A *nice* story."

"I have read that," Libby said, "before the great forty-niner gold rush, the Spanish missions were very beautiful with fountains and many lovely flowers. They were covered with roses in the springtime, and the Indians who worked for the padres sang hymns and prayed to Jesus and Mary."

"What else did they do?"

"They wove cloth and harvested the fields and the orchards," Libby said. "They butchered the mission cattle and tanned their hides for sale. They also made tallow from the fat."

"And it's warm there, not like here, right, Mama?"

"Of course. Even in these short days of autumn the flowers still bloom in California and there is fresh fruit

45

on the vine and in the orchards. They have many festivals, always with music and lots of color."

"Beside the Pacific Ocean?"

"Oh, yes," Libby assured her daughter. "You see, everyone except the gold prospectors choose to live close to the Pacific. That way, the weather is never too hot or too cold. Also, the people of California like to go down to the oceanside where they dig for clams and fish."

"Are ocean fish good to eat?"

"Very," Libby said. "And clams and oysters are equally delicious. The biggest are called abalone and I've read that they must be pried from the rocks, then beaten into a softness. When dropped in batter and cooked slowly, they are sweeter than honey and chicken."

A weary smile formed on Fay's lips. "When Pa and Matthew come to find us, will we all live beside the Pacific?"

"Definitely," Libby promised. "And I have heard that, in the summer and winter, giant whales, as long as ten Conestoga wagons, swim up and down the coastline. We can watch them blow mist from their backs and swim and play with big fish called porpoises."

"Do the Californians catch and eat whales and porpoises, Mama?"

"Yes," Libby said, "the whales have always been hunted for their oil and I suppose that the dolphins are good to eat."

"Once," Fay said, "you told me that porpoises are beautiful creatures and very playful. You said that sailors believe them to be friendly."

"Yes."

"Then I would not eat porpoise or whale," Fay said with conviction.

"Clams and oysters are very delicious," Libby said. "And we'll have plenty to eat when we live in California."

"I've been dreaming a lot about food," Fay admitted. "I dream of the Thanksgivings we used to have on the farm and those big Sunday afternoon picnics when everyone gathered behind the church."

"Sometimes," Libby said quietly, "I dream about food too."

After that, they lay quietly side by side for a time on the little desert river island, thinking about feasts from the past and all kinds of wonderful things to eat. Anything was better than thinking about Indians and Pa and Matthew and dying. How long they lay in the damp river grass and daydreamed Libby did not know but when they shook themselves out of their fanciful reveries, the sun was going down.

Libby dug some crusty bread and salt pork out of their provision sacks, which they chewed with little relish. "My darling, as soon as it is dark, we will wade across the river to the north bank and hike just as far along the river as we can before daylight before we hide again."

"But without Bob . . ."

"We'll do fine," Libby interrupted. "The Indians may have gotten our last horse but not our last weapon. I'm sure they *don't* know that a pepperbox is practically useless beyond a couple of dozen feet. I pray that, now that they have taken Bob and almost everything else that we own, they'll not risk getting shot."

"But, without Bob, how will we carry everything?"

"We'll have to leave a few things behind."

"What?"

In the vanishing glow of sunset, Libby studied the pitiful few possessions they had managed to retain. She had brought a frying pan, kettle, and a few eating utensils. Must she leave them? Yes, except for maybe the kettle, which was neither large nor heavy. They were already wearing almost all of their extra clothing but would need to keep their extra blankets and the big square of oilskin tarp that Libby had brought to protect them from a heavy rain. Also high in the order of priorities was the last of their traveling money, now less than

three hundred dollars, and a pair of canteens which they
would need to cross the forty-mile desert when this river
finally ran dry. What else could be abandoned? Not the
ammunition for the pepperbox and certainly not the
food or the old daguerreotype of her parents.

"Mama, you didn't answer my question."

Libby was jarred out of her deliberations. "We'll
start off carrying just the food, blankets, a kettle, and
the canteens . . . oh, and the oilskins and extra
clothes."

"Can we really carry *that* much?"

"I'll wrap up everything in a couple of sacks," Libby
explained. "When it gets very dark, we'll sneak away
and wade in the shallows for a while so that the Indians
can't follow our tracks."

"That's a good idea."

"It's not original," Libby confessed. "As I child, I
read all about it in one of James Fenimore Cooper's
books. Maybe *The Last of the Mohicans*, or *The Deer-
slayer*."

"Did they escape the Indians?"

"Of course! And we will too."

Twenty or thirty minutes later, Libby and Fay saw
their chance when the moon slipped behind clouds and
it grew very dark along the Humboldt. Gathering up all
their belongings, they waded quietly downriver. The
footing was treacherous and they both fell into the water once or twice, immediately turning nearly blue with
cold. It was grim business but Fay did not complain and
they did not leave the river until they had struggled several miles downriver.

Fay was shivering violently when they crawled back
into the sage. Libby helped her daughter change into
dry clothes and then she did the same but neither one of
them could get warm again. The only thing that helped
was movement but it seemed forever until a frosty dawn
finally edged over the eastern horizon.

Libby surveyed her surroundings, eyes settling on a
high prominence less than a half mile north of the Hum-

boldt. "We'll sneak up to that rocky peak and rest in the brush until evening," Libby said, taking her daughter's hand as they slowly began to work up to the higher ground. "From up there, we'll be able to see if any Indians are coming."

As it turned out the prominence was farther north and quite a bit higher than expected. It took nearly an hour to reach the peak, which was littered with broken red rocks, many of which had soft, flat bowls holding clear, sweet rainwater. Libby emptied their canteens of the bitter river water and replaced it with the rainwater after they each drank their fills. The delicious water raised her spirits and there was enough of it to wash their hair and faces.

"I feel better now," Fay said, drying her face.

"So do I," Libby replied, noting the dark circles around her daughter's eyes and realizing again the extreme physical and emotional toll that Fay was being made to suffer.

"Honey, just lay down and sleep for a little while and I'll keep a lookout for trouble," Libby said, wrapping her daughter in a blanket.

Fay was so tired that she fell asleep in an instant. Libby stayed down low behind the rocks as she began to survey the vast, empty panorama that stretched for hundreds of miles in every direction. Nothing moved except the wind and the dust devils. Libby had halfway expected to catch sight of poor Bob or a few wild horses but it was if every living thing had been swallowed by this ocean of rock and sage.

Libby felt overwhelmed by the size of this empty land. She felt weak, vulnerable, and insignificant. A craziness in her almost wished to see some other form of humanity, even Indians.

Stop it! she told herself. *They are probably out there, but you just can't see them.*

But, if that were true, where were her poor horses? Could they also be hidden from view? Libby did not think so. She felt a glimmer of hope. Perhaps . . . per-

haps the Indians really had settled for the Conestoga
wagon, and almost all of their worldly belongings except
the few hundred dollars she carried. That made perfect
sense. After all, there would be little to gain and much
to lose by risking being killed in a wild, smoky fusillade
of bullets—unless they badly wanted Fay to raise.

Libby shivered as a fresh blast of icy wind lifted
from the valley. *Dear God, we're about at the end of our
hope and strength. Please, help us. Deliver Elias and Matthew to us and then deliver all my suffering family from
this terrible wilderness.*

Libby took one last look to the east, eyes tracing
the watery ribbon and reaching up to the distant col-
umns of hazy lavender mountains. She watched immense cloud shadows race across the landscape and
wondered how Indians could survive in this cruel country. Libby had been raised in eastern pine forests. After
her marriage to Elias and their move to Indiana, she
had never grown accustomed to the open midwestern
plains. Now, however, even they seemed like paradise
compared to this tortured, thirsty desert.

Libby turned a half circle to the west, trying to
imagine that she could see the Sierra Nevadas even
though they were still impossibly far away. The wide
river valley stretched on to the end of the horizon and
Libby clenched her hands together, struggling not to
lose heart. There must always be hope.

Always.

Hours passed and she rested, dreaming again of
food, of her husband, and of little Matthew. Tears
leaked from her closed eyes and she started into wakefulness when a fierce gust of wind blew her hat from her
head. Libby retrieved the hat, then started to rouse Fay
but an impossibly faint movement caught her eye. A
dust storm? No, it was too cold and damp for dust devils
to play. Then what? Wild horses, perhaps even that
same band led by the proud and feisty chestnut stallion?

Libby ground her knuckles into her eyes. Something *was* moving out there but her eyes were too weary to really focus.

"Fay?" she said, reaching for the child. "Fay!"

The child roused with a fearful start, head whipping back and forth with sudden alarm. "Indians, Mama?"

"I don't think so," Libby said, pointing westward along the river. "Look closely. Am I imagining things, or do you see something moving right about where the river takes a sudden bend south? Don't you see something?"

Fay froze with concentration and Libby anxiously held her breath. "Well?"

"There *is* something moving out there!"

"But what!"

Fay drew her knees up to her chin and sat as still as a sphinx. Libby squinted so hard that her eyes watered. The only sound up on their rocky lookout point was that of the wind wheezing through the sage . . . and the blood rushing through Libby's ears.

"It is . . ." Fay said, slowly rising to her feet, "a flock of sheep!"

"Sheep?" Libby's hand flew to her mouth. "Sheep! Darling, are you sure!"

Fay nodded, chin quivering. "Yes, Mama. I *am* sure."

Libby crushed her daughter and they rocked together in a jubilant embrace even as Libby asked herself what sheep would be doing out in this horrible country.

Time passed and during the next hour, the gray, woolen haze gradually took on a definite form. They *were* sheep! Hundreds and hundreds. Maybe a thousand! It was impossible to tell because they blended in so perfectly with the sage. Fay squealed with joy when she recognized two men riding donkeys.

"We're saved," Libby whispered hoarsely. "Fay, we *are* saved!" They became so excited that they forgot about the Indians. Had there been any hidden in ambush, Libby later realized, she would have been killed and her daughter taken captive. But the Indians were nowhere to be seen as she and Fay ran headlong down to the Humboldt River.

"Try hard to stay calm," Libby said, leaning over to catch her wind. "We know how these distances are deceiving. That band of sheep could actually be miles and miles away."

"No," Fay said, not nearly so out of breath. "They're much closer than that."

"What makes you think so?"

"Because, if we listen we can *hear* them!"

Despite the sound of her labored breathing and the pounding of her heart, Libby listened and then she did hear the blessed bleating of sheep. "Let's collect our belongings and go to meet them," she said, combing her hair with her fingers and then swatting away dirt from the seat of her husband's old pants.

"Mama, will these sheep people be kind enough to help us find Pa and Matthew?"

"I'm sure that they will! They must be taking that huge band of sheep to Salt Lake City, although I can't imagine how they'll get them across the desert after they pass beyond the headwaters of this river."

"Maybe they expect it to rain or snow."

"Yes," Libby said, realizing that was a very logical explanation. "I'm sure that must be how they intend to do it."

"But . . . but if they're going back to Salt Lake City, how are *we* ever going to get to California?"

Libby shrugged because she just didn't have an answer. "Let's just hear what they say. Until a few moments ago, our chances of getting out of this desert alive were impossibly slim. Now, with the help of these people, we can at least survive and be delivered. After that, we'll find a way to search for Matthew and your father. We can't ever give up hope."

"We'll find them someday, Mama!"

"Of course we will," she replied as they shouldered their sacks and marched forward to greet their rescuers.

CHAPTER

SIX

Old Xabin Arostegi was riding a donkey because of an infected toe, but he would rather have booted the donkey in his behind and walked. Xabin's hooked nose resembled the beak of a hawk. His stern and weather-chiseled face, coupled with his oft scarred but still handsome features, were evidence of his fighting blood.

Xabin smoked cigarettes, rolling them expertly despite his thick, crooked, and calloused fingers. His hair was silver, his skin tanned leather. Xabin was not a tall man, but his mass of humped shoulder muscle was the result of sixty years of hard labor and made him appear rather formidable, even among much younger men.

"Yahh, donkey," he kept grunting around his cigarette, kicking upward with his heels at the soft underbelly. "Move!"

Other than to occasionally wag his immense ears back and forth with annoyance, the donkey paid scant attention to Xabin because the old man's heels were harmless. Xabin weighed 165 pounds, all of it tough and sinewy, but the donkey did not fear the old man, knowing he was always preoccupied by the welfare of his sheep.

Xabin's eldest son, Augustin Arostegi, was cut from the same granite mold as his father, only he stood taller and his disposition was far more temperate. Augustin was twenty-seven, and now he gaped as the sheep flowed around him like a dirty gray river. Several times, he blinked before finally shouting, "Father, I see two people!"

Xabin didn't hear his son. He was glaring suspiciously at a ewe that was dragging its hind foot and showing no interest in grazing. Xabin knew that a ewe without appetite would quickly weaken and die. Therefore, the ewe needed to be caught and examined. If she was found to be sick or seriously injured, the animal would soon rest in Xabin's huge cast-iron Dutch oven. She would simmer and roast in garlic, wild onions, and her own succulent juices.

Their sheepdogs also saw the two approaching figures and began to bark a warning.

"Lata! Emo!" Augustin commanded. "Be still."

The dogs fell silent, then wagged their tails fretfully and turned their attention back to the flock. They were sensitive creatures who had never been whipped or cuffed and very much took to heart even the slightest hint of their masters' disapproval.

"Father," Augustin said with a hint of exasperation, "we will catch that ewe and look at her later! Look what has risen from the land to greet us!"

With a foul imprecation, Xabin tore his eyes away from the ewe and followed his son's pointing finger. He was afflicted with failing eyesight so he could not see anyone coming. Xabin chewed his tobacco-stained mustache with irritation.

"Where?" he growled.

"Along the river. See?" Xabin nodded, but only because he did not want to appear blind. He believed his son and that was enough. "Indians?"

"No," Augustin said. "I think they are white people."

"On foot or mounted?"

"On foot!"

"Impossible," the old man grunted. "They must be Indians . . . or outlaws."

"But one is very small."

"Then a *small* Indian or outlaw. No matter. Get your rifle," Xabin ordered, dragging out his own Navy Colt pistol. "Anyone on foot in this desert is not to be trusted."

"But the small one looks to be a woman, or maybe even a child."

"Or an evil dwarf. Be ready, Augustin!"

Augustin obeyed although he thought it unlikely that an evil dwarf could survive in this desert. Like Xabin, he was powerfully built with a cleft in his chin like a fissure etched deeply in granite. Unruly raven-black hair escaped from his shapeless old hat. Augustin had an aquiline nose, bent slightly to the left, compliments of an enemy long ago forgotten but never forgiven. His heavy brow shielded piercing black eyes and his muscular neck was protected by a red and white checkered bandanna. His feet and hands were small, his knuckles scarred and fingers heavily boned, all with torn and blackened nails.

Augustin didn't hurry as he strode over to one of the family donkeys and yanked free a heavy Sharps .45 caliber breech-loading rifle. Like his father, he was already wearing a cap-and-ball Navy Colt six-shot, .36 caliber. Augustin could fire and load his pistol almost as fast as Palo, his younger brother.

Old Xabin drew his own pistol and dismounted, at last detecting the hazy figures. After several long moments, Xabin conceded that Augustin had been right. They were white people, but he had been right too, because one was surely an evil dwarf.

"I think the short one is *very* dangerous."

"Or maybe," Augustin said, "the tall one brings

along a boy to make us think they are harmless, while others hide to ambush us and take our flock."

The old man glanced back over his shoulder but their sheep wagon was still missing. "Damn your brother! Where is Palo whenever he is most needed?"

"Palo will be along," Augustin said, never taking his wary eyes off the approaching pair.

"We stay with our flock and let them come to us," Xabin decided. "This is *definitely* a trick."

Augustin glanced nervously aside at his father. "Just don't shoot them until we know for sure."

"I don't like the looks of this." Xabin glanced back over his shoulder a second time, muttering, "Where *is* your worthless brother? Palo was supposed to have overtaken us hours ago after mending that wheel."

"He will be along," Augustin promised. "Maybe he just took a little nap."

"He *is* worthless," Xabin snapped before blowing twin streams of smoke from his thick nostrils, then grinding the butt of his cigarette under his worn heel. "Maybe the Indians caught him sleeping and took his scalp."

"I don't think so," Augustin said, a little shocked by the hopefulness in his father's voice. "Palo has too many weapons and uses them too well."

"And look at the trouble that has gotten us all into!"

Augustin said nothing. He was not interested in rehashing the unfortunate circumstances that had forced his family to leave California as wanted fugitives.

The two shepherds kept moving forward as they watched the intruders closely, half expecting them to draw weapons and open fire. Xabin whispered, "What would a man and a dwarf be doing out here without horses or supplies?"

"Maybe they are prospecting for gold. They are thin and ragged."

"Like most thieves and murderers."

Suddenly, Augustin's jaw sagged. "Father, I think the dwarf is a little *girl!*"

"Your eyes deceive you."

"No! It *is* a girl and . . . and the taller one is a *woman!*"

Xabin stopped so suddenly that his sleepy donkey bumped him forward. Xabin stumbled, slashing the barrel of his pistol at the beast but missing.

"Damned donkey!" he muttered without passion as he stared ahead. "I see an *ugly* woman, Augustin."

"Well," Augustin said, trying to look at the bright side of things, "at least we won't have to protect her from Palo."

"This might be true," Xabin agreed, nodding his stubbled jaw. "But, remember, it has been weeks since Palo has seen *any* woman, even an ugly one. Therefore, he is still not to be entirely trusted."

"Hello!" Augustin called, sweeping off his hat and waving it in greeting.

Libby waved in return. Her step quickened.

"Mama," Fay said hopefully, "they look friendly."

"They look like criminals," Libby said, making sure that the pepperbox was resting in her coat pocket where it could be quickly brought into action, "but this is no time to be critical as long as they are honorable shepherds."

"What are you going to say to them?"

"I am going to say hello," Libby decided out loud. "And then I am going to ask them to help us find Matthew and Elias."

"How could they not?"

"I don't know."

"Their dogs are beautiful!" Fay exclaimed.

"Don't go near them until we learn if they bite."

Biters or not, Libby had already decided that the pair of sheepdogs were far more handsome than their scruffy owners. The dogs had shiny black and white coats. Libby was surprised that there were only two given such a large flock. But then again, she knew little about sheep.

"We should smile," Libby said as they drew nearer. "Considering our desperate and pitiful circumstances, that should be easy."

Fay forced a smile. "You are right, they do look rough and scary, Mama. And one of them is carrying a rifle."

"Let's hope that they are at least friendlier than Indians."

Libby could only imagine what these two heavily-armed and grim-visaged men must be thinking of her and Fay as they drew closer. After all, it was not every day that someone would find a white woman and child walking alone amid a thousand square miles of desert wilderness. Then again, she could not imagine why anyone would be trailing a flock through this country unless they were Mormons heading back to the Utah country after purchasing sheep in California.

"Hello," Libby called to the men, before whispering, "Fay, let's stop and curtsy."

"Dressed in old pants?"

"Yes."

They curtsied.

"At least," old Xabin said under his breath, "they have manners. They are probably crazy . . . but they do have manners."

Augustin had nothing to say about that. His own mind was working hard to unravel this interesting mystery. He kept raising his eyes to the country from which the pair had appeared, expecting to see the woman's husband or at least some friends with horses or cattle. But there was nothing. Just this thin, haggard pair. It simply did not make sense.

At last, both parties grew close and halted to speak.

"Good afternoon," Libby said.

"Good afternoon," the two sheepmen replied almost in unison, bowing slightly and raising their hats before lapsing into a curious silence.

"It . . ." Libby struggled for something more to say. In desperation, she cast her eyes at the heavens. "It looks like it might storm today."

Augustin's thick black eyebrows shot up and he glanced sideways at his father, who dipped his chin in agreement. "Yes, it could rain."

Libby was encouraged. These men were not Spanish speaking as she had first supposed, but they did have a strange foreign accent. "I have never seen so many sheep. Are they all yours?"

"Yes," Xabin said, eyes pulled down to regard the girl. "And what is your name, Miss?"

"Fay." She extended her hand. "Fay Pike. This is my mother, Libby Pike."

"We are pleased to meet you," Xabin said before he introduced himself and Augustin. "I have one other son, Palo. He is coming with our sheep wagon but he is not to be trusted by women . . . or even young girls."

"Father!" Augustin was appalled.

Xabin shrugged and added, "Augustin, I am only telling them the truth."

Libby did not know how to respond to this naked revelation. Like the entire ordeal that she and Fay had suffered this past week, this meeting seemed a bit unreal. She was faint from exhaustion and the air felt suffocating.

"You look unsteady," Augustin said, taking a wary step forward. "We could sit down on those rocks and talk. Would you like food?"

"You are very kind," Libby heard herself say, aware that she did feel unsteady.

"Here," Xabin said, gallantly offering her his arm. "We have wine, cheese, and bread on the donkeys. If that damned Palo ever comes, we can offer you much more from our sheep wagon."

Libby allowed the old man to escort her over to some rocks where she could sit and rest. She was embarrassed by this sudden infirmity. It was uncharacteristic of her to feel light-headed like some fragile Southern belle.

When they were seated, Fay said, "Do your dogs bite?"

"Oh, yes," Xabin said. "They bite at the heels of the sheep all day long."

"I meant, do they bite *people*?"

"Some people," Xabin admitted. "They are not pets, those dogs."

"They are pretty."

"They work hard and ask little," Xabin answered. He decided that this woman wasn't so ugly after all. In fact, washed and brushed, she would look very fine. Such a woman was sure to arouse Palo.

"I suppose you're wondering why we are out here alone and afoot in this wilderness," Libby said, searching their rugged faces for kindness and compassion. "I appreciate that our circumstances appear very unusual."

"You are in trouble," Augustin said, which seemed very obvious.

"Yes," Libby confessed, swallowing hard and wondering how much she should or should not reveal. She decided that she might as well make a full confession and then beseech these men for their assistance in helping to find Matthew and Elias.

"Here," Augustin said, offering the woman and her daughter the bread and wine from his knapsack and goatskin bag. "This will give you quick strength."

Libby and Fay were famished and accepted the food but declined the goatskin bag in favor of their own sweet rainwater. While Fay ate ravenously, Libby nibbled and began to explain.

"Soon after reaching the Humboldt River trail," Libby told them, "Indians stole one of our best wagon horses."

The bread and cheese stuck in her throat and she tried to wash them down with water.

"The wine is better," Augustin said, again offering her the skin bag. "If I had a cup, I would squeeze you some but it is easy to squirt it from the bag."

Augustin demonstrated and did not spill even a drop of the dark wine as he threw back his head and squirted until his mouth was full. Libby thought the act quite repugnant. She had only drank wine once, at her own wedding, and it had been awful.

"Where are you from?" Augustin asked.

"Indiana. We sold our farm and were on our way to California."

"California is very nice."

"That's what everyone says. But we have heard the gold is all panned out."

Augustin shrugged. He had never been interested in prospecting and had little use for those who did, most of whom were now destitute. Augustin saw his father begin to roll a cigarette. He felt like rolling one of his own but did not want to be distracted.

"I lost my husband," Libby said, feeling it important that she give a complete and honest account of their sad circumstances. "He rode off after the horse the Indians had stolen. Mr. Pike never came back."

"How long ago?" Xabin asked.

"Almost two weeks."

"Then he is probably dead."

Fay expelled a long, shuddering breath and then sniffled. Xabin looked over at the girl, noting the sudden tears in her eyes. "Then again," he added quickly, "it is entirely possible that Mr. Pike is very much alive and well. Just lost, eh?"

Fay brightened. Xabin gave her an approving smile and it occurred to him that sons were fine but it was a man's daughters that could always play melodies on his heartstrings.

"My son went to find his father a couple of days later and he never returned either," Libby said, in a voice that threatened to break.

"Here," Augustin said, taking the skin bag and leaning close. "Open your mouth and I will squirt in some wine. It will help."

Libby did not want to drink wine but felt she dared not offend their sense of hospitality. To her surprise, the warm red wine was not so awful after all. In fact, it was quite good and it soon stoked a glow in her empty belly. Libby decided that she would have more of the wine, if it were offered. But until then, she must finish her sad tale.

"Matthew was a good boy but was devoted to his father and rode away at night while I was asleep."

Libby was overcome by emotion and had to stop. After another squirt of wine from Augustin, she recovered enough to continue. "I truly believe that both my husband and son are still alive. This is why I am now begging you to help me find them."

Xabin forgot about the lame ewe and took a long squirt of wine for himself. Clearing his throat, he said, "We share your sorrow, but we cannot leave our flock unprotected."

Libby had already anticipated this objection. "You are going back toward our wagon. I don't know your destination but you could stop for a few days. Maybe . . . maybe if we could just search out a little farther, we would find my son and his father. Just a *little* farther, Mr. Arostegi! You could remain with your flock and perhaps your sons . . ."

Libby's plea was suddenly interrupted by the clanging of pots and pans as a strange looking wagon hove into view. The sheep wagon was much smaller than her beloved Conestoga. The wagon was painted dark green and the wheels were white like the canvas top. It was pulled by four big mules, all of them stouter than Libby's stolen wagon horses.

"Hello!" the driver yelled, tearing off his hat and waving it around and around overhead. "Hello!"

"Who is that?" Fay asked as the young man began

to slap the mules with the lines and drive them into a fast trot.

"That is my younger brother Palo," Augustin explained. "He is twenty-three."

"And worthless except in a fight," Xabin added, regarding Libby closely. "Beware of him."

"Why?"

Xabin glanced at Augustin, eyebrow cocked. When Augustin colored and looked away suddenly, Xabin turned back and replied, "Palo has too much Basque."

Libby frowned, not at all sure what that meant. She had heard of the Basques and thought them natives of somewhere in Western Europe.

"Do you know anything about our country?" Augustin asked, looking as if he wanted to change the subject or distract Libby from his brother's typically boisterous appearance.

"No."

"It is in the beautiful Pyrenees Mountains between France and Spain." Augustin's head lifted proudly. "We are neither of those peoples, though. We are our own rulers, always free."

Libby had the feeling that Augustin would have said more about the Basques but Palo was shouting and his wagon was almost upon them so that she could not help but be distracted. It soon became obvious to Libby that Palo was the handsomest man that she had ever laid eyes upon. He was slender with black eyes, wavy hair, and perfect teeth. His smile caused Libby to forget her sadness for an instant and when Palo jumped down from the wagon, swept off his hat, and bowed with a flourish, Libby's cheeks warmed with appreciation.

"Who are these beautiful ladies!" he cried, grinning and looking very animated.

"This is *Mrs*. Pike," Augustin said. "And her daughter, Miss Fay. They have come seeking our help to find Mr. Pike and a missing son."

Palo's wide smile dimmed and he suddenly looked very upset. "What happened?"

"The Indians stole our horses back upriver," Libby explained. "My husband went to find them but never returned. My son went to find his father and he also vanished!"

Unbidden tears spilled from Libby's eyes and it was Palo who offered her a clean handkerchief. "Please don't cry. If they are alive, we will save them."

"Thank you."

"No matter how long it takes, we will find them even if we have to go to the ends of the earth," Palo vowed, his voice ringing with conviction.

Xabin scowled. "Palo . . ."

"But Father, we could not live with ourselves if we do not find them," Palo argued, eyes never leaving Libby. "It will become for us a matter of honor!"

Xabin muttered something under his breath but, when Augustin nodded in grudging agreement, the old man relented. "All right. We will look for them."

"Thank you!"

Palo bowed slightly. "It is our pleasure!"

Augustin started to say something, but then he changed his mind and marched over to the sheep wagon and began to rummage around for something inside.

"Go help your brother," Xabin said to Palo.

Palo's cheeks darkened but he obeyed. When he was gone, Xabin said, "Remember what I told you about Palo."

"He only wants to help."

"No," Xabin argued, "he only wants to win your trust and then steal your heart."

"Nonsense! I am a married woman and that is an insult!"

Xabin opened his mouth to say something, then changed his mind and went to catch the lame ewe to see if she should be saved, or cooked.

"Mama?"

"Yes?"

"Is Palo bad?"

"No," Libby said.

"Should I be afraid of him?"

"I don't think so," Libby told her daughter, "but it would be foolish to trust any of them completely."

"I think they are good men. Don't you, Mama?"

Libby nodded. "Yes," she said, "and I even think they are honorable . . . to a point."

CHAPTER

SEVEN

The Arostegi men rested almost two hours beside the Humboldt enjoying a leisurely meal of cold bread, meat, wine, and dried apples before Xabin finally caught up his riding donkey. Nothing much was said, but Libby could tell that it was time to leave and it was all she could do to mask her own growing impatience. Though good-hearted and capable, to her way of thinking, these Basques moved far too slowly. Didn't they understand that Elias and Matthew might yet be saved if everyone displayed a greater sense of urgency and initiative?

"My husband and then my son both headed out in an easterly direction when they tried to recover our horses," she informed Xabin after he'd mounted the donkey.

The old man had a little difficulty getting his big, round-toed work boots through his stirrups. He scowled, saying, "Mrs. Pike, your husband acted like a fool. He should have stayed with his family."

Libby bristled. "People make mistakes, Mr. Arostegi. My husband had quite a temper but he was brave and a very good man. He realized that our four horses

were already overburdened with the Conestoga and he had his family's welfare in mind when he tried to get our horse back."

Xabin watched as Augustin whistled for his dogs to start moving their flock. Only then did he return his attention to Libby. "You know," he began, "my late wife also had a bad temper. That is why, when we fought, it was a terrible thing."

"You would strike each other?"

"Sure! Once, she broke my nose with a frying pan and another time she almost bit my ear off." Xabin clucked his tongue and a smile played with his lips. "She was a *good* fighter and I admired her spunk. I still miss those fights."

Libby shook her head in amazement. "I can't imagine why."

"My Rosalinda had spirit! I had spirit. Life was more interesting then."

Libby gave up trying to understand this man or to even imagine what his marriage must have been like. "Did your wife die in your Basque homeland?"

"No, many years ago in California. I brought her and my two little sons to help the Spanish padres raise sheep at the missions. Only, when I got here, the Mexicans had taken over California and the missions. So I raised sheep myself in the foothills of the coastal mountains. And I prospered."

"I have heard it is very beautiful everywhere in California. I imagine that you will go back once you deliver these sheep to . . . whomever."

"No," he said, eyes clouding. "The missions are all gone. The damned Mexicans destroyed them. The Indians are gone too, killed off by the Americans. California is not the same anymore. The Americans have ruined the land, ripping it apart in their mad search for gold."

"I am sure that it is still beautiful," Libby said, not wanting her daughter to hear such bad talk.

"It is too crowded now," Xabin complained. "Everywhere you go there are people. The gold hunters are

rootless, godless people. Most are lost souls without
families. There are very few good women in California.
Mrs. Pike . . ."

"Libby. Please call me Libby."

He ignored her request. "Mrs. Pike, if I am right
and your husband is dead, you will have ten . . . no
fifty California men asking for your hand in marriage."

"I don't want another husband, Mr. Arostegi. I will
remain true to Mr. Pike."

Xabin crooked a finger, indicating that Libby
should lean closer so that no more of his words would
be overheard by the girl.

"Fay," Libby said, "why don't you go over and see
if Augustin needs any help?"

"Yes, Mama."

When Fay was gone, Libby looked up at the rugged
old man with suspicion. "What else do you want to tell
me?"

"I can tell that you are a good woman. I appreciate
that and so do my sons. But you must be prepared to
accept that your husband is dead. And that your son is
probably dead too. This country is cruel and unforgiving
of mistakes."

"Mr. Arostegi," she said in a low, firm voice. "I
can't tell you *why* I know that my son is alive, but I do.
Perhaps my husband is lost—but not my boy. Not my
fine son, Matthew! I say this because I know that Indians often take white children to raise."

"I have heard this too. And so you are right. The
boy might have a better chance than his father." Xabin
began to expertly roll a cigarette without even looking
down at his gnarled hands. "And you would rather the
boy live than the father, eh?"

Libby was appalled that anyone could ask so rude
and insensitive a question. "Why, I . . . I couldn't possibly choose!"

Xabin returned the tobacco to his shirt pocket and
licked the brown cigarette paper, twisting it slightly. "Of

course you could, Mrs. Pike. A woman will always choose a son or a daughter over her husband."

"That's *not* true."

Xabin shrugged. "It is true. I admit that I would have chosen Augustin over my Rosalinda, except at the very first."

Libby blushed when he winked and grinned. This man was incorrigible! It was all that she could do to ask, "And how about Palo? Would you chose Palo over your wife?"

He laughed, knowing that she had trapped him and then he jammed the cigarette between his lips without an answer.

"Well?"

He struck a match with his thumbnail, then inhaled deeply, and exhaled through his nostrils, all the time carefully considering her question. "I don't know, Mrs. Pike. That would have been a hard decision to make. Palo has been a great disappointment, but so too has life."

The anger left her as quickly as it had arisen. "Mr. Arostegi, I know nothing about your family and that is probably for the best. However, I do believe that a parent never should favor one son over the other."

Xabin pulled on his cigarette, then said, "You have a strong spirit, Mrs. Pike. Tell me something."

"If it's not too personal."

"Didn't you ever beat *your* husband with a frying pan?"

"No!"

"Then hit him with a rock or maybe a broom hard enough to break a few of his bones?"

Libby couldn't believe she was hearing these insulting questions. "Of course not!"

"Didn't you at least threaten him with a gun or a knife?"

"Don't be ridiculous!"

Xabin squinted through smoke. "Then I think your

husband was small or so weak that you could whip him bare-handed."

"Why, you old . . . !"

Xabin's bushy gray eyebrows arched, he peered down his hawkish beak and looked very pleased with himself. "Admit it, Mrs. Pike, you *could* whip his ass, eh?"

"You . . . you are insane!"

The old man cackled and leaned far out of the saddle to pinch her cheek. She doubled up her fist and took a wild swing at Xabin's craggy face but he leaned back, booted his sleepy donkey and rode away surrounded by his own demented laughter.

Libby was so furious that she felt like screaming but that might have caused the sheep to stampede, if sheep ever did such things.

Instead, she went over to join her daughter, who was watching Augustin work the sheepdogs. He directed them using whistles and gestures that caused both dogs to sometimes bark or yip like soldiers jumping at an officer's sharp commands. The dogs worried the sheep but did not crowd them too closely or cause them to bolt in panic. When several of the sheep attempted to charge off into an inviting arroyo, the larger of the dogs laid his ears back and streaked forward, easily cutting off the escape and driving the truant sheep back into the main bunch by nipping at their hocks.

Watching the dogs work allowed Libby to calm down. She noted how, in places where the sagebrush grew tall and thick, the dogs would leap into the air to see Augustin make his rapid hand and arm signals.

"They are remarkable, aren't they," Libby said, smothering the last of her anger concerning the old devil sheepman.

Coming up to join them, Palo followed their eyes. He must have read the admiration on their faces because he said, "Our dogs want only to please."

"How many sheep do you have?" Fay asked.

"A little over two thousand. There will be many more in the spring after lambing season."

"Two thousand," Fay said, looking very impressed. "What are you going to do with all of them?"

"Sell some, butcher others, but mainly we will raise even more. We will raise *ten* thousand and split them into three bands."

"Then you will probably need a lot more dogs."

"This is true," Palo agreed. "There is a place in California where we can buy more, but even pups are very expensive. A highly trained sheepdog such as Lata or Emo is worth more than a fast horse."

"Really?" Libby asked.

"Certainly," Palo replied, folding his arms across his chest. "Why should this be a surprise? Without a horse, a man can always walk or choose to ride a donkey or a mule. But without a dog, a shepherd has no hope of keeping his flock together. Also, the dogs will fight off coyotes, bears, and even cougars."

"I would like to have a dog like those someday," Fay said.

"They are bred to work sheep," Palo told her. "But despite what my father would tell you, they also make fine companions. And maybe someday we can get you a pup."

"I would *love* that!" Fay breathed, looking happier than she had in weeks.

Palo chuckled and then he sauntered over to his sheep wagon. "You can both ride up there with me and I will tell you everything about sheep and sheepdogs. How does that sound?"

"It sounds good," Fay said, looking very happy that she would not have to walk any farther, at least not the rest of this day.

But Libby changed her mind when she really looked up at the driver's seat. "There is obviously not enough room for three on that bench, so I'll walk, Mr. Arostegi."

"Palo!" he corrected. "And I would rather cut my

wrists and bleed to death than allow such a thing! *Palo* will be the one to walk."

"But . . . but don't you need to drive?"

"I will lead," he said. "So, Libby, how is that?"

"Are you sure?"

"Of course!"

Libby started to tell him thank you but before she could, Palo swung her up to the driver's seat as easily as if she were a stuffed rag doll.

"Now you," he said to Fay. "Up beside your mother!"

Fay squealed as Palo swung her completely around before depositing her on the driver's seat.

"You both look good up there!" he said with a laugh. "And I am happy to walk."

"Are you sure?" Libby asked.

"Yes," he said, patting the lead mule, "this is a very smart fellow and we will have a good conversation."

When the little sheep wagon jolted forward, all the pots, pans, and utensils inside began to bang and clatter again and it quickly became apparent that the wagon was heavily loaded. This explained why it took four big mules to haul it across the desert. Libby squeezed her daughter's hand and, despite the jarring, they both breathed a deep sigh of relief.

"Before we fall asleep tonight," Libby said, "we must remember to thank God for the arrival of these fine Basque sheepmen. It is a miracle that they found us before the Indians."

"I know," Fay agreed. "Do you think the Indians will also try to steal their mules?"

"I doubt it."

Libby breathed deeply of the pungent sage and gazed all around. She had forgotten how much finer the view was perched upon the seat of a wagon where she could see over the tallest sage.

"Mama, with the Arostegis helping us to look, don't you think it will be easy to find Matthew and Father?"

"We'll just have to wait and see. But I do know this, we'll all do our best. These men have guns and pistols and I've no doubt that they know how to use them."

"They don't seem a bit worried about Indians."

"No," Fay agreed. "They don't."

Had Libby and Fay not been so physically exhausted and mentally drained, they would have enjoyed the remains of that afternoon. Over the din of the pots and pans, Palo tried to carry on a conversation. That was quite impossible but Libby thought his animated gestures were quite entertaining.

Libby was very curious why Palo and his family had traded California for this hellish country. But, unless she was very much surprised, her questions would be satisfied before too many days. These Basques were not a bit shy or secretive. Libby still bristled at the memory of Xabin's galling impertinence but told herself that the man was old and irascible. Most likely, he was only trying to get her goat. Well, he'd succeeded today but he darn sure wouldn't tomorrow.

Libby avoided being alone with old Xabin for the next few days. She was more than content to be in Palo's company and might have even enjoyed herself had the circumstances been different. As it was, all of her thoughts were focused on locating her husband and her son.

"There it is!" Libby cried when they finally saw the Conestoga. "The Indians must have overturned it in the river!"

"I am surprised that it was not burned to ashes," Xabin called, as he urged his donkey ahead by beating it with his hat.

The sheep began to graze and the dogs watched them while everyone rushed to examine the overturned wagon. What remained of precious furniture had been smashed beyond recognition, and much of it had been burned in their old campfire. Their trunkful of extra clothes had been sacked and scattered and Libby was embarrassed to see many of her undergarments hanging

from the sage in what she supposed was a form of Paiute mockery. Augustin seemed embarrassed too, but
Palo collected everything that had not been defiled and
returned it to the trunk.

Fay was saddened to find that her dolls were missing as were all of Elias's tools, extra harnesses, ropes,
the ax, a pike, and a shovel. In truth, there wasn't much
left of value.

Despite Libby's resolve to keep up a brave front,
her composure nearly cracked and she hurried away to
the edge of the camp and had a good cry. Soon, Fay
arrived to comfort her, saying, "Xabin, Palo, and Augustin say they can right our wagon. They're already starting to hitch up those big mules."

Libby scrubbed away her tears. "They're going to
right it? Why?"

"Augustin and Palo said that they would pull it out
of the river so that it would dry off and we could live
inside of it while they hunted for Pa and Matthew."

"I ought to help," Libby said, heading back to camp
and feeling foolish for displaying such weakness.

The Basques went right to work, asking only that
Libby and Fay give them a wide berth. They hitched up
the mules and used a chain and a rope to pull the heavy
Conestoga upright. The mules really had to strain for
solid footing in the shallow river, but they had remarkable power and, when the wagon did tip upright, Libby
smiled so wide that her lips split again.

She didn't care. And when the wagon was dragged
back to the camp, water pouring out the drop tailgate,
Libby was able to forget her sorrows by setting her
house back in order.

By nightfall, the Conestoga was livable. Since their
bedding had been taken by the Indians, the Arostegis
gave them extra blankets. When Libby and Fay climbed
under the canvas top, it seemed ever so familiar, safe,
and fine.

"Maybe things are going to change for the better
now that we have the wagon back," Fay said, hugging

her mother. "Maybe all the bad stuff is over, huh, Mama?"

"I feel . . . hopeful," she said, hearing the Basques laughing softly beside their campfire and the occasional bleating of a sheep.

They prayed to God that tomorrow they would be able to find or at least learn the fate of their menfolk. And they thanked Him too, for sending along the Arostegi family and giving them fresh hope.

"Libby?"

She had just been about to doze off when the whispered voice roused her into wakefulness.

"Libby, are you awake?"

"Yes," she whispered, Fay's soft, even breathing telling her that the child was asleep. "What do you want, Palo?"

"I just wanted to make sure that you were all right. You know that those same Indians who stole your horses are likely to still be around somewhere."

"I have a pepperbox," she told the young man. "And with you men close by, I'm not worried."

There was a long silence, then Palo said, "I'm happy to hear that, Libby. I was thinking, though, that maybe I should sleep close to you and Fay."

"That's not necessary."

"I didn't mean inside the wagon. I meant under it."

"Really," Libby said, "we're all right."

He pulled back the canvas and studied her in the moonlight.

"What are you doing? Go away!" Libby ordered in a hushed voice.

"I . . . I just wanted to say that I'm sorry that you and Fay had to suffer so much misery. And . . . and that I'm sure that we can find your husband and son. Father won't want to stay put here very long, but Augustin and I have talked it over and we're determined to take enough provisions to ride out for at least three, maybe even four days just to hunt for 'em."

Libby sighed, collecting her thoughts. "Palo, I want you to go, but I also want you both to be very careful."

"Oh, we will!" He cleared his throat. "Course, there's no way to say for sure that we won't run into a big band of Paiutes or Shoshones and come to a sad end."

Without thinking, she reached out to touch his hand. "Palo, please don't take any chances! On top of everything else, I don't think I could bear the deaths of you and Augustin on my conscience."

"It's all right," he said. "We can take care of ourselves. Augustin is a dead shot, almost as good as I am. I'm going to be more worried about you, Fay, and my father than you will be about us."

"Why?"

"Well," he said, leaning closer, handsome face bathed in the moonlight. "Once those Indians see us leave this camp, they'll know that my father is the only man still here to protect you, Fay, and the flock."

"Then maybe you both shouldn't go!"

"Have to," he said, dredging up a brave smile. "I'm the best tracker and fighter. And Augustin wouldn't allow himself to be left behind. But don't you worry about a thing. I won't let anything happen to you and Fay, no matter what."

Libby squeezed his hand.

"Libby," he said, pulling away, "I want you have something that my mother gave me before she died."

"What?"

"It's a religious medal. It was blessed by a cardinal or bishop or something back in our homeland and it's always brought me luck and protection."

Libby shrank back. "Then for goodness' sakes, you should wear it when you leave!"

"No," he said stubbornly. "I want you to wear it around your neck for me. You see, that way it'll have twice as much power."

He'd lost her. Bewildered, Libby said, "Palo, I don't understand."

"You will someday," he said. "Just . . . just wear it, Libby, and keep me in your thoughts and in your heart."

"I will," she promised. "And Augustin too."

His brow furrowed. "Sure, Augustin too," he said. " 'Bye, Libby."

"I'll see you before you leave, won't I?"

"Maybe not. Augustin and I want to leave early in the morning before first light so that, if the Indians are watching this camp, we'll be gone before they can see which way we went."

"I see."

"Libby?"

"Yes?"

"I don't suppose you could climb out of that wagon and sort of point in the general direction where your husband and son disappeared?"

Now she saw his clever game and realized everything he'd said and done had been leading up to getting her to join him outside of the camp.

"You'll see the tracks just to the east."

"Washed out, Libby."

"Then look due east and you'll see a low bench and a rocky prominence. It's several miles distant and that's where the tracks disappeared. Palo?"

He was a long time answering. "Yeah?"

"You and Augustin hurry back and we'll pray for you."

"Do that," he said, sounding discouraged as he left her alone in the night.

CHAPTER

EIGHT

Augustin Arostegi waited until his brother had saddled and bridled his mule. He glanced up at the dying stars and checked his rifle before saying, "Palo, did Libby give you any specific landmarks for us to follow?"

Palo slung his canteen across the saddle horn and then mounted. He thumbed his hat back on his forehead, grinned, and pointed toward the shadowy silhouette of a prominence that he judged to be a good ten miles to the east. "She said to head for that tall pile of rocks and look for tracks."

"That's all?"

The grin widened. "Do you mean, about where to start the search, or about the strong feelings she's already got working for me?"

Augustin shook his head. "She doesn't have any 'strong feelings' about you, Palo. Xabin warned her off."

Palo chuckled and then glanced back at the wagon. "Gus, she's a very lonely and helpless woman."

"She's a very *married* woman," Augustin shot back, "and I don't think there is anything 'helpless' about Mrs. Pike."

"Shhh!" Palo cautioned with exaggerated alarm. "If you speak so loud, you'll wake her and I can tell she needs her rest."

"Of course she does," Augustin said, reining his own mule eastward. "It's a good thing that Xabin warned Mrs. Pike and Fay not to trust you."

"He warned Fay!" Palo exclaimed. "Dammit, did he really warn that little girl too?"

"Yep." Augustin forced his mule into a trot, letting it pick its own way through the heavy sage.

Palo was still angry when they finally reached the rocky prominence soon after sunrise. "I can't believe that Father would warn little Fay! She's only a child and I would offer my life to keep her from harm."

Deep inside, Augustin knew that this was true. Think what you might about Palo, he was a gentleman in the company of children and treated them all with deep affection.

"Palo, our father was not serious."

Palo looked away quickly to hide the pain in his eyes. "Sometimes I think that I will never be able please him. That it is useless to even try."

"That is not true."

"Isn't it?" Palo turned around, angry now. "He favors you in everything. He always has and he always will."

Augustin said nothing because it was the truth. Even when they were boys it had been this way and there had been many times when he actually had tried to fail so that Palo would look better by comparison. Actually, there was much good and admirable about his brother. Palo had a great heart. He was generous to a fault, open and honest, except in affairs of the heart. Palo was also courageous. Augustin knew of no one— not even Xabin—that he would rather be standing side by side with in a bad fight. And while his only brother might lack brute strength, Palo more than compensated for that with cunning, quickness, and his fighting skills with both a gun and a knife.

"You don't even try to deny the injustice anymore," Palo said, his anger cooling.

"No," Augustin admitted, "but I think that some-day you will show our father he has been wrong. It is just that you need to try and please him a little more. Work a little harder and . . ."

Palo shook his head. "I won't do that, Gus. Not for him, not for you, and not for anyone. Our father is a workhorse. You are also strong and steady, both sheep-men to the core. But I don't even *like* the stupid sheep."

"It is not a matter of liking them or not liking them," Augustin said. "It is all that we know. The Basques have always been sheepmen. We do it well be-cause it is in our blood."

"Not my blood. I could raise horses, or cattle, or even chickens and they wouldn't be in my blood either."

"You talk crazy."

"Everyone is at least a little bit crazy," Palo said. "But I am finished with sheep. I hate both the sight and the stench of them. And, if I don't leave soon, I will even begin to hate our father. Can you understand that?"

"Yes," Augustin said, "I can."

"You do?" Palo was surprised. "I thought you also would be angry when I leave."

"No, not angry. Sad, but not angry."

Palo tugged his hat back down and rolled a ciga-rette. "You should come with me."

"Don't talk stupid!"

"Augustin, you could . . ."

"We should hunt for the tracks," Augustin said, cutting off Palo's foolish words. Did he really believe they could both leave their father, the sheep, and their dogs to fend for themselves in this hard country?

"Any tracks they made will be long gone because of the wind and the rain," Palo said, touching a match to the cigarette and squinting through the smoke and the heightening sunrise. "So what are we supposed to do?"

"We look for bodies, or the marks of a battle. Maybe we'll see some Indians."

Palo looked amused. "And then?"

"If we do not have to kill them all, we try to find out if they know the fates of Mr. Pike and his son."

"Now, why didn't I think of that?" Palo said with a grin.

"Because you would rather dream of women than think out a problem."

Palo chuckled. "I think your plan is worthless, but let's search this cruel country for a couple of days. I could not face that woman or her daughter again if we do not give this a good try."

"Me neither," Augustin said, urging his mule on up a dry wash toward the rocky prominence.

"Look," Palo said a short time later as he dismounted and squatted on his heels. "Here is where Mrs. Pike came in search of her husband. I can still see the mark of a shoe."

Palo gazed up toward the rocky prominence. "She must have climbed up there to look around. I think that I will do the same."

"We will *both* look around," Augustin said. "Palo, if you go alone, you might decide to take a long nap and leave me waiting."

"I would not do such a thing," Palo said trying to look offended as he tied his mule and dragged his rifle out from his saddle scabbard. "But come along, if you are up to the hike."

Augustin also collected his rifle and followed Palo up the side of the rocky slope. They did not stop until they reached the rocky summit. The view was unexcelled. Far to the west they could see the Humboldt and, in every direction, ranges of mostly barren mountains. They were not able to locate either the sheep or the Conestoga wagon.

"Libby calls her wagon 'Rambler,' " Palo said with a half smile. "Did you know that?"

"No."

"And last night she begged for something of mine to treasure while we hunt for her husband."

"What do you mean, 'to treasure'?"

"She wanted something to remember me if we are also killed." Palo winked. "In truth, the woman pleaded for a lock of my hair. But I thought she ought to have something more, so she is wearing my saint's medal next to her heart."

"You lie."

Palo whirled around and unbuttoned his coat and shirt to expose his bare chest. "Look for yourself!" he challenged. "Do you see a saint's medal resting next to *my* beating breast?"

"No."

"That is because it is next to *her* beating breast," Palo said triumphantly. He wiggled his black eyebrows. "Yes, right next to her warm, soft, beating breast."

"Palo, you are a raving idiot."

"No," Palo said, brushing aside the insult as he might a fly, "I am a romantic dreamer."

Augustin had heard more than enough of his brother's drivel. Palo's medal was probably stuffed deep into his pocket and he was just trying to make up for his bad feelings about what Xabin had said concerning the girl.

"Let's go back down and ride," he ordered.

"To where?"

"To the east," Augustin said. "Toward those high, green mountains. If I were an Indian, that is where *I* would go to live."

"But they are at least twenty or thirty miles away."

"Then we have a hard ride ahead of us."

"And," Palo said, rebuttoning his shirt and jacket, "what if I say riding that far would be a big waste of time?"

Augustin turned and looked back up the prominence toward his brother. "If you have someplace better to look, then by all means do it! As for me, those mountains are where I am going unless I see something that tells me to do otherwise."

"All right," Palo said. "I can see that you are determined, so I will go along. But it is not good to leave our camp so unprotected. Our father's eyes are not so clear that he could drive off a big Indian attack, eh?"

"The woman would help. Probably even the girl. Between the three . . ."

". . . Between the three they might hold off six or ten Indians. But if there were more, it'd be dicey at best and the Indians might even put the torch to the flock."

"Lata and Emo would go straight after them," Augustin said quietly, even as he realized that the dogs wouldn't have much chance.

"Then we'd be without sheepdogs," Palo said. "And you know what that would mean."

Augustin knew. Without dogs, they would be exposing the flock to all manner of dangers. They would lose a good many sheep, especially lambs in the spring. The coyotes would have a feast.

"Let's go," Augustin said. "The sooner we reach those mountains and have a look, the sooner we can get back and tell Mrs. Pike that her son and her husband are dead."

"Maybe, maybe not," Palo replied. "Maybe the boy was taken alive by the Indians. But I agree that the stupid father is probably dead."

That was how Augustin saw it as well as they returned to their mules and pushed on to the east, riding about a hundred yards apart and weaving back and forth in the hope of chancing upon the hoofmarks of shod horses, which could only belong to the Pike family.

Several hours later, Augustin called out to his brother, "All I see are lots of mustang tracks."

"Me too," Palo shouted. "I expect that they might have trampled out the ones we're looking for."

An hour later, Augustin saw the body. "Palo, over here!" he shouted, kicking his mule forward.

Elias Pike was riddled with bullets. His coat, shirt,

hat, and boots had been stripped from his angular body and his eyes were open wide and staring at the sky. His nose, ears, and a piece of his scalp had been cut away as had his ring finger. Even though Augustin was accustomed to harsh realities, he shivered at the grisly sight, and the sweet stench of decaying flesh made his stomach flop.

"Do we take him back?" Palo asked, dismounting to join his brother.

"No," Augustin said quietly. "We'll bury him as best we can. We're not going to let his wife and daughter see this."

Palo nodded and looked around. "Maybe the boy is close."

"Maybe."

"I'll take a look around while you dig the grave."

"Sure," Augustin said as his brother moved away.

The ground was hard and rocky, the grave ended up being very shallow but Augustin covered it with heavy rocks. No doubt the coyotes and vermin would find and consume poor Elias's flesh, but there was no help for that. They had to go on and find the boy, if there was anything left to find.

"No sign of the kid."

"Then let's ride," Augustin said.

"Ain't you going to say a few words over him?"

Augustin tossed his reins over the head of his mule. "I already did."

They rode all the rest of that day and still came up a few miles shy of the mountains. They could even smell the pines because a cool breeze flowed down from the higher elevations. A thin, gurgling stream trickled into a small, grassy basin where it seeped into the earth.

"This is as good a place as any to camp," Palo said hopefully. "Plenty of grass and water for the mules."

"But if we were attacked, this would be a poor place to defend," Augustin said, raising in his stirrups. "I think we should push on to the mountains and camp in those pines."

"It'll be midnight before we reach them."

"So be it," Augustin said. "Tomorrow, we can split up and ride both ways along these mountains searching for tracks. If we don't find anything, then we can both look Mrs. Pike in the eye without shame and tell her with certainty that her husband and son are dead."

Palo wasn't happy, but Augustin's plan made sense. So far, he'd seen no sign of Indians, but that sure didn't mean they weren't sneaking around someplace, perhaps even very near. And Augustin was right about it being too dangerous to camp in the little valley. The Indians could encircle and rain arrows down upon them from higher ground.

"All right," Palo said. "Let's ride."

Augustin was pleasantly surprised. Usually, Palo liked to argue, especially when he felt like someone was telling him what or what not to do. So they rode on up the mountain as darkness fell. Accustomed to stopping with the flock well before sundown, the mules became balky and irritable. Both brothers had to cut switches from the sage and use them frequently in order to push the mules as they followed the little stream higher and higher.

"Now *this* is country," Augustin said when they finally entered the pines and chose a good place to make camp.

Palo didn't say a word. He just unsaddled then hobbled his mule before climbing into a bowl of rocks to eat a cold meal of bread and mutton.

Augustin rolled a cigarette, still not quite ready to settle down to their supper. And although he did not want to consider the issue, Augustin wondered if Libby Pike really had consented to wear Palo's medal close to her sweet breast.

The possibility left a bad taste in Augustin's mouth. He doubted that Libby Pike would consent to do such a thing. Still, Palo was incredibly persuasive and women had always baffled Augustin. He did not understand how Palo could capture their hearts, outwit and usually seduce them given that all women represented such deep mysteries. And now Palo would tell the woman that she was definitely a widow. In her grief, he would probably comfort and then seduce her.

Augustin happened to look up and see a shooting star. He smiled, enjoying the scent of the pines. He had not smelled them since they had crossed the Sierras and that seemed like a long, long time ago. Augustin well remembered a woman in California, a good woman like Mrs. Pike, who also had lost her husband. Augustin had found her very attractive and she had looked at him with what he had thought was real interest. But then, just when he had been about to pay her a social call, Palo had done it first and that was the end of the matter. No doubt, the same would happen with Mrs. Pike.

"Hey, Gus! What are you doing out there?" Palo said much too loudly because his words echoed up and down the mountainside.

"Smoking and thinking," Augustin answered, deciding that he ought to return to their camp before Palo shouted again and awakened every Indian for a hundred miles.

"I'm going to sleep," Palo announced. "You aren't thinking of keeping a watch all night, are you?"

Augustin hurried back to their camp. "I was."

"Hell, there isn't anything up here on this mountainside other than us, the mules, and a few wild animals. If there were Indians about, the mules would be braying."

"Maybe," Augustin said, thinking that Indians would be smart enough to stay downwind so that the mules would not catch their scent.

Palo yawned. "I am going to sleep."

"I'll wake you in time so I can get a few hours of sleep," Augustin said, giving his brother fair warning.

Palo muttered and immediately went to sleep. Augustin stayed awake as long as he could keep his chin off his chest. When that became impossible and he was tired of attempting to decide whether or not the woman had consented to wear Palo's religious medal, Augustin roused his brother and fell into a dreamless sleep.

The sun was well above the eastern horizon when Augustin roused into wakefulness. He lay still for quite some time and then he knuckled his eyes and sat up.

"You should have awakened me sooner, Palo," he said groggily. "We are not going to get a good start on this day, and that's for sure."

Palo didn't answer and when Augustin swayed to his feet, he saw why. Palo was slumbering and . . . and dammit! The mules were both gone!

"Holy Mary!" Augustin whispered, scooping up his rifle and hurrying over to boot his brother almost hard enough to break his ribs. "Palo! Palo, we have been robbed of our mules!"

Palo jerked into wakefulness, hand dropping to the six-gun on his hip. "Huh?"

"They're gone!" Augustin hissed. "Grab your gear and let's get after them!"

Palo didn't have to be told twice. He left his saddle and blankets, but snatched up his saddlebags as well as his rifle. Augustin was already hurrying up the mountainside, anxiously searching for tracks.

"Here!" he shouted when he came upon the slashed hobbles. "They went this way!"

The tracks were very fresh and, less than a mile up the steep slope, they came upon mule dump so fresh that it was still steaming in the cold mountain air.

"Look at that," Augustin said when they crested a divide and gazed out onto a mountain valley dissected by a fast-flowing stream. "These Indians aren't very concerned about pursuit."

Palo agreed because the brown valley grass was tall and they could easily identify the trails along which both Indians and mules had traveled. They appeared to be headed toward a big gorge up higher in the mountains.

Palo was already winded and it took him a moment to gasp, "How long are we going to chase 'em?"

"To hell and back, if we have to. You know what Xabin will say if we return to the Humboldt camp without our mules."

"Yeah," Palo said, "he'd have lots to say but there might be a lot of Indians up ahead."

"The wonder is that they didn't kill us in our sleep. Dammit, Palo, you were supposed to be on guard!"

"I must have nodded off."

"And it's going to cost us plenty."

"Maybe not. After all, these aren't Apache or Comanche warriors. They're just Diggers."

"That kind of thinking will get us killed for sure," Augustin argued. He decided it would be smart to skirt the valley and keep to the high brush where they had at least some cover in case they were attacked. "Palo, these so-called 'Digger' Indians have fought and killed a lot of emigrants. And while they might not be as dangerous as Kiowa or Apache, they've proven themselves to be damn fine horse and mule thieves."

Palo grumbled but had no reply as they moved forward at a slow, steady pace. Augustin thought they'd never get around the mountain valley, which was pretty as a picture with ample water and grass. Its upper end was ringed by a large stand of tall timber out of which tumbled the clear, icy stream. Augustin considered it all the more amazing that such a lush and picturesque country was hidden in the middle of a desert wilderness.

"This might be the kind of place that Xabin has been looking for us to settle in," Augustin told his brother the next time they stopped for a breather.

"Out here?" Palo straightened at the waist and gazed down at the basin. "Why, Gus, there isn't a white man or woman within five hundred miles of this valley!"

"That would suit me and Xabin just fine. But there's no time to waste. Let's hurry before we get so far behind we'll never overtake those mules."

When they finally passed around the big valley, they entered the rocky gorge they had seen much earlier. Its walls soon grew steep as the gorge narrowed. They could smell smoke and burning flesh.

"We're bound to be walking right into a trap," Palo told his brother in a hushed voice. "And, while I know that Xabin will skin us alive without those mules, I'm not ready to be ambushed and scalped."

"Shhh!"

Augustin crouched and listened.

"Do you hear something, Gus?"

"I think so. Stay low and be ready to shoot."

They left the Indian footpath they'd been following and struck directly through tall willows and bushes. Suddenly, Augustin detected movement and dropped to his knees. Palo did the same. They both crept forward and then flattened when they saw at least fifty Indians camped under the overhang of a water-stained cliff that was at least two hundred feet tall. At its base yawned the dark abyss of a huge cave where perhaps two dozen women and children could be seen huddled around a big fire.

"Holy Mary, they're roasting and eating our mules!" Augustin breathed, clenching his fists. "Xabin's going to *kill* us!"

"It's not Xabin that I'm worried about," Palo said, gripping his rifle. "What color did Libby say those horses were that her husband and son rode off on?"

Augustin's eyes shifted to the Indians' horse herd. Most of the animals were undersized and probably mustangs. But not the four Pike horses that Libby had carefully described. And not five other animals that were very obviously Thoroughbreds, unless Augustin was badly mistaken. They were magnificent horses, all black, four mares and a stallion.

"Now *those* are my kind of horses," Palo whispered.

"Yeah," Augustin agreed. "Some poor devil must have been planning on delivering them to California hoping to establish a racing stable or breeding ranch."

"What a waste of horseflesh."

Augustin thought about that for a moment.

"Maybe not. In a few years, their blood will have improved that of the mustangs."

"Nope," Palo said with conviction. "The blood of five Thoroughbreds would be like spit on the ocean. Wouldn't mean a thing and would all be diluted away. In ten years—or less—you wouldn't have seen even a trace of that Thoroughbred blood."

"Well," Augustin said, "I expect we've bigger things to worry about."

"Yeah. What do we do about those Pike horses?"

"I don't know," Augustin admitted. Augustin was not a man who made rash decisions, especially ones that were crucial.

"We've got to do *something*."

"We wait," Augustin finally said. "We wait until we find out if these Indians are holding Matthew inside that cave as a hostage."

"Not likely. But what if they are?"

Augustin removed his hat and flattened out on a slab of cold rock. He wished that Palo had some answers instead of so many questions.

"Well?" Palo demanded.

"Well then, dammit, Palo, we figure out some way to get the boy out of there!"

"And you said *I* was crazy!"

"You are," Augustin said, trying but failing to get comfortable as they began what he suspected might be a long, tedious vigil.

CHAPTER

NINE

It was almost sundown and Augustin was thinking they ought to begin their long walk back to the wagons when they finally saw Libby's son emerge from the Indians' dark cave. The boy was hobbled by a short length of rawhide.

"That's *got* to be him," Palo whispered.

"Shhh!"

They both watched as a short but powerful looking Paiute dressed in rabbit skins and carrying an old rifle escorted Matthew Pike down to the stream to drink. The boy appeared steady and in control of himself. He was dirty but warmly dressed.

"Gus, what are we supposed to do now?"

"I don't know."

Palo eased his rifle forward. "I could drill that guard and . . ."

"No!" Augustin shook his head. "Don't even think about it."

"Why not? If I shoot him, the boy might be able to reach us before they cut him down."

"He's hobbled! He'd never make it and neither would we."

"You can't be sure. Gus, I could drill that Paiute right through the heart at this range. You could run down there, cut the kid's hobbles, and we'd be on our way back to the Humboldt before those Indians knew what hit 'em."

"We'd never make it out of this canyon alive. The Paiutes would overtake and kill us. We're in no shape for a footrace."

"Maybe not," Palo grudgingly conceded. "The kid wouldn't be able to keep up."

"I wasn't talking about the kid," Augustin said as the guard prodded Matthew back toward the cave.

"There he goes," Palo said, "back inside. We'll never get him now."

"I'm not willing to say that."

Palo frowned and scratched the stubble of his beard. "Maybe we should return to the Humboldt and get Xabin and the other pair of mules. We could . . ."

"No," Augustin said, shaking his head. "Xabin wouldn't risk leaving his flock or losing our last two mules. And, once we told Mrs. Pike about finding her son, she'd probably come running and get *us* killed trying to save her."

"Gus, you're a real drench of cold water. From the way you've just outlined this predicament, we might as well give the kid up and sneak back to our flock like a pair of whipped dogs."

"Not yet. We're just going to have to figure out some way to better the odds."

"Fine. And when you get around to figuring that out, wake me up and tell me all about your great plan," Palo said, rolling over on his back and closing his eyes. " 'Cause, to my way of thinking, the only way to free the Pike kid is to shoot his guard the next time they come down for a drink, then make a running fight of it."

"Go to sleep, Palo."

"You ought to do the same. You look awful."

Palo fell asleep almost instantly. Augustin ate a piece of cheese and some bread while the Indians huddled around their big roasting fire. Shadowy fire-dancers cavorted across a stage of stone. Augustin's exhausted mind played tricks on him and the fire-dancers took on a mesmerizing and ethereal quality as they weaved a silent, ghostly dance upon the pocked face of the high, rough cliff.

"Damn!" Augustin muttered, pressing his thumbs against his temples hard enough to cause pain. He shook his head and refocused, driving away the demons of his twisted imagination. Augustin thought he could identify Matthew Pike but the boy had been shoved deeper into the murky shadows.

Augustin reasoned that, because Matthew was hobbled and closely guarded, he must have attempted at least one escape. Augustin just hoped that the boy was blessed with his mother's spunk because he was sure going to need it if he had any chance of surviving this ordeal.

The night took on a deep chill. Augustin shivered a little, envious of the Paiutes' warm fire. Soon, weariness overcame shivering and Augustin's eyelids began to droop. At first, he struggled to stay awake, but soon abandoned that as being impossible. So he closed his eyes because his mind and body felt drugged. Augustin told himself that he would need to be in possession of all of his faculties if he was to think of some way to free the boy and engineer a safe return back to the Humboldt River. Furthermore, Augustin was sure that he and his brother were in no danger of being discovered because of their excellent hiding place and the fact that these Indians didn't seem to be at all concerned about an attack.

And why should they be? Their numbers were so large that only a pair of total fools would attempt to retaliate. Furthermore, in the Indians' minds, there would be no connection between the boy and the unwary pair who'd allowed their mules to be taken while they slept.

Augustin awoke hungry with the sun. He rolled

over, knuckling his eyes and yawning. The Indians had
refueled their bonfire and were getting ready to roast
more mule meat. Augustin's empty belly rumbled with
envy and he dug into the saddlebags for some bread and
cheese. There wasn't much.

The Paiutes were smiling and crowding around the
fire with hunks of bloody meat impaled at the end of
long, green branches. When they began to roast the
meat, the aroma was so tantalizing that Augustin's
mouth watered. A man could not live on bread and
cheese, especially without wine.

The sun finally warmed the air and the Indians
gorged. Augustin paid attention, noting that they did
not even bother to guard their horse herd. What would
these Indians do with the draft horses and Thoroughbreds? Trade them for weapons, blankets, or some other
goods? That seemed very likely because the Paiutes or
Shoshones, Augustin didn't know which these were,
would certainly not roast that superior horseflesh. He
hoped.

Palo began to stir into wakefulness.

"We need to stampede that herd and get those
Thoroughbreds and Mrs. Pike's four wagon horses
back," Augustin decided out loud as his mind again
grappled with the issue of rescue and then escape.

"Huh?"

Palo squinted up into the sun. He yawned,
scratched, and then rolled over to stare at Augustin.
"Any sign of the boy this morning?"

"I think I can see him just inside the cave."

"Have you figured out what we are going to do
besides lay here until we die of boredom or starvation?"

"We've got to stampede *all* their horses," Augustin
said. "If we can drive off the mustangs and then mount
those Thoroughbreds, we stand a good chance of getting back to the river alive."

"Hell yes we would! And, after that, we could gallop clear over to San Francisco on those Thoroughbreds," Palo said sarcastically.

Augustin wasn't listening. "But I expect that Thoroughbred stallion might be a handful."

Augustin felt a little hopeful this morning. Sunlight always brought more hope than darkness. "Palo," he began, "I think we should try to capture and ride those tall Thoroughbred mares. Then we could drive the stallion along with Mrs. Pike's four big horses, and as many of the mustangs as we could hold together. Drive the whole bunch right back down to the Humboldt."

"Sounds good except that the draft animals would slow all of us down," Palo complained. "And, if any of the mustangs escaped—as they are likely to do—the Indians would catch us on 'em."

Augustin reluctantly agreed. Even at this distance, it was very evident that the Pike horses were heavy boned and built more for pulling than running. They'd be slow, all right.

"Well, then," Augustin said, thinking out loud, "we'll just have to get every last animal running for the river."

"And if the mustangs break off?"

"Then we scatter 'em into the hills."

Palo shook his head. "That sounds like a damn tall order considering we're trying to save our scalps as well as that of the kid."

"I agree," Augustin said. "That's why we had better expect a lively chase."

"I like our chances with us on Thoroughbreds and them on foot."

"Me too. But I'm worried about these Indians taking revenge on our camp. They could raise hell with our flock."

"And pick us off, one after the next."

"Yep," Augustin solemnly agreed, "but it's a chance we have to take. Having seen the kid, we can't turn our backs on him now."

"All right," Palo said. "When do we strike?"

"When they bring Matthew out for a drink, same time as last evening."

"And if they don't?"

"I expect that they will," Augustin predicted. "Everyone I ever knew lived according to their daily habits. I'm betting that they let the boy drink, stretch his legs, and do his personal business every evening."

"We'll just wait and see."

"No," Augustin said. "Starting now, we're going to get ourselves in position. One of us has to hit the herd, the other go for the kid."

"I'll take the horses," Palo offered. "Seems like the healthier thing to do. What about the kid's hobbles?"

"I'll have to throw him a knife and hope he doesn't freeze," Augustin answered. "And then we'll both have to run for your horses."

"The whole plan sounds shakier than hell."

"You got a better one?"

"I guess not."

Augustin glanced up at the sky. "Nary a cloud. I sure wish it was fixing to storm. Might give us a little edge. Palo, you'd better start crawling. Get as close to the horses as you possibly can before sundown."

"Gus, I haven't even got a catch rope, let alone bridles or reins."

"Figure some way to catch and bridle us a pair of horses after they've stampeded," Augustin said without sympathy, "unless you'd rather take your chances snatching the boy."

Palo shook his head. "The way I see things, dead is dead and that's most likely what we'll *both* be after attempting this great scheme."

"*Now* who is a drench of cold water?"

Palo managed a weak grin. "Before we part, I want to say that it's been a pleasure just knowing you, Gus."

"Get out of here," Augustin growled. "And I don't care how you do it, but get us a pair of horses to ride. Any pair. The Thoroughbreds, if you can, but if not, a pair of those big wagon horses or even a couple of well-broke mustangs. Just have them ready when we come running to meet you down near the mouth of this gorge."

Palo opened his mouth to say something, then changed his mind and began to slither toward the stream, which, as far as Augustin could tell, emerged from the base of the cliff. The gorge was still draped in morning shadows and that would help to conceal movement until they could both get into position. Even so, Augustin thought their chances of grabbing the kid and surviving were slim to none.

Dusk found Augustin curled up behind rocks within fifty feet of where the boy had come to drink the evening before. Augustin had lost sight of Palo but knew his brother must be hiding somewhere near the horses. The Indians had kept their cooking fire going all day and twice Augustin had almost been discovered by women collecting firewood. Augustin had emptied then concealed both rifles under some brush and rocks, knowing that he would have to rely on his six-gun. Grabbing Matthew, cutting away the boy's thick rawhide hobbles, and then making a desperate run for the mouth of the gorge and the waiting horses would not only require extraordinary luck, but also the use of both hands.

Earlier that afternoon, Augustin's heart had begun to race when six or seven of the Indians left the cave and rode their mustangs away. Soon after their disappearance, Augustin heard the echo of rifle fire. At first, he'd nearly panicked, believing that the warriors had flushed and then killed Palo. Augustin had suffered mental agony for the next two hours until the hunters had returned with two slender does, which their women quickly butchered and added to the roasting fire.

Now, the sun was long past the rim of the canyon leaving everything in deepening shadow. The air was turning cold and Augustin knew it would soon be dark. And just when he was beginning to lose hope of seeing the boy, two figures emerged in the heavy gloom. Augustin recognized Matthew's silhouette and there was no mistaking the boy's awkward shuffling. The same stocky guard was bringing the boy down to the water and Augustin could distinguish a rifle cradled in his arms. It would be loaded and Augustin took for granted that the Indian could hit whatever he aimed for.

Augustin unholstered his Colt. He felt slightly sick and did not know if this was caused by lack of food, sleep, or gut-chewing fear. He said a quick, silent prayer and, as the light began to fail, squinted, trying hard to see if Palo was sneaking into the horse herd. But Augustin saw nothing and the horses gave no indication of being bothered. Where was Palo! If he had not managed to reach the horses, what sense was there in making a try to grab Matthew Pike? Without horses, they would be slaughtered. Augustin could still see Elias Pike's bullet-riddled and mutilated corpse lying in the brush. The vision made his blood run cold.

The twilight was suddenly shattered like crystal by the explosion of Palo's six-gun. Augustin saw the shadowy figures of Indians leaping away from their cave fire. He heard women shriek and men shout. An instant later, muzzle flashes flickered like candles. Augustin jumped up and sprinted for the boy.

"Matthew!"

The boy had been kneeling beside the stream. Now, his head shot up and he saw Augustin. With a cry of his own, he tried to run. Thin arms flailing, he charged for the stream, shuffling and hopping and falling.

The guard shrieked a warning, which was drowned in the thunder of beating hooves and gunfire. Augustin saw the guard lift his rifle and he aimed his own Colt. They both fired at the exact same instant. Augustin's shot went wide, the guard's bullet burned past Augustin's face, and both raced forward. But the guard was closer. Augustin tried to thumb back the hammer of his six-gun and fire again as the guard overtook Matthew. He even shouted an unintelligible warning as the Indian whipped the butt of his rifle downward. When it struck the back of Matthew's skull, a bone-crunching sound caused Augustin's hair to stand on end.

"No!" he bellowed, firing again and watching the guard slam over backward.

When Augustin finally reached Matthew, the boy was probably dead. There was no time to be sure. Augustin jammed his six-gun into his holster. He bent to pick up Matthew, but a bullet hit his upper left arm and he staggered. Augustin looked up to see a wave of howling Indians charging toward him. There was nothing to do but turn and run for his life. He crashed blindly into the brush, fighting it like he would a wild beast. He broke through, fell, climbed up and ran blindly onward toward the mouth of the gorge. His own tearing breath and pounding heart did not drown out the sound of the Indians close on his heels.

"Palo!" he gasped. "Palo!"

Palo appeared astride the Thoroughbred stallion like a dark angel of mercy. Even more amazing was that he led two extra horses, also tall Thoroughbreds. The mares were crazy with excitement. Augustin tried to grab one of them but she began to whirl and spin, trying to escape.

"Go!" Augustin shouted. "My arm, I've been shot!"

But Palo jumped from the stallion and somehow managed to help Augustin onto the back of one of the mares. The stallion broke free, then the other horse, so Palo swung up behind his brother and turned their mount toward the desert.

"Hang on!" he shouted into Augustin's ear.

Augustin *did* hang on. His left arm felt numb and he could feel a river of warm blood flowing down his fingers into the mare's mane, which he clenched with all his might.

"What happened to the boy!"

Augustin was so overwhelmed by his sense of failure that he was unable to speak.

"Never mind!" Palo shouted.

Augustin was not an accomplished rider. It was all that he could do to hang on to the mare while it pounded down the gorge. When they overtook the horse herd, Palo began to shout and fire his gun. He had fashioned a simple Indian bridle around the muzzle of the mare and the crude reins were enough to guide their mount so that they could drive the entire horse herd across the mountain meadow and on down the mountain to the Humboldt.

At some point, Palo drew in the mare and mounted one of Mrs. Pike's draft animals. He twisted around and yelped in triumph.

"I got *all* of them stampeded out of there, Gus! Those beaten devils will never catch us now!"

Augustin could not share his brother's elation. The air was cold, the moon a wedge of shimmering gold, and the stars brilliant and brittle as ice pellets. He stammered his painful confession. "I fired but missed the boy's guard and that cost him his life, Palo."

"Don't talk about it now."

"The guard smashed Matthew's skull with his damned rifle! I heard it crack like the shell of an egg. I should have stopped and taken careful aim. If I'd have done that, maybe . . ."

"How bad are you hit?" Palo interrupted. "We should bandage that arm."

"It is not so bad."

"There is blood all over the shoulder of your horse," Palo argued.

Augustin expelled a deep, ragged breath and whispered, "Just like there is blood all over this hard land."

"Rein up!"

The horses stopped. Palo dismounted and Augustin sat still on the sweaty, steaming mare. He could see the stallion racing back and forth among his mares. The mustangs were already breaking away to flee back into the hills, their paths marked by wisps of dust floating against moonlight.

"Get down," Palo ordered.

"You always did like to give the orders."

"But I never had much practice," Palo said, gently easing Augustin from his horse. "Now, let's get your coat off and bandage that arm."

Augustin was too weak and heartsick to argue.

"You are right, Gus, it is not so bad," Palo said after a quick examination. "I think you have too much blood anyway."

"The Basques have always shed a lot of blood."

Palo tore his silk handkerchief into strips and bound the arm. "Don't bleed so much anymore or you will faint and then I will have to leave you behind."

"Okay."

"Here," Palo said bending low and cupping his hands. "Put your boot in my hand and climb back on your horse. We have a long way to ride yet."

Augustin grunted with pain when he was hoisted back on the hot mare. "What am I going to say to that woman, Palo? That I had a chance to save her son but missed my aim and saw his skull crushed?"

"Tell her the boy died quickly and . . . and that he was very brave," Palo said, remounting. "And that you did your best to save his life. That we *both* did our best."

"But . . ."

"Never mind all of that!" Palo was really angry. "Don't you tell her anything. *I* will tell her instead."

Augustin nodded with relief. Palo had a way with words, guns, and women. He would do it much better.

CHAPTER

TEN

It was almost sundown the next day when Augustin and Palo finally drove the horses into camp. Shouting with excitement, Xabin, Libby, and Fay hurried out to meet them.

"Where'd you get those Thoroughbreds!" Xabin yelled, head swiveling back and forth as he took stock of the new arrivals. Before Palo could answer, Xabin demanded, "And what happened to my mules!"

Palo dismounted, eyes touching Libby, then returning to his father. "Long story. Augustin has been shot."

"It's nothing," Augustin said, but he almost toppled from the horse and, when they helped him dismount, he realized his legs were as weak as those of a newborn lamb. "I'll be fine. Just a flesh wound."

"It's more than that," Palo said, helping support his brother on the way into the sheep wagon.

Libby could tell by the sallow color of Augustin's skin that he had lost too much blood. She wanted to ask about her husband and son but knew those questions could wait a few minutes until this brave man had received proper care. The canvas-topped sheep wagon was surprisingly comfortable with a potbellied stove near the front Dutch doors and two long, hinged-top side benches to sit, eat, or sleep upon. Under the side benches were immense storage spaces where the shepherds packed supplies, blankets, and utensils.

"Put him on my bed," Xabin ordered. "Easy now, son. Just try to get comfortable."

"I'll be fine," Augustin assured them, although he did not look fine at all.

Libby rolled up her sleeves and surveyed her surroundings with a trace of envy. The Arostegi wagon was weathertight and there wasn't a square inch of wasted space. Libby had to admit that it was a far more comfortable home than their faithful Conestoga.

"We'll need some hot water and bandages," she told the two men. "Palo, is the bullet still buried inside Augustin's arm?"

"I don't know. It was dark when I wrapped my bandanna around the wound and there was no time to strike a match and have a close look."

"Are the Indians coming?" Xabin asked, backing outside and peering back through the doorway.

"They might be."

"Then I'll have our dogs crowd the sheep in close."

Palo wiped a hand across his sweat and dust-streaked face. He looked to have aged ten years. "After I'm through helping Libby, I'll help you load all the weapons and get ready for an attack. Gus and I hit 'em hard last evening."

"Where are your rifles?"

"Had to leave them," Palo said, eyes dropping to his hands.

"You left them!" Xabin exclaimed. "In two days, you've cost me a couple of good Sharps rifles and prime mules!"

"Pa, we had *no* choice." Palo's hands knotted into fists. "Dammit, Augustin was wounded! We barely escaped with our lives. And besides, the Thoroughbreds we took from the Indians are worth far more than the rifles and mules we lost."

Xabin wagged his shaggy head back and forth. "Not to me they're not."

Augustin had apparently heard more than enough. "Father, leave Palo alone. *I'm* the one that got us into that fix, not Palo."

Xabin's anger washed away. "All right, it looks like we're sure going to need those two rifles when the Indians attack."

Libby had heard more than enough wrangling. "Mr. Arostegi, will you *please* go away! Fay, help him get some water to boiling."

"Yes, Mother."

"And don't let him bully or shout at you."

"No, Mother."

Muttering imprecations, Xabin disappeared. Augustin gazed up at Libby saying, "Don't be too upset with our father."

"It's hard not to be. His concern ought to be for you, not for a couple of mules and rifles."

"He knows that I'm too ornery to die young."

Libby unwound the bloody bandanna and studied the damage. At least the wound had stopped bleeding.

"How's it look?"

"I think the bullet nicked a vein."

"No wonder I bled so much."

"If it had been an artery, you'd most likely have bled to death."

"Is the bullet still in my arm?"

Libby gently lifted the arm and studied it closely. "No. Here's the exit wound."

Augustin sighed with relief. "Good. That simplifies things. Why don't you just bandage it again so that I can fight if we are attacked tonight."

"Do you think that will happen?"

"I don't know." Augustin looked at Palo. "We don't even know if they're Paiutes or Shoshones. I've heard that both tribes claim this basin."

"I thought it was the Paiutes that had taken our horses," Libby said.

"They could just as easy have been the Shoshone." Augustin took a deep breath. "Mrs. Pike, Palo and I have something to tell you."

Libby's heart dropped. Not trusting her voice, she whispered, "I have a feeling that you found Elias and Matthew."

"I'm afraid so."

"Maybe," Palo said, leaning between them. "It would be better to go into that outside—after you are finished here."

"Yes," Libby said, trying to keep her voice even, "Palo, you are quite right. Now, would you please get me some water and rags?"

"Sure," Palo said, looking a little hurt and disappointed. "But . . ."

"*Warm* water would be better," Libby interrupted.

"Okay," Palo said, backing out of the wagon.

Augustin's eyes never left Libby's face. He watched tears begin to slide down the woman's cheeks and when they were alone, said, "Mrs. Pike, if it's any comfort, neither one suffered."

Libby scrubbed the back of her hand across her eyes. "Thank you."

"We found your husband up in the hills and buried him proper."

Augustin had no intention of telling her about the condition of Mr. Pike's mutilated body. "And we saw Matthew in the Indian camp. I tried to grab your son but an Indian clubbed him with his rifle's butt."

Libby had been staring at a place on the canvas, but now her head suddenly snapped back. "Did you say, 'clubbed him'?"

"That's right. And by the time I shot the Indian and reached Matthew's side, it was just too late."

"But you can't be *sure* that Matthew was dead, can you?"

"I'm *pretty* sure," he said, wondering what she was

driving at. "I mean, the light was poor so I couldn't see real well but I heard the sound of the club breaking your son's skull. He wasn't even twitching when I tried to scoop him up. That's when I got a bullet in the arm and had to run. I'm sorry, but I couldn't help him."

"Augustin, don't feel so badly. From what you've told me, Matthew might only have been knocked unconscious."

"Oh, no, ma'am! He was *brained*."

"But he could still be alive!"

Libby's words caused Augustin's heart to sink. Maybe he should even have lied and said that the boy had been shot to death. Creating false hopes was no kindness. None at all. And now, dammit, he could see the woman actually trembling with excitement. "Listen, Mrs. Pike."

"Libby," she corrected, "and are you absolutely sure that Elias was dead?"

"He'd better have been because we buried him."

She dipped her chin in acceptance. And just when Augustin thought she was going to turn the talk back to Matthew, she said, "And why didn't you bring in my husband's body?"

"We were tracking Indians and figured it was a whole lot more important to do everything we could to find your son."

"I see." Libby nodded. "Yes, that was certainly the right thing to do under those very extreme circumstances."

"Yes, ma'am."

"Please, call me Libby. You and Palo proved yourself my dear friends when you risked your lives trying to rescue my family."

"I should have been able to rescue that boy and deliver him back here alive."

"Augustin, I'm sure that you did everything humanly possible and I'll be eternally grateful."

"But I missed my shot and it cost your son his life."

Libby shook her head emphatically. "I'm just not

willing to accept that Matthew is dead. I've felt from the beginning that Elias was killed but that my son had survived. Nothing you've just told me alters that conviction."

"But I was there and I heard and saw what happened! I know you want to believe he's alive, but wishing won't make it so—it'll only drag out the pain."

"Augustin, you heard gunfire and shouting. You were fighting for your life and things were happening very fast. There was confusion and the light was failing. Who could blame you for not being able to help Matthew out of that terrible fight or to think he was dead when he really was not?"

"But . . ."

Libby clasped her hands together and breathed deeply. "Augustin, please say no more. I choose to believe that my son *is* alive."

Augustin digested that and while he knew that he ought to drop the subject, there was something important that he had to confess. Something that just might get through to this poor woman.

"Libby, I was away when my own mother died years ago. I was with Fremont and the Americans and we were a wild bunch bound to seize California from the Mexicans. When word came about my mother dying, I wouldn't believe it. Someone else's mother had died, not mine. I left the fighting and started for home believing with all my heart that I'd find her still rocking on the porch the way she liked in nice weather."

"But . . ."

"Let me finish," Augustin insisted. "You believing that Matthew is dead is the same as I felt about my mother. I hurt myself by not accepting the truth. Wishing and hoping just made losing Mother all the harder. Don't you see what I'm trying to save you from?"

"Of course. But that was far different."

"Not so I can see it." Augustin started to say more but just then, Xabin appeared. "Here's some water. It isn't very warm yet, but I figured that you needed some in a hurry."

"This will do for a start," Libby said.

Xabin looked closely at his son. "Augustin, did they really *eat* my mules?"

"I'm afraid so."

The old sheepman slammed his fist against the door so hard that the entire wagon shook. "Gawddamn them!"

Augustin pushed himself up on his elbows. "Those people were ragged and hungry. I'm not making excuses, but their women and children looked half starved."

"I can't help that! The wonder is that they didn't also eat those Thoroughbreds."

"They'd recognize such exceptional animals," Augustin said.

"Yeah, I suppose they would."

Augustin turned to Libby. "Mrs. Pike, your draft horses are thin, but they're still sound enough to pull your wagon."

"That's a blessing."

Xabin scrubbed his stubbly beard. "So I guess you'll be returning to Salt Lake once we get everything in good traveling repair."

Libby did not bat an eyelash when she said, "Mr. Arostegi, we're not going back to Salt Lake City."

"What?"

"You heard me," Libby said. "I've no intention of returning east."

"You have to! That forty-mile desert is a killer and who is to say that you won't run into more Indians on your way to California?"

Libby supposed that she might as well get it all out. "We're not going to California, either."

Augustin stared. Xabin's jaw dropped and he stammered, "Well . . . well where the hell *are* you going!"

Libby squeezed her hands together so hard that her knuckles turned white. "I haven't decided."

"Are you addled?" Xabin asked, concern replacing amazement.

"No," Libby said. "At least, I don't think so."

Xabin made a visible effort to be reasonable. "Mrs. Pike, you got a fine little girl to think about. You can't afford to make another bad mistake."

"Where are *you* going?"

The question caught him by surprise. "Huh?"

"You heard me." Libby's chin lifted. "I asked where you, your sons, and this flock of sheep are going."

"Don't know for certain."

"Well," Libby said, "I'll give you the same answer. *I* don't know for certain either."

"I think you *are* addled," Xabin said looking disgusted as he backed out of the wagon.

"Mr. Arostegi, my son is still alive and I won't abandon him."

"He's dead! Your son was brained."

"No!"

Xabin composed himself. "Mrs. Pike, I'm real sorry, but Palo just told me everything that happened in that Indian camp. You've got to get a better grip on your mind."

But Libby wasn't listening. Turning back to Augustin with the basin of water cradled in her hands, she said, "It would help if I stitched up this wound."

"Why?"

"The bullet tore a nasty gash. The wound would heal better and faster if I could sew the flesh together with a needle and thread. We had both in the wagon before the Indians sacked it. But maybe I could use a fish hook and some line."

"I'd rather you just cleaned it out and bound it up tight as anything. It'll be just fine that way."

"You'll have a much bigger scar."

"Doesn't matter. I got scars everywhere anyway."

"Very well," Libby said. "And while I do that, would you mind telling me exactly how my boy is looking?"

Augustin closed his eyes. "Well, he was . . ."

"*Is*," Libby corrected. "Not was."

"He *is* kind of thin."

"Yes, but isn't Matthew handsome?" Libby finished cleaning and bandaging the wound. Then she turned back toward the door and called, "Fay!"

The little girl appeared almost instantly. "Yes, Mother?"

"I have some very good news. Matthew *isn't* dead."

Her eyes widened with surprise, then joy. "He isn't?"

"No. I'm sure that he was just knocked unconscious."

"Oh, Mama!" Fay rushed into the wagon and hugged her mother.

Watching them, Augustin felt nothing but pity.

"When can we see him?"

"Not for a while. For the time being, it would be better just now not to risk anyone else's life. Matthew *is* hurt but I have read that the Indians use very powerful natural medicines. They'll take care of Matthew, perhaps even better than we could. And they'll help him recover as good as new."

"When will we be able to get him back?"

"I'm thinking next spring, if not sooner."

"But Father is dead, isn't he?"

"Yes, and they gave him a decent Christian burial." Libby's eyebrows arched in Augustin's direction. "You did say a few words over my husband, didn't you?"

"We sure did."

She patted his good arm. "Fay, run along while I finish up here. I'll join you soon. We have a lot to be thankful for when we say our prayers tonight."

Augustin waited until the little girl was gone before speaking his mind to this headstrong woman. "Xabin was right when he said you can't stay out here alone and unprotected. You have to either return to Salt Lake, or find someone to escort you to California."

"And leave Matthew? Never!"

Augustin gave up. Xabin was right, the poor woman was completely addled.

"Before you make any more plans, Libby, I think we're leaving this river."

"Leaving it? For where?"

"To those mountains off to the east. We found a valley and maybe even a new homestead."

Libby was incredulous. "Are you serious?"

"Completely."

"But I thought you were driving this flock to Utah to sell to the Mormons."

"Nope."

Libby didn't understand this at all and confusion must have shown on her face.

"It's a long story," Augustin said, struggling to keep his eyes open. "And not a very happy one. We got into some trouble. We're Basque sheepmen and California already belongs to the settlers and the cattlemen. We need lots of land and we need it cheap."

"But *this* kind of land?" Libby could not believe anyone would settle in this dangerous, sage-covered wilderness of their own free choice, but that's what Augustin seemed to be implying.

"You see," Augustin began, forcing his eyes open, "our sheep can thrive out here where no one would ever attempt to farm or plow. And I saw a fine mountain valley when we were tracking those Indians. It had grass, water, and lots of surrounding timber. It was blessed with everything we would need to build a sheep empire. Up in these mountains, we'd never have to worry about cattlemen or farmers again."

Libby's brow knit. "What about the Indians?"

"Maybe we could make peace," Augustin said. "Those people were in pretty tough shape. You should have seen the way they devoured our mules."

"And might do the same again after killing all of us."

"Yes," Augustin admitted. "Don't forget that I buried your husband and I'm not about to underestimate the danger. But at the same time, from what little you've told me about Mr. Pike, I expect that he overtook the Indians and opened fire. He probably even shot a few before they got to him."

"I expect that Elias did."

Libby studied Augustin before saying, "For someone that has just been shot by Indians and barely escaped with his life, you have a curious attitude."

Augustin yawned. "I have dealt with the few Californians left after the Spaniards, Mexicans, and Americans finished with them. They generally have sound reasons for wanting to kill whites. I've heard that the Indians in these parts have themselves been murdered by the emigrants, especially the forty-niners."

"Why don't you go on to Utah or Wyoming?"

"There are even more hostile Indians up in that country," Augustin told her. "And their winters are far worse. Besides, if we could make peace with the Indians in this country and build a ranch in the valley that Palo and I found, then we could sell sheep to the California emigrants. Maybe a few cattle and horses as well. The big gold rush is over, but an even greater strike has been found in a place called the Comstock Lode so I expect that more will keep coming."

"Have you told Xabin about these thoughts?"

"No, but I will. My father has a curious mind. He will want to see this valley for himself. Once that happens, he'll know that it is the right place for us to settle down once and for all."

"If the Indians do not kill you," Libby said, immediately regretting the remark.

"They're on foot and couldn't possibly get here until late tomorrow," Augustin predicted as he sat up and examined the bandage on his arm. "Ma'am, you need sleep."

"So do you," Libby said, noting the dark hollows around his eyes as she gently pushed him back down on the bed. "You and Palo are exhausted. But you look worse than your brother because of the blood you've lost."

"Rested or tired, Palo will always look better'n me. Now, hand me my pistol before I fall asleep."

"I thought you said that the Indians couldn't possibly arrive before late tomorrow."

"Sometimes I make mistakes," Augustin admitted with a wry grin.

Libby placed Augustin's Colt at his side and turned to leave.

"Watch out for Palo," Augustin whispered as his eyelids drooped. "We both think you are beautiful and now you are a widow."

She shrugged. "That changes nothing."

One of Augustin's eyelids struggled open. "We will see, Libby. We will see."

A moment later, Augustin was snoring. Libby retreated from the wagon with the washbasin. She tossed the crimson-colored water into the brush. Xabin and Palo had a large fire blazing and beyond its yellow circle the night was very dark.

Fay hurried over to her mother and hugged her waist. "I'm so happy about Matthew but sad about father."

Libby knelt, setting the washbasin aside. She wrapped Fay in her arms and breathed in the sage. "It's going to be all right," she promised with Augustin's lofty vision of a sheep empire weighing heavily on her mind. "I have a very good feeling that everything is going to be just fine."

"And the Indians won't kill us like they did Pa?"

"No," she said, finding comfort in the sharp barks of Lata and Emo, the now familiar bleating of the sheep, and the occasional shouts of Xabin and Palo as they brought the flock in close to bed down during the long anxious night to come.

CHAPTER
ELEVEN

Augustin awoke early the next morning, just as the sun was struggling to break off the purple skyline of eastern mountains. He felt a dull ache in his arm and it was stiff, but he knew it would heal just fine. Libby and Fay were asleep on the side benches of the wagon and Augustin allowed himself a few precious moments to watch them. They shared the same straight nose, wide, generous mouth, and determined jawline. Fay was going to be taller and not quite as sturdily built as her mother but the girl had inherited plenty of spunk and determination.

Augustin fixed his gaze on Libby and noted faint worry lines etched across her brow. They didn't detract at all from Libby's appearance and neither did the small scar on her right cheekbone. The amazing thing was that Libby didn't have a lot more worry lines, given the ordeal that she'd just suffered.

It would be nice, Augustin thought, to have such a wife and daughter. Augustin could not help but ask himself if they possibly might become his wife and daughter.

"Probably not," he whispered, knowing that if Libby stayed around for a while, Palo would win her heart. Anyway, the best thing for Libby and Fay would be to go away because, even if a genuine and lasting peace could be made with the Indians, the mountain valley of Augustin's dreams was too rough and isolated. Libby and her daughter deserved to live in a town with a church, a school, and shops where they could visit and enjoy the company of other wives and children.

Augustin swung his feet to the floor, then tiptoed out of the wagon. Xabin was waiting. The old man was tending his biscuits and frying lamb chops and potatoes. Augustin did not fail to notice that three loaded rifles and two Colt revolvers were propped up and in easy reach.

"Are you hungry, son?"

"I am." Augustin looked around. "Where is Palo?"

"Sleeping under the wagon." Xabin used a glove to lift the lid of his oven. "Biscuits are done and so are the chops. Grab a plate, pour some coffee, and get to eating. Damned Indians could hit us at any minute."

Augustin took his breakfast and ate without comment. He was famished and Xabin just sat smoking until Augustin had finally consumed his fill.

"When will they come?" Xabin asked, tossing Augustin the makings for a cigarette after he'd finished his meal.

Augustin rolled his smoke and then used a brand from the fire to light it. The tobacco was so strong that it made him feel giddy in his weakened physical state. He smoked for a few moments and said, "I'm not even sure that the Indians will come."

"You killed some of them and stole all their horses. Why *wouldn't* they attack?"

Augustin shrugged. "I don't know. But they could have killed Mrs. Pike and her daughter at any time after they stole her horses. And they could have killed young Matthew instead of taking him captive."

"But they *did* kill Elias Pike."

"That's probably because he shot a couple." Augustin glanced up from the fire. "If you ask me, those Indians are a whole lot more interested in stealing than in killing."

"So you think they will only come to steal our livestock and sheep?"

"Yes, if they come at all. And they'll want their horse herd back."

Xabin considered that for several minutes before saying, "If we give back Mrs. Pike's horses or those Thoroughbreds, they'll think us weak and rob us until we've nothing left."

"I know that."

"So we fight!"

"But maybe," Augustin said, "we can strike a deal."

"What kind of a 'deal'?" Xabin asked suspiciously.

"We'll give them back all the mustangs that didn't run away into the hills last night."

"But no more mules, or Mrs. Pike's draft horses or those fine Thoroughbreds."

"That's right."

Xabin poured himself more coffee. "Can you believe that crazy woman saying that she won't leave until she has her son?"

Augustin said nothing.

Xabin squinted across the smoky fire. "The boy *is* dead, isn't he?"

"I think so."

"Last night you said he *was* dead."

"Maybe I was wrong," Augustin answered. "If so, we will trade sheep for the boy."

"Not *my* sheep, we don't!"

"Then mine," Augustin growled.

Xabin brooded for several minutes, then said, "Your mistake was in not telling that woman her son was definitely dead."

"And what if he isn't?"

"He is dead, all right. I think that you just want the woman to stay with us."

"Sure," Augustin admitted, "I'd like that."

"But so would Palo."

"I don't care about Palo!" Augustin lowered his voice. "Go or stay, it's Libby's choice, not ours."

"Why?"

"Why?" Augustin demanded. "Because we can't just run the woman and her daughter off. Even you wouldn't do that to save a few damned sheep."

Xabin muttered into his coffee cup and Augustin didn't want to hear the old man's words. "Father," he said, "did Palo tell you about the big mountain valley?"

"A little."

"We could prosper there. It has everything we'd ever need to raise sheep."

"Including starving Indians to steal and eat them."

Augustin ignored the sarcastic remark. He launched into a flattering description of the mountain valley that had so impressed him in spite of very grim circumstances. Knowing the way of Xabin's mind, Augustin listed the various types of grasses and feed that would nourish and fatten their sheep.

Augustin ended by saying, "Father, it is exactly such a place that you have always talked about and . . . perhaps best of all . . . it is too remote to attract the attention of ranchers and farmers."

The sheepman poured himself more coffee and Augustin knew he had the old man's complete attention. Finally, Xabin said, "So this is why you hope to make peace with these thieving Indians."

"Yes," Augustin confessed. "But consider this—we have already fought with the cattlemen and the settlers. I think our chances are better with these Indians."

"Who would always steal us blind."

"Not if we give them a few sheep every week."

"Every week!"

"Or two," Augustin quickly added.

"That could be more than a hundred each year!"

"But they would only be the weak among the thousands of healthy," Augustin countered. "I promise you our flock would multiply like locusts. We could even use the sheep as payment to the Indians for protection."

"Maybe you've been eating locoweed!"

Augustin refilled his coffee cup. "No."

"That would never work," Xabin said, making a sour face.

"It could, if we do not shoot them before we bargain for peace. Father, these people are not stupid, just hungry. They might be made to see the wisdom of getting to eat two of our fat sheep every week."

"Oh, now it is *fat* sheep!"

"When you see the valley I've just told you about with your own eyes, then you will know it is the kind of place where you have dreamed of settling all your life. In such a place, far from all others except a few Indian friends, we could prosper in peace."

"So you say."

"I *do* say! And, in the winter, if there were ever deep snows, we could trail the bands down to this river. In the spring, after the lambs, we could sell our fattened old rams, ewes, and our wethers to the emigrants for mutton."

"What makes you think they would eat mutton?"

"They would!" Augustin exclaimed. "If the Comstock strike is as great as everyone thinks, then thousands more will follow this river and such men are *always* hungry."

Xabin scrubbed his beard. "This is true. Perhaps even we could make some money hauling good water down from the mountains. This river water tastes like goat piss."

Augustin's mind was racing. "We could find plenty of empty water barrels out in the forty-mile desert less than three days from here. The best of them were tossed away by thirsty emigrants just last summer."

Xabin's head was beginning to nod now. "But maybe there is one big problem besides the hungry Indians."

"What?"

"Hungry coyotes. This is bad country for them, Augustin."

"Coyotes!" Augustin scoffed. "As our flocks multiply each year like insects, we buy . . . or breed more dogs."

"With two males?"

Augustin almost laughed out loud. "Father, why are you trying so hard to think of reasons why this would not work? Only a few weeks ago, wasn't it you that said this would be fine sheep country?"

Xabin's eyes came to rest on their wagon and then on his youngest son sleeping so soundly underneath. "Palo would never accept this land. There are no women, except for Mrs. Pike and I am not even sure that she would have him."

Augustin said nothing. It would serve no good purpose to confide in his dreams for Libby and the girl but it would not have surprised him if Xabin had already guessed his fantasies. This was confirmed a moment later when Xabin added, "I would not let a woman come between my sons."

"I promise," Augustin said, "that would never happen."

"Then don't think of her so much."

"How do you know I think of her?"

"I can see it in your eyes. They are like a *cow*'s eyes when you watch her."

"Oh." Augustin felt his cheeks warm for he never doubted that this was true.

"I will wake up Palo," Xabin said.

"Let him sleep."

"So you can be alone with the woman?"

Augustin grinned. "She still sleeps."

Xabin tossed the dregs of his coffee into the fire and called his dogs. Lata and Emo came in to be fed. They gobbled their breakfast of mutton and biscuits and then the old man took up a rifle and pistol and followed them toward the sheep.

"Wait up a minute," Augustin called, arming himself.

"You are worried I will be caught by surprise?"

"Your eyes are not what they used to be."

"They are still good enough."

"Then maybe," Augustin said, "I am more worried that you will kill an Indian and our chance for peace will be lost."

"Peace?" Xabin passed wind and grinned coldly. "That is what I expect of this peace."

But Augustin paid the old Basque no mind. He could tell that Xabin was a little excited about the idea of a beautiful mountain valley far, far away from ranchers and farmers because the old man's step was a little quicker and his chin was raised a little higher. But mostly, Xabin could not help but look up every few moments toward the eastern mountains.

Later that morning, Palo rode out on the stallion to scout for Indians. He was gone only a few minutes before he came flying over a low ridge and shouted, "Indians!"

Palo hurriedly dismounted and turned the stallion back into the rope corral they'd fashioned between the Conestoga and the sheep wagon. The sweating horse joined his mares, the donkeys, draft horses, a few mustangs, and Xabin's mules.

"Libby," Augustin said, "you'd better get into the wagon with Fay and keep out of sight until we see what's going to happen."

"No," she said, clutching the pepperbox. "But Fay, you need to get inside."

"I can fight too!"

Palo stepped between them. He scooped Fay up and swung her into the Conestoga. "Your mother said to get inside."

Fay disappeared.

Thirteen Indians, all of them on foot and heavily armed with bows as well as rifles, came to a halt less than a hundred yards east of the wagons.

"I'll go speak to them," Palo said, checking his

Colt, and producing a white silk bandanna to tie on a stick.

"No," Augustin said, "this *is* my idea. I'll go."

"They would recognize you as the one that shot the guard and tried to steal away the boy," Palo told him. "You'd be dead the minute they got you into their range."

"He's right," Xabin agreed. "Let Palo go. Because of all the husbands he outran in California, he's a lot faster than you, Augustin."

Palo didn't appreciate that cutting remark. He started to say something but changed his mind and marched out waving his flag of truce.

Augustin gripped his father's Sharps rifle while Xabin held a trusted old Hawken. Both of them were wearing six-shot revolvers.

"Look at Palo. He's bold as brass," Augustin said as he watched his brother casually stroll toward the Indians.

"Yes," Xabin said with rare admiration, "at least he has our courage."

As Palo waved the white bandanna in his left hand, Augustin noticed that his right hand stayed very close to the butt of his six-gun. The Indians came to a halt, weapons up and ready.

"There's exactly thirteen of 'em," Xabin said. "Bad luck."

Augustin didn't respond. He knew that, if worse came to worst, Palo could only kill two, maybe three before they could retaliate. If their intention was to kill, Augustin had already told Palo to turn and run for the camp. He might even make it because Palo really was exceptionally fast.

"They're talking," Libby noted. "That short one wearing the red flannel shirt seems to speak English."

"That's good," Augustin said. "Very good."

Palo and the Indians, many of whom were dressed in white man's clothing, talked a long time while the morning slowly wore on. Finally, the red-shirted Indian who was doing all the talking grabbed and began to pump Palo's hand.

"Maybe they have a deal!" Augustin exclaimed.

"Not until I hear it first," Xabin replied. "Here they come."

A smiling Palo led the Indians over the Humboldt River where they seated themselves in a loose half-circle facing the wagons. They were of all ages, some little more than boys while others were silver-haired and frail looking. Their straight black hair was long and more of them than not wore headbands. The younger ones carried mostly flintlock rifles while older ones seemed to prefer the more traditional bows and arrows.

Despite the rough and rocky ground, a third of them were barefooted. Others had moccasins, and the rest shoes they had no doubt stolen or traded from emigrants. All of them were short, most not much more than five feet tall. Dusky to dark, they were uniformly thin with high cheekbones and impassive expressions.

"What were you talking about?" Xabin demanded when his youngest son rejoined them at the wagons.

"Food. Mules. Guns."

Palo looked back over his shoulder and waved. The Indians waved back. "That's what they want."

"No guns or mules," Xabin vowed.

"Food first then," Palo said, turning to Libby. "Will you help us get those people fed?"

"Of course," Libby said, rushing over to throw more wood on their small, smoldering fire. "Did you ask them about Matthew yet?"

"Not yet," Palo said, "but I'm sure that they expect the subject to come up. Along with wanting to kill Augustin for shooting their guard."

"I'll see them in hell first!" Xabin shouted.

The Indians jumped at Xabin's sudden outburst. One of them became very upset and began to rant and rave.

"Now look and see what you've done to our dinner

guests," Palo said, face taut with strain. "Father, would you just put a noose on that temper!"

Xabin growled something low in his throat but it was clear that he wouldn't make the same mistake again.

Augustin said, "Palo, how do you read them?"

"So far, so good. I told them we want to be friends, maybe even live in that valley in peace."

"And what did they say?"

"They wanted to know if we intended to shoot what little game is left in these hills or to cut down more pinion pine. I told them we would not hunt the game or cut down their source of food."

"Who is the one that speaks English?"

"His name is Miguel. His mother was a white woman."

"Don't you mean an Indian slave?" Xabin growled.

"I don't expect we ought to go into his family background," Palo said. "I think what we ought to do real quick is to stuff them full of juicy mutton so that they can know how good it tastes when it's stewed with wild onions and a little sage."

"Agreed."

In record time, huge portions of steaming mutton were dished out to the Indians who exhibited ravenous appetites. Palo joined the Indians beside the Humboldt River and ate with them but warned Augustin and Xabin to keep their distance. The young Basque and half-breed Miguel carried on their rambling negotiations, which was maddening because it could not be overheard from the wagon camp.

After several more hours of talking, Miguel and Palo left the half-circle and walked over to the wagons where Palo introduced the stocky and grinning half-breed with more than the necessary amount of formality.

"This is Miguel," Palo said. "He wants you to know that his tribe is always hungry and that they like the mutton but not as much as mule meat."

"They should become better hunters," Xabin said coldly.

"Not much left to hunt," Miguel replied, eyes losing their friendliness. Miguel might have been thirty but he looked much older. His skin was deeply wrinkled and he was missing many of his front teeth. His dark eyes wandered so that Augustin was constantly trying to judge exactly where the man was looking.

"All right, Miguel. What do you and the others want in return for peace from us?" Xabin demanded.

"We've already gone over that," Palo said between clenched teeth. "We've agreed on two *fat* sheep a week . . . or three skinny ones."

"But no mules?"

"Yes," Palo said wearily, "they insist on eating our last two mules."

"No!" Xabin thundered. "By gawd those mules cost me a hundred dollars apiece! You know that!"

"*In exchange for,*" Palo said testily, "the Thoroughbreds and Libby's big draft horses."

"They are not part of any deal because they already belonged to Mrs. Pike."

"Not to these Indians' way of thinking."

Libby, who had been going quietly crazy with anxiety over Matthew's fate, could wait no longer. "What about my son? What about Matthew?"

Miguel reached down and collected a pinch of dirt between his thumb and forefinger. He rolled the dirt around until it was dust, then let it filter away. The meaning seemed ominously clear.

"No!" Libby cried. "Matthew can't be dead!"

"He *is* dead," Miguel said, looking deep into her eyes.

Libby sobbed and ran back to join Fay in the wagon. Augustin yearned to go comfort the woman but dared not. "Miguel, what about the guard that I shot?"

"That was very bad."

"Can we still make peace?"

"That is what Palo and I have been talking about. The answer is yes. We killed the other man."

"And what about the mountain valley?" Augustin asked.

Miguel rubbed his belly and showed his gums. "Sheep meat very good. Shoshone want more. We be good friends."

"But no guns or rifles," Xabin vowed.

Miguel tensed. "And what if we chose to *take* them from you?"

Xabin slipped his Colt out of his belt, and damned if it wasn't already cocked and ready to fire. "Then I will blow a hole in you."

Miguel did not even blink, much less tremble in the face of death. He appeared to take Xabin's threat at face value, which was good because Xabin never bluffed.

"If you kill me," Miguel said, voice dropping, "they will kill all of you."

"I don't think so," Xabin said.

Miguel threw his hands up to indicate that this matter was not worthy of talk. "Then some of you now, the rest tomorrow, or next week. Either way, they would steal back your horses, or shoot them from the brush. You would all die, except the girl."

Xabin laid his gun in his lap. His great shoulders slumped and he said, "If we agree to your terms, can these people be trusted?"

"Can *you* be trusted?"

Xabin's chin dipped. He glanced at his flock and Augustin could read his father's thoughts and knew the price was steep. But Xabin turned back, spat into the palm of his hand and then extended it out to Miguel.

Miguel giggled. His eyes wandered a full circle and then he spat in his own hand and shook. The Indians saw this and they smiled too.

And, just like that, the tension was gone. Everything would have been just fine except that they could all hear Libby and Fay sobbing from their Conestoga. Augustin sighed. Now that they knew for sure that the boy was dead. . . .

"Miguel," Palo said, leaning forward. "There is one more thing."

"Yes?"

"The boy. We will want to move his body in order to give him a Christian burial according to our own customs."

"That is not possible." Miguel wasn't smiling anymore.

"Why?"

"It . . . it is too late."

"No. When we leave to see the valley, show us where he is buried and we will do the rest."

Miguel squeezed another pinch of dirt, only this time, he crushed it between his forefinger and thumb so tightly that none escaped.

"Miguel?" Palo asked, eyebrows arching.

"The boy lives," the half-breed confessed in a low voice even though Libby was gone. "He was taken away by the Paiute."

"Paiute?"

Miguel's eyes rolled around like black beads. "Sometimes we trade with them. This time, we trade for the boy."

Even Palo was getting excited now. "Then Matthew *is* alive!"

"Yes," Miguel admitted. "He has a very bad head but Indians have strong medicine. Paiute take him far away. Maybe trade him, maybe he die. Only get two bad eating horses from Paiute for boy. Leave horses for women and children to eat now."

Augustin started to jump to his feet to tell Libby about this wonderful news but Xabin ordered, "Augustin, your brother won the right to tell her."

Augustin was stung. He twisted around to see Palo

disappear into the wagon and then, an instant later, he heard Libby's cry of joy.

So, he thought, Matthew was really alive, but his own chances of ever winning Libby now were completely nonexistent. In a single bold and intuitive stroke, Palo had captured Libby's heart.

CHAPTER

TWELVE

There had been a great deal of discussion about how to go see the mountain valley without exposing their wagons and flock to dangers and hardships. But, in the end, everyone had realized that the only sensible way to do the thing was for them all to leave the Humboldt and journey together into the mountains.

Libby especially would hear of no other solution. "I'm going to find my son," she declared to the Arostegi men. "At first Miguel told us that he was dead, now he says that Matthew was traded to the Paiutes. I don't believe he was traded to anyone. I think he is probably still at that cave, too injured to travel. I mean to find him, with . . . or without you."

"And foolishly risk the life of your daughter?" Xabin snapped.

Libby dipped her chin in assent. "Fay and I have talked this over and we're willing to take the risk."

"She is just a child and you are foolish," Xabin declared. "But since we do want to see that valley, it is probably for the best that we all travel together."

"Then it's settled."

"Yes, except that I only have two mules, which I might have to give to the Shoshone. That means that we haven't the stock to pull both that heavy Conestoga and my sheep wagon up into the mountains."

"I have the four draft horses. I am sorry that you no longer have a team of mules. But I insist that we take Rambler."

" 'Rambler'?"

"Yes," Libby said. "That is what we call our wagon."

Xabin looked to his sons for help. Palo just shrugged, but Augustin stepped forward doubting he could change the woman's mind. "Libby," he began, "the Conestoga is too heavy for the trail we must follow. You've been up part way and know how it becomes very steep and narrow. Our sheep wagon can make it to the valley, but not your Conestoga."

"I disagree."

"Be reasonable!" Xabin exploded with exasperation. "We're taking *our* wagon!"

Libby had anticipated this impasse and she knew that she could not really oppose Xabin. After all, his family's help and protection was indispensable. She had already been told about Augustin's idea of settling in the mountain valley to build a sheep ranch. Libby thought it sounded crazy, but it was exactly the sort of thing that would appeal to Xabin.

"Maybe," Libby said grudgingly, "we could make a trade."

"A trade, Mrs. Pike?"

"Yes."

The wrinkled flesh at the corners of Xabin's eyes tightened. "What kind of a trade?"

"My draft horses for your mules and the Thoroughbreds."

He blinked, then threw back his head and roared. "You are insane!"

Libby remained impassive. She could feel the sons staring at her but she did not shift her attention from

Xabin for even a moment. "Then you would take my horses without my permission? Steal them like the Indians?"

Before he could explode again, Libby added, "Are you really a thief, Mr. Arostegi?"

"No!"

"Then I want those mules and Thoroughbreds."

"Not the mules. I promised them to the Indians."

"Give them more sheep instead. Or your donkeys."

"They wouldn't do that," Palo told her. "They liked mule meat even better than our mutton. And as for the donkeys, well, they are too thin and tough."

"All right," Libby finally conceded, "then I'll trade my draft horses for the Thoroughbreds, your Sharps rifle and best six-shot pistol."

"No!" Xabin shouted. "The Thoroughbreds alone are worth five, maybe even ten times the value of your four miserable workhorses."

Libby folded her arms across her chest. "That may be, but not to you. So, either accept my offer, or else become a thief. Which is it going to be?"

The old sheepman was so angry that his entire body shook like a wet dog. He looked to Augustin who merely shrugged.

"All right, dammit! But what are you going to do with that stallion and those mares?"

"I expect that I'll need them to save Matthew. They, along with your rifle and pistol, might be the only hope for us to escape this country. And when we get to California, we can sell them for enough money to help us get established."

Palo cleared his throat, capturing their attention when he asked, "Libby, how much do you think the stallion is worth?"

"I haven't a clue. Why?"

"I'll buy him from you."

"Palo!" Xabin warned.

Palo ignored his father. "My offer is one hundred dollars."

"Where would you come by that much money?" Xabin asked.

"A third of the flock is mine, isn't it?" Palo stared at his scowling father. "You could advance me one hundred dollars on my share."

"No!"

Palo flushed with humiliation as a deep, angry silence settled in between them.

"I have some money," Augustin offered. "You could borrow it against a small part of your share of the flock."

Xabin was so furious that he turned on his heel, bellowed at the dogs, and stomped away.

"He'll cool down," Augustin said.

"I'm not so sure of that," Palo replied. "We both know the way our father carries a grudge. Augustin, you've finally taken my side against his."

"I haven't taken anyone's side. And, anyway, your share of the flock is worth thousands of dollars. So what's such a big deal about the loan of a hundred dollars?"

"It's not a big deal at all," Palo agreed.

"But *why*," Augustin asked, "do you want the Thoroughbred?"

"Because I'll be leaving soon," Palo told them. "Just as soon as Xabin decides where to settle."

"Where will you go?" Libby asked.

"To the Comstock Lode," Palo grandly announced. "I mean to become rich!"

Libby had to smile, for the idea of Palo swinging a pick was almost ludicrous. "As a miner?"

"Of course not! I'll race the Thoroughbred. Maybe he's fast enough to win me lots of money which I can invest in mining stocks."

Augustin sighed. "Palo," he said, "you don't know a thing about investing or mining."

"I can learn."

He turned his dazzling smile on Libby and then

bent to address Fay. "Would you like to go to the Comstock Lode? To the famous and exciting Virginia City?"

Fay shook her head. "We have to find Matthew."

Palo's smile slowly dimmed. "Yes," he said, straightening, "I forgot. Libby, will you accept Augustin's loan of one hundred dollars for that stallion? I refuse to ride a donkey or a mule to the Comstock. A Thoroughbred, however, does suit my fancy."

"Palo, I had thought that perhaps I might breed that stallion to the Thoroughbred mares and . . ."

"Not a good idea," Palo interrupted.

"Why not?"

"Because such horses are too temperamental and delicate for this hard country. You would do far better to crossbreed the Thoroughbred mares to a mustang. Find a big stud with a handsome head, intelligent eyes, straight legs, and a deep chest. I'll bet that such a cross would give you horses that not only would survive in this country, but prove very valuable. They'd have the mustang's toughness and stamina and the Thoroughbred's size and speed. Libby, such animals would have the best of both breeds and prove to be a superior combination."

Libby realized that she was nodding her head. "Yes," she said, "you are right."

"Of course I am!" Palo laughed. "I am the best judge of horseflesh in this sheep-loving family, though that is not saying much. Eh, Gus?"

"True enough," Augustin admitted. "Father and I live and breath sheep. Horses are handsome yet secondary to the flock. But, Palo, I hope you'll give this idea of leaving more thought."

He shook his head. "I've been thinking about it for years. I got you into trouble back in California, but once I've helped you settle, I'll consider the debt paid and be on my way."

"If you leave," Augustin said, "you'll have no claim on our ranch."

"If I *don't* leave," Palo said, "Father and I will finally have our showdown and he'll drive me away in anger or shed family blood. Which is the better choice? To leave now with him only angry? Or to stay and end up leaving in bad blood?"

"To leave now," Augustin said with resignation. "I'll make sure that you get your share of whatever comes out of the flock as it now stands."

"I appreciate that," Palo said. "I may need to borrow funds in the future and it will be nice to know that you will honor my share."

"Goes without saying."

"For you, maybe."

Augustin frowned. "Father too. You know he's difficult, but he's fair. We'll figure a value of your share of the flock and it'll be held in trust. But whatever lambs . . ."

"I understand," Palo said. "When I leave, that's it."

"Yes. But, if you stayed through spring and helped us with the lambing, then . . ."

"It wouldn't work," Palo interrupted. He turned to Libby. "Maybe by then we'll have Matthew back."

She almost felt heady at the prospect. "You'll help me?"

"I will," he promised. "Gus and Father will be busy tending the flock and building a cabin and then with the lambing. I think I'd rather spend my time helping to track down and find your boy."

"Can I come too?" Fay asked.

Libby nodded. "If it seems safe, I suppose there's no reason why not."

"I'm afraid it won't be a bit safe," Palo told Libby in a grave tone of voice. "We'll have to travel fast and light on the Thoroughbreds. We could be ambushed by either Paiutes or Shoshone."

"Mama, I want to stay with you!" Fay was upset. "I want to help find Matthew!"

"We'll see," Libby told her daughter.

Augustin thought he saw the way of Palo's mind. His brother would seduce Libby during the perhaps long and dangerous search. Maybe they would find Mat-

thew and be able to rescue him from his captors but
Augustin was pretty sure that would be secondary to
Palo. His brother honestly wished to leave for the Comstock, but Augustin knew that Palo also desired Libby
before he turned his back on his family and the monot-
ony of raising and tending a huge flock of stupid, helpless sheep.

"Thanks for the loan," Palo told his brother. "Now,
I guess we had better get hitched up and ready to go see
that valley, huh?"

"Sure," Augustin said, resisting a strong impulse to
grab Palo by the throat and choke him into admitting
his devious scheme of seduction.

Within four days after leaving the Humboldt River,
Xabin had struck his deal with the Shoshone and now
stood overlooking the vast, hidden valley where they
were intent on building a sheep empire.

Tears of joy actually coursed down Xabin's leathery
cheeks. "This is what I had dreamed of from the very
start," he said in an emotion-filled voice. "Augustin, this
is where we'll make our stamp on the land."

On each of the two previous occasions when Augustin had seen the valley, he had been in a state of high
anxiety about the Indians. First going to find them and
the second time galloping away wounded and desperate
to save his life. But now, with a fair wind blowing from
the tops of the higher peaks and with the scent of pine
needles in the air, Augustin took a deep breath and
knew that this place was right for them. A good, hardworking sheepman could prosper in this Nevada wilderness. The only thing lacking was the prospect of having
a family to raise, love, and protect.

"What do you think," Xabin said, coming to stand
before his eldest son, "about locating our ranch over
there at the far end near the pines?"

"Yes," Augustin agreed. "Right where the stream
bends and that sandbar glistens like gold. We'd want to

be out of the pines and into the valley far enough so that we could see anyone approaching."

Xabin patted the gun on his hip. "I'm sure that we are both thinking about our Shoshone friends."

"Them and others," Augustin said. "We just need a clear field of fire in all directions. We ought to be near the stream and I think I can even see a building site on a patch of slightly higher ground in case it ever floods in springtime."

Xabin looked as excited as a kid at Christmas. "Let's get down there and start to work!"

They drove the wagon into the valley and paused to watch as their sheep flowed across its dry winter grass like ocean foam. The flock made familiar sounds of contentment as they grazed.

"I knew they'd like it here," Xabin said, eyes bright with the pleasure that always came upon him when his sheep were happy. "Where is that spot where you want to put up the cabin?"

"Over there," Augustin said, pointing.

"Then let's sharpen our axes!" Xabin roared, pounding his son across the shoulders hard enough to stagger a lesser man.

On a bright, breezy afternoon the following week, Libby and Palo used one of the dogs to drive four old wethers up to the Shoshone cave. The wethers were called "gummers" or "broken mouths" because they were missing teeth and therefore not able to forage as well as younger animals. Xabin reckoned that such small infirmities would not matter in the least to the Indians. That might be true, but Libby was nervous at the prospect of entering the Shoshone village and possibly finding her son grievously hurt or even unconscious.

"Relax," Palo said. "These Indians need our sheep and fear our guns. I got a good feeling about them being willing to keep their share of the bargain."

"Is that why you don't feel guilty about leaving?"

A muscle twitched along his jawline and Palo

dipped his chin. "The way I see it, these Indians can overrun all of us and take whatever they please. My gun wouldn't make any difference."

"That is one way to look at it," she said, thinking that Palo's outlook was rather self-serving.

Leaning forward on the Thoroughbred stallion, Palo raised a hand and pointed. "The cave the Indians use is just up ahead. I also saw some brush tepees over there near that brown patch of cliff. I expect the Shoshone offer those shelters to visitors in milder weather."

"Augustin said that these people were very hungry."

"That's right. I was talking to Miguel, who said that the Shoshone call themselves the Newe."

"Which means?"

"The People. He said that the Newe weren't always so desperate for food. In earlier generations, there were a lot more of them."

"What happened?"

"They've been shot by emigrants for sport." Palo shook his head. "It was no different in California. Miguel said that the Newe welcomed the first white men who followed the Humboldt River. But then they saw how these men killed all the beaver, which were valued by the people for their warm, thick fur."

"We saw old beaver dams, long ago abandoned."

"Miguel said the last beaver disappeared over twenty years ago. And when the beaver were gone and the trappers vanished, the forty-niners came and chopped down thousands of pinion and juniper pines. That's the main food of these people and they soon knew great hunger. Just as bad, emigrant oxen, mules, and horses grazed the river grass to the roots so that what deer and antelope that weren't shot by the whites also vanished. Miguel says that the Humboldt River used to be a favored hunting place of The People, but no more."

Libby was well-read. She knew what had happened to many of the eastern and midwestern tribes and there was a sad and upsetting familiarity to this Nevada scenario. "So the Shoshone are now hungry and steal from anyone who passes through their traditional lands."

"That's right. Miguel also said that bands of both Shoshone and Paiute are having to relocate more often in order to keep from starving. This is causing friction and fighting among the Indian peoples."

As they neared the end of the canyon, Palo pointed out the cluster of brush tepees. These crude shelters were only about eight feet high and conical shaped with their brush tightly woven over poles.

"The cave is right up ahead," Palo told her.

Libby's heart really began to hammer the moment she saw the big cliff and the Indians' cave. When the Shoshone saw them approaching, they all came out to catch up the sheep offerings.

Palo dismounted and Libby did the same. She was shocked at how thin these people were, especially troubled by the women and children. The wethers were slaughtered on the spot but Libby hardly noticed for her eyes were jumping from one person to the next, hoping that they would light upon her Matthew.

"Maybe they're hiding him inside that cave," she said, starting forward with every intention of going inside to investigate.

"Wait a minute!" Palo called, grabbing her arm and pulling her close. "These people would be offended if you just marched in there without an invitation."

"But Matthew might be hurt inside!"

Miguel must have overheard her outburst for the little half-breed came over and said, "I told you that your son not here. Now, I show you."

Libby could barely contain her emotions as she was led into the gathering. The women and children wore both skin and cotton dresses, several of which had come from Libby's own trunk of clothes. She didn't care a whit about any of that now. And when she entered the cave, she discovered that it was only about ten feet deep, cold, and damp. Its only inhabitants were an old couple as well as a mother dressed in Elias's coat holding a nursing infant. Libby stared at the woman, who appeared to be a little frightened.

"No Matthew," she whispered, crushed with disappointment.

"I told you your son taken away by the Paiute," Miguel said, his voice faintly accusing.

"But where is he?"

Miguel led them back outside. "Maybe to the east where sun rises. Or to south. More Paiutes there."

"Was he . . . was he hurt bad?"

"Could walk, but not straight."

"Will they take good care of him?"

Miguel nodded. "Good care."

"Why did they take him?"

Miguel gazed up at the clouds and considered the question at some length before answering. "Maybe help trade with whites. Maybe other things."

Libby knew she didn't dare to ask what the "other" things were. She felt so depressed not to have found Matthew that she nearly collapsed and she had to bite her lip to keep from crying.

"Let's go before they take to the notion of catching and eating our horses when we're not looking," Palo urged.

Libby agreed. She managed a thin smile of farewell to Miguel and the others, especially the children. Then she hurried to their horses.

Once they had ridden a short distance, Palo reined in and said, "Libby, don't worry about Matthew. I'm going to come back here tonight and dig up the two rifles that Gus and I had to leave behind the first time when we tried to grab your son. Then I'll offer Miguel a trade for one, if he'll give us more solid information on your son."

She took heart. "Do you think he knows more?"

"I sure do," Palo said. "I think he knows a whole lot more but is just waiting for the chance to strike a deal of his own. Tonight, I'll give him that opportunity."

Libby's throat went dry. "If he tells you where to find my son, when . . ."

"We could leave tomorrow," Palo said. "Xabin won't like it, but to hell with him. He's always favored Gus . . . and for good reasons. But I mean to help you find Matthew and then head out of this wilderness."

Palo leaned out of his saddle and slipped his arm around Libby's waist. "And honey, I'm expecting that you and your kids will come with me to Virginia City. This is no country for women and children. I guess you saw that just now."

Libby was shocked at his boldness. She froze, not daring to offend him and risk losing his help and support.

"Thank you," she managed to say.

"Then you'll go away with me?"

"Yes."

He tried to kiss her mouth but now she did lean away. Rather than be offended, Palo smiled. "I guess that you're still feeling married, huh?"

"I am."

"Only natural." Palo straightened in his saddle and lifted his reins. "Every good woman needs a mourning period. I'd think less of her if she didn't. But, out here in this country, sometimes things have to happen fast. You suffer, get hurt, get back on your feet, and go on real quick. You follow me?"

"I do," she said, unable to hide the tremor in her voice.

"Good!" Palo reached out and stroked her shoulder. "You're a decent, God-fearing woman and I am an honorable man. Don't worry, we'll find that boy and we'll get out of this country. That's a promise, Libby."

"Thank you," she said as a flood tide of powerful and conflicting emotions pushed her this way and that.

CHAPTER
THIRTEEN

"I don't like this," Augustin said as he helped Libby and his brother prepare to go off searching for young Matthew and the nomadic Paiutes. "We don't know a thing about the country out there and . . ."

"Miguel will be our guide, interpreter, and negotiator," Palo said, checking his cinch before mounting. The Thoroughbred stallion and Libby's Thoroughbred mare were both stomping and always a handful. And their two donkeys were packed with food, grain for the animals, miscellaneous cooking things, supplies, and trade gifts that they would need to free Matthew.

Augustin shook his head. "But, if you were ambushed or tricked . . . well, how the devil would Xabin or I have any idea where to find you?"

"I fear you wouldn't," Libby said, tying a bedroll behind one of the saddles that they'd gotten from the Shoshone. It was a fine saddle with a stamp in the leather saying it had been made in St. Louis. Libby could not help but wonder if, like her husband, its previous owner had been ambushed and killed by the Shoshone.

"Well, dammit!" Augustin said with exasperation. "What about Fay!"

"Nothing will happen," she managed to say.

Libby knew the inadequacy of her answer but there was nothing else she could say. If worse came to worst, Fay would be the last survivor of the Pike family. Augustin and Xabin would make sure that Fay would not go wanting or be sent to some poorhouse or orphanage. Fay had relatives back East, but none that Libby trusted or thought as honorable as Augustin.

"But what if it does?" Augustin pressed. "You know as well as I do that there are no guarantees out here."

"Leave her alone!" Palo warned. "Can't you see that leaving is difficult enough for Libby without you badgering her about the child?"

Augustin swung around toward Palo. " 'Badgering' her!"

"That's right!"

It took all of Augustin's considerable self-control not to erupt in anger. "If anything happened to the pair of you, this is *not* a fitting country for a girl to be raised in! I don't even have a relative's name to notify."

Libby could feel her self-control slipping as she finished lashing her bedroll down. The last thing in the world she wanted to do now was to reveal her fear and anxiety to anyone, especially Fay. Her knees were actually shaking in Elias's baggy old pants and she wasn't even sure which she feared the most—savage Indians, or Palo with his dark, hungry eyes.

"We've got to ride," Palo said, full of impatience, as he dallied his lead rope to the donkeys around his saddle horn. "I told Miguel we'd meet him outside Shoshone Canyon at noon. It's almost that time now."

Augustin stepped over beside his brother. "Just don't get into a damned fight out there because you won't win!"

Palo's voice turned to ice. "I'm about to get into a fight *now* if you don't back off, Gus!"

Augustin turned away shaking with fury. As Libby prepared to mount up, he saw that her stirrups were going to be far too long and in need of adjustment. "Libby, those stirrups need to be shortened. Mount up and let's take a look."

"I can help her adjust them later!" Palo snapped.

"No," Augustin said tightly. "You know as well as I do that Libby could take a bad fall if this hot-blooded mare whirled or shied. And at the very least, she'll suffer from saddle sores. Palo, what is eating you?"

Palo took a deep breath and expelled it slowly. "The weather is looking bad to the north. We need to cover some ground in case we get rain or snow."

"You'd do better to hold off a few days until the weather clears."

"Wait here?" Palo made a disdainful face. "There's no shelter in this valley."

Xabin had vowed to hold his tongue, but now found that he could not. Bitterness roughened his voice as he said, "Palo, if you'd stay for even another damned week or two, we'd have our cabin! But then, you always were one to run when it was time to get down to hard work."

"So long, Xabin," Palo grated as he reined the Thoroughbred away and leading their heavily burdened donkeys toward Shoshone Canyon.

"I'll have Palo help me with the stirrups at our first rest," Libby promised as she struggled to control the mare who was dancing and fussing in its need to overtake the stallion. Augustin grabbed the mare's bit and held it firmly saying, "Libby, if you were willing to wait just a month or so, maybe I could go with you before the lambing."

"A month or so could mean the difference between saving or losing my son," Libby told him with a sad shake of her head. "I'm sorry, Augustin. I know that we're leaving you in a fix. But you're the only man I'd trust with my daughter."

Libby waved to Fay and then reined her mare after

Palo. It was fortunate that she was a very good rider because the mare exploded out of their camp and she almost lost her seat because her feet could not reach the stirrups.

When she caught up with Palo, they both pushed the animals for another mile and then they drew them down to a walk. The donkeys were upset and continued to bray to the flock of sheep they had left behind.

"I've caused a lot of trouble already between you and your family, Palo. I'm sorry."

"It's been coming a long time before you and Fay walked into the picture. I've always been the black sheep of the family. The wild one and the quitter. My father loves sheep and I've always believed he wants me to act like one."

"I don't think so."

"I do."

"But Augustin doesn't act like a sheep."

"Oh, no?" Palo gave her a tolerant smile. "My brother almost always dances to Xabin's tune. Augustin sometimes thinks that he's in charge but only because Father gives him a little slack. But when it comes down to important things, Xabin rules the roost."

Libby saw no point in arguing. So they rode over to Shoshone Canyon where they met Miguel. Libby couldn't resist asking what she suspected was a foolish question. "Do you have any idea where the Paiutes who took my son are, and how long it will take to find Matthew?"

"They go east to far mountains," Miguel told her, throwing an arm out in that general direction.

"I'm hoping," Palo told the old half-breed, "that we can catch them before they go too far."

Miguel looked amused.

"What's the matter?" Libby asked.

"No catch Paiute," he said. "Paiute see us first."

"Are they on foot, or mounted on mustangs?"

"Some both. Mostly on foot."

"Good," Libby said. "Any women and children? Besides Matthew?"

"Some both."

Libby wanted to ask Miguel more, but she didn't seem to be getting much information so she resolved to be still and to keep her spirits high, always hoping and expecting the best.

Just before sundown, Palo and Miguel picked up the tracks of the Paiute, tracks already blown faint and filled with dust.

"How long after the fight did these people leave with the boy?" Palo asked.

"Next morning. Same as me when we come to your camp."

"Then they've got better than a week's head start," Palo said. "No wonder the tracks are so poor."

"Get worse very soon," Miguel said, gazing up at the boiling cauldron of storm clouds that had filled the northern skies.

"Yeah," Palo said as the wind began to freshen. "I'm afraid that you're right."

The storm broke just before sundown. Jagged bolts of lightning began to spear the dark clouds and highest rocky peaks. The temperature plunged.

"We're going to have to find some cover," Palo yelled as the wind began to howl and the first icy blast of snow struck them like a frozen fist. "Miguel, find us shelter!"

Miguel didn't need to be told. He was already reining and forcing his mustang higher into the pines and rocks. The wind intensified and the snow thickened to the consistency of gravy, coating them all. The mare, who had been rambunctious at the start, now lowered her head and tucked her tail between her legs, as miserable as anything. Behind them, the two donkeys grew stubborn making it necessary for the stallion to pull them up the mountainside. Palo yanked the brim of his hat low and ground his teeth together. He was wearing a pair of old work gloves but his hands were still freezing and, when he glanced back over his shoulder, he could barely see Libby.

The footing grew very slippery. The Thoroughbred, which was not accustomed to rough trails, began to flounder badly and Palo knew that its shoes were in poor shape. He wondered what he would do if the animal threw a shoe or went lame. He'd either have to wait out the storm and lead the valuable animal back to the sheep camp, or . . . or what?

"Dammit, Miguel," he shouted into the intensifying storm. "How much farther?"

Miguel did not bother to reply and just when Palo was about to push on up and grab ahold of the man, Miguel ducked under an overhanging pine and the wind and flying snow were gone. The light was poor, the air freezing but Palo realized they had entered an old Indian camp tucked into a shallow cleft in the mountainside. Closely spaced brush-covered huts could be seen and even a solid cedar pole corral.

"Nice going," Palo yelled as he swiftly helped the Indian unpack the donkeys, then unsaddle and feed their shivering animals from sacks of grain. "Let's get inside and get a fire going. Come on, Libby!"

Libby was freezing despite the fact that they were sheltered from the wind. She looked at the brush-covered huts and wondered if they could possibly be watertight. "Miguel?"

But he was already dragging his blankets and gear into the smallest hut and then hurrying back out to gather firewood.

Palo attacked one of the brush huts, tearing away its sage and pine limbs to hurriedly select what he wanted to start a fire. "Libby, throw your stuff in there beside mine and come and help me get enough to burn!"

She jumped at his command and began to help him carry armfuls of brush and wood into the largest of the shelters.

"Damn," he whispered, dropping to his knees and

tearing off his wet leather gloves, "I'm about to freeze to death. It's going to be *cold* tonight, Libby!"

She nodded and started to leave but he said, "We've got enough wood. Didn't want to have to tear that other place apart, but there's no time to be out hunting wood."

Libby watched as he struck a match that sputtered and then died. It was almost dark and it took him three more matches before he could get a fire started.

"Won't be long now," he said, tearing off his heavy leather coat and wrapping the empty arms through each side of the doorway poles to try to block the wind and the cold.

The sage was damp and smoky but there was a fire hole in the top of the tepee and soon the smoke was venting upward. The interior of the hut warmed and Palo spread his bedroll close to one side of the fire while Libby spread hers on the other side of the fire.

"Where are you going?" he asked, when Libby started to duck under his coat and go outside.

"I thought I'd see if Miguel was all right and maybe it would be warmer if we were all together and only had to tend one fire tonight."

"Miguel is fine," he said. "Probably prefers his own company. Don't worry about that half-breed, he's old and tough enough to know how to keep warm and dry."

Palo reached into his saddlebags and produced a bottle of whiskey. "Want a little pull to warm your insides?"

"No."

Palo shrugged and took a long drink. He gritted his fine teeth and shook his head. "I hope this storm passes by morning. If it's a big one, we could be stuck here for a couple of days."

"Maybe we should have stayed at the sheep camp after all."

"Naw! We're in luck here and I doubt the snows get so deep we can't get back out when the weather clears."

Palo raised the bottle in a toast. "Plenty of food, plenty of whiskey and wood. Plenty of each other, Libby."

"No," she said, shaking her head.

Palo studied her like a cougar might a deer before he attacked. "You just relax and everything will be fine. I'm the one that can help you find Matthew. Xabin wouldn't leave his flock and Augustin showed his true colors."

"What do you mean?"

"Never mind what I mean," he said, shaking his head and setting the bottle down to rub his hands briskly over the flames. "I just mean that you couldn't have found a better man for going after young Matthew. I'm a good trapper and fighter. If your son is alive, I'm the man that can find and get him back for you, Libby darlin'."

She took exception to his calling her "darlin' " but wasn't about to challenge him for taking that liberty.

Palo stretched and sipped at his whiskey. "Why don't you tell me all about yourself?"

"Why?"

"What else is there to talk about except us? We've got a lot of time now to get well acquainted."

Libby drew her bedroll up and around her shoulders. "Palo," she said, "I don't know if you think something is about to happen between us or not, but it isn't."

He cocked an eyebrow. "Is that right?"

"Yes, it is."

"Okay. Whatever you say."

Libby's jaw almost dropped. "Do you really mean that?"

"Sure! I just want to be friends for now. That's all."

She studied him closely. "I *hope* you mean that."

"Oh, I do! But I also hope that you and I can get to know each other a lot better. I've been around Augustin and Xabin so long that I know what each of them is thinking even before they know. I'm sure that they can say the same. It gets wearisome, Libby."

"I suppose."

"You said you were on your way to California?"

"Yes."

"Any particular part?"

"Near the coast," Libby told him. "I've read about the missions and the ocean. The whales that migrate up and down the shore and warm, salty air."

"It gets real foggy too." Palo smiled. "I like the western Sierra foothills better. They get hot in the summer but it never gets this cold in the winter. But the prospectors and miners messed that country all up, especially when they took to hydraulic mining."

"What is that?"

"They use big high-powered hoses to blow away mountainsides with streams of water. The power comes from gravity pulling the water down from up above and sending it through these little nozzles. The water shoots out so strong it just blows the side of a mountain clean away. Makes a terrible mess and fouls up the rivers and streams for miles and miles."

"I imagine it would."

Palo sighed. "California isn't so much anymore. I mean to live on the Comstock. One thing I hear, it wasn't much to begin with so the miners can't foul it up much."

"I see."

"I guess they got saloons and gaming halls that will rival anything that was ever in San Francisco. Might be that you'd want to take a look at it."

"I don't think so."

"Might like it," he persisted. "You see, wherever there is big money, there is big opportunity. People are getting rich in Virginia City. You didn't see that happening back East on the farms and in the little towns where you came from, did you?"

"No."

"Well," Palo said, looking as if he'd been vindicated, "it happens all the time on the Comstock Lode. It happened in the Sierras too. Trouble is, even if you do get rich, it's tough to hang on to all your money. People are always out to take it from you."

"People like you?" Libby could have bit her tongue. The question had just popped out of her mouth, completely unexpected.

He laughed. "Yeah, people like me! How'd you guess?"

"I just did," she said. "But I didn't mean to say that I thought you were dishonest or anything."

He was amused. "Well, I am honest, with those that I like. Would you like me to prove that to you, Libby?"

She swallowed. "What do you mean?"

"I'll be real honest with you right now." Palo took another pull on the bottle. "I admire you, Libby. You're a good and God-fearing woman. And you've got a lot of grit and courage."

"Thank you. But . . ."

"You're welcome!" he said with a big smile. "And another thing that I really like is that you are a very *practical* woman."

"What do you mean?"

He dragged another small limb to feed the fire. "I mean that you understand the long odds we are facing when it comes to finding Matthew and getting him back in good shape."

"I understand the dangers," she said woodenly. "And I appreciate the risks you are taking."

"Well," he said, "that's what I was getting at."

She blinked across the fire at him. "I don't understand."

"It's plain and simple. I thought it all out today while we were riding up here and I want you in return for the boy."

Libby bit her lower lip so hard she tasted blood. "I . . . I can't do that."

"Sure you can!" He rubbed the stubble of his jaw. "You're getting the better of the trade but I'd be satisfied."

"No!"

"Yes," he said quietly.

She jumped to her feet. "I'll go on with Miguel. We don't need you!"

"Without me, you'd be taken and sold, the same as your son. You'd be enslaved and your life would be worse than anything you could imagine. And you wouldn't get the boy back alive. Oh, no! You could forget him."

Libby shivered and turned to the doorway.

"You're no blushing virgin, Libby! You're a woman and I'm a man willing to risk my life to save your son. Willing to try and make right the mistakes of your foolish damned husband!"

Libby turned back to the man. "I could find my way back to Augustin and your father. I could *tell* them what you just said."

Palo shrugged. "Fine. Do it! My horse's feet are bad and there are good blacksmiths in Virginia City. As soon as the storm blows by, I'll go there and you can go back to Augustin with your dignity. But, by then, you're son's trail will be old and cold. Augustin had his chance to help, but he chose to stay with Xabin. He'll make the same choice when you go back and beg him to come out here and leave his father and the flock. Trust me, Libby. I know. It's a fair trade."

Libby clenched her hands into tight fists and stood trembling with fury and cold just inside the door of the brush shelter.

"Well," he said, taking a swig. "Cat got your tongue?"

"I thought you were honorable."

"They told you I wasn't." Palo sighed like the chill wind high above their shelter of rocks and trees. "I never said I was anything I wasn't. No promises. Something for something. You for a chance at saving your son."

"I could get help in the spring," she said. "I have money hidden away and I could *buy* help!"

"Then do that," he said, corking the bottle. "And spend the next six months wondering about Matthew. Is he alive? Is he suffering? Is he . . ."

"Stop it!" she screamed.

They studied each other and, in the end, Libby's eyes dropped to her clenched hands and willed them to open. "I wouldn't be able to trust you to keep your promise. You'd run and leave me, Matthew too, if we got into real trouble."

"No!" he shouted. "I might not be honorable, but I am *not* a coward and I will not run out on you. I didn't run out on Augustin and I never ran out on *nobody*!"

He lowered his voice. "Libby, a man has to have something that he likes about himself. I like my looks, my brains, my fighting ability, and my way with the women."

She scoffed with derision. "You call this a way with women?"

"You're more lady than you are woman," he reasoned. "That's another thing that I figured out riding up here today. Of course, I'd like to see if I could change that tonight."

Libby thought she might get sick. Suddenly, the air seemed entirely too smoky and she needed fresh air. Tearing Palo's coat away from the opening, she rushed outside and the sweat on her brow turned to ice. She stumbled over to the cedar pole corral and ducked between the poles. One of the donkeys, hoping for more food, hurried over to greet her. Libby hugged its neck and buried her face in its hair, then began to sob.

And that's where Palo found her a short while later. She was shivering and crying and sniffling.

"You're the most stubborn and prideful woman I ever met," he said, leading her back to their brush shelter. "And you're going to be a dead woman if you don't let me warm you up."

Libby thought of Matthew and then of Fay. And
that made it all right to go back inside to the heat. To let
him lay her down close beside the fire and then to strip
and rub Libby's chilled body until her flesh burned and
he was ready to mount.

CHAPTER

FOURTEEN

Palo abruptly lifted his hand and reined up his thin, trail-weary stallion. Libby watched as he slid the Sharps rifle out of its scabbard and dismounted. She pushed her equally thin mare up to silently accept Palo's reins. Their eyes met, clashed really, then Palo edged forward into the pinion pines. Libby could not see any deer, antelope, or bighorn sheep, but she knew that Palo must have spotted something to hunt.

Just behind them, Miguel sat stoically on his tough mustang. The man's eyes were not so keen and he had already learned that Palo was an expert rifleman. Miguel glanced at Libby and she imagined she saw pity in his expression. Miguel knew very well what she was being forced to do every night with Palo.

Libby tilted her face up to the sun, letting its warmth soak into her skin. She had come to accept what she had become with Palo. It *was* all for the chance to rescue Matthew. And besides, Miguel said they were getting very close to the Paiutes that had taken her son into this wild but surprisingly beautiful country of pines, mountains, and high desert sage. In the three weeks they had been traveling steadily southeast, Libby had

come to see this land with a less jaundiced eye. Yes, it
had caused her and their animals a great deal of suffering. They had been forced to slaughter one of the donkeys for food and their supplies were running
dangerously low. And yet, at times such as in the late
afternoon when the sun fired the western horizon, or
during the glimmer of first sunrise, or when the sun
poked through storm clouds and shafts of light played
across the still valleys and soaring peaks, Libby keenly
appreciated real physical beauty.

Now, however, she dismounted. Their two
Thoroughbreds, both of which had once been nervous
and excitable, drooped their heads and rested. These
two animals had suffered. Their long, slender legs were
covered with scabs and scars and their feet were
chipped and tender. It was a miracle that they had not
gone completely lame.

Please, she thought, *let Palo be successful this time.
We need the meat.*

She loosened the cinches. The Thoroughbreds nibbled without enthusiasm at a few wisps of available
grass. Studying them, Libby knew that they must soon
find another river or meadow and give the animals a few
days to rest and feed. But that meant that she would
have to spend a lot of time in the blankets with Palo.
And while he was a skillful and practiced lover, he had
also proven himself a man without honor. Deep in her
heart, Libby despised him for holding her in bondage.

A half hour passed before the silence was shattered
by the crash of the big hunting rifle. Even expecting it,
Libby jumped and the Thoroughbreds bolted, heads lifting, nostrils dilating.

"Easy, easy," Libby crooned, stroking the animals
and calming their fears as she listened to the rifle's
heavy boom echo up and down the lonely pine-studded
mountainsides.

Libby retightened their cinches and climbed back
into the saddle just as Palo appeared with a wide grin.

"Finally got one of them bighorns," he happily answered, "so we'll damn sure feast tonight."

Miguel licked his lips and smiled in his funny, shy way. They all rode up the trail and when they came to a rock slide, Palo dismounted and motioned for the Indian to come with him while Libby would stay and hold the horses.

The bighorn that Palo killed was small and probably less than two years old but its meat was delicious and quite tender as they feasted that evening over a hot cedar fire. Palo's whiskey had long since been consumed but they had good water and some potatoes left to boil. Also, the weather had warmed and the stars were a diamond blanket suspended across the broad sweep of sky.

"How much farther?" Palo asked after dinner as they sat around the fire.

"Not far."

"You've been saying that for the last two weeks, dammit!"

Miguel shrugged. "Maybe Paiute know we are after them."

"Even if that were true," Libby said, "why would they run? We are only three. They are many."

Miguel shrugged. "Maybe not want to fight. I don't know."

Palo ground his teeth and Libby expelled a deep breath as the night silence deepened.

And then Miguel asked a strange question. "Do you believe in God?"

"Sure," Palo asked, looking up from the ribs he was chewing. "But what the hell kind of a question is that?"

Miguel turned to Libby. "And you?"

"Yes."

"In Jesus and his mother Mary?"

"Of course."

"I don't believe that anymore," Miguel said, shaking his head so that his long dark hair shook around his face.

"Why?"

"Woman *must* know man to have baby Jesus."

Before Libby could speak in defense of her own Christian beliefs, Miguel continued, "You want to know what the Newe believe?"

Libby clamped her jaw, but Palo said, "Why sure, Miguel. If you Shoshone have a different explanation for the world's creation, tell us about it."

"It is very simple, yet, makes sense," Miguel began. "You see, long ago, the Creator, whose name is Uteen Taikwahni, gave Coyote a large woven basket to carry across all this Newe land and deliver to Rabbit. The basket was heavy and the Creator told Coyote he must *never* open it."

Miguel actually rubbed his hands together he grew so excited in retelling his people's story. "But Coyote was very curious about what was in the basket. And, as he struggled to carry it across this hot, dry land, he began to think that maybe the basket held a pot of cool water to drink. But maybe too it held a trick, like being full of snakes or lizards . . . for Coyote was sure he could feel it wiggling inside when he laid the basket down to rest.

"Finally, Coyote opened the basket and out jumped some of the Newe people. Coyote was surprised. He tried to catch them but they ran too fast and he was very tired. So Coyote picked up the basket and hurried on but again he grew thirsty and tired. He opened the basket and more of The People escaped. The basket, of course, grew lighter each time this happened. When Coyote finally delivered the basket to Rabbit, who waited by the far mountains, it was empty."

Miguel grinned to show his missing teeth. "And so you see," he explained, looking quite satisfied, "that is how the Newe became scattered across all this country. Makes more sense than your Jesus and Mary, eh?"

"Yeah," Palo agreed, eyes darting to Libby, "I guess it does at that."

"It's a childlike story," Libby said. "One without any basis of fact."

"You have something of Jesus to show Miguel?"

"Jesus's words are in our Bible."

Miguel giggled, which caused Libby to bristle with indignation. "What's so funny?"

"I can't read your words so I believe in Uteen Taikwahni and how Coyote scattered our people. Your Jesus is *dead*." Miguel opened his arms wide and gazed all around, saying, "But Coyote still lives everywhere!"

"He's just a big, wild dog," Libby argued, not caring if she did sound mean-spirited or narrow-minded.

Miguel did not take offense and had difficulty trying to stop giggling. Then, he shrugged his narrow shoulders and tossed his gnawed bones into the brush. "I just feed Coyote. He comes tomorrow and eats those bones. Your Christ, you *eat* him!"

"You mean when we take communion?" Palo asked as he stopped chewing.

"Yes," Miguel said before he collected his rabbit skin blanket and slipped away into the night.

"Huh," Palo grunted, tossing a rib into the brush, "never quite thought of things that way."

Libby was so upset that she had not been able to better defend her religion that, when Palo came over to enjoy her, she threatened him with a knife. "No more!"

He retreated around the fire, dark eyes flashing with anger. "Then maybe I'll just leave you out here with Miguel. Would you like that?"

"Yes!"

Palo's anger died and he sounded almost concerned now. "Libby, that half-breed would sell you out. He'd leave this very minute if he could steal our weapons and our horses. The only reason he's stayed this long is because I've promised him my Sharps along with plenty of ammunition if we get young Matthew out safe. Miguel knows the Sharps will keep him and his people well fed. It's a better weapon than any of them have now and it will give Miguel even more importance among his people."

"And that's the *only* reason he's staying?"

"Yep."

Libby lowered the knife. "Palo, you can go, or stay and help me rescue Matthew. I don't care anymore and I'm finished being your captive whore."

His jaw sagged. Palo looked offended. "Is that how you think of yourself?"

"Yes!" Libby screamed. "And if you ever touch me again, I'll kill you."

"Jeezus," he breathed. "You really *hate* me, don't you?"

"I do," she confessed as tears began to spill down her cheeks. "I've lost my husband. I may never see my daughter again. I'm worried sick about my son. And do you offer sympathy? No! All you do is take advantage of my misfortunes."

"Christ," Palo whispered. "And I thought. . . ."

"What? That I enjoyed being blackmailed? Or would love you for giving me no choice but to submit to your rutting?"

Palo jumped up, grabbed his bedroll, and shouted, "That ties it! Libby, I'm leaving. I've been risking *my* life every damned day for you. And I've never even met this wayward son who must have been as stupid as his father to have ridden off alone into Indian country."

Something snapped in Libby and she hurled the knife at Palo. Missing badly, she grabbed a hot rock from the fire ring, ignoring its burn. "Go on! Get out of here!"

"I'm gone," he vowed, scooping up his saddlebags and rifle. "This is fine thanks for what I've gone through for you up to now. Well, no more!"

And, just like that, Palo wheeled around and disappeared.

Libby collapsed beside her fire. She could hear Palo cussing and fuming around the horses and she wondered if he would take all of their animals. And then, she heard Miguel's voice followed by Palo's. They were arguing. Fiercely.

"Miguel, just let him go!" she cried, afraid that Palo might injure or even shoot the smaller man.

Minutes later, Libby heard the drum of hoofbeats fading into the night. Miguel reappeared. He looked worried as he sat down across the fire from Libby and stared into the flames.

"Are you going to run out on me too? Or sell me to the Indians?"

Miguel said nothing. He just shook his head and stared into the flames.

"Are you still willing to go on however long it takes to find my Matthew?"

Miguel did not answer. Libby cried into the night and then fell asleep. But in the morning, when she awoke, the fire had been rekindled and Miguel was humming a song and roasting more sheep meat.

Libby and Miguel hardly spoke for the next two days after Palo's sudden departure. It was clear that the half-breed was troubled about something and Libby hoped it was because he had lost his chance to own the Sharps. At midmorning of the third day as they walked across a high mountain meadow flanked by a northern line of mountains, Miguel pointed to a thin trail of smoke.

"Is that them?" Libby asked.

The little man nodded. "I think yes."

Libby tried to calm her emotions. If this *wasn't* the right camp, she knew she was going to be crushed with disappointment.

"These Paiutes sometimes bad," Miguel warned. "I go alone to speak with them."

"Not on your life."

"You stay!"

Libby was momentarily stunned by this un-characteristic outburst. "Miguel, why?"

"These bad Paiutes," he repeated. "I alone speak for boy."

Libby had to turn her head away in bitterness and

confusion. Admittedly, she did not understand Indians and there was a very real possibility that Miguel had good reasons why he should go in alone in order to have the best chance of bargaining for Matthew's freedom. On the other hand, Palo had predicted that Miguel would betray her and he might want her to remain here so that he could bring reinforcements.

"Miguel," she said, "how long will I have to wait here?"

"Maybe half day. Maybe to sundown."

"All right," she decided, "but I want you to fire a single shot when I can safely join you. And, if something is wrong, fire two shots as a warning."

"Okay," he said, drumming his moccasins against the mustang's flanks. "You stay here!"

"I'll give you until sundown," Libby shouted, not at all sure what she would do if Miguel did not return or was about to betray her trust.

Libby dismounted, hobbled and unbridled her mare. The animal was famished, and the grass, while withered and brown, was still thick and nutritious. Their only donkey again began to demonstrate that it could consume more feed in a shorter time than any hoofed animal that Libby had ever known.

She had her pepperbox, of course, and Augustin had insisted that she take a cap-and-ball Navy Colt revolver so Libby had plenty of firepower in the unlikely event that she was being double-crossed by Miguel. Libby did not loosen the mare's cinch before she scaled a tall boulder where she had an excellent vantage point.

The sun was warm and it helped to calm her worst fears and imaginings. Libby waited patiently through the rest of the morning and into the afternoon. Her stomach churned with anxiety and she felt slightly nauseated, probably due to exhaustion and nerves. The day was growing short and so was her patience when the Thoroughbred mare threw up her head and whinnied.

Libby scrambled up to a higher rock and saw Miguel and three other riders approaching at a trot. Libby squinted into the weakening light, wanting to believe that one of the other horsemen was Matthew.

She ran down to the mare and bridled her, then removed the hobbles and mounted. She let the hungry mare continue to graze as the figures grew larger against the sky. When they were less than a quarter mile away, Libby's heart fell because there was no sign of Matthew. The first thing that came to her mind was that she had been tricked.

Libby checked both of her revolvers and slid one into her husband's heavy coat pocket. Holding it in her right hand and the reins in her left hand, she rode forward to greet Miguel and his companions.

Miguel drew rein early, before they were close enough to comfortably talk. Libby tried to offer a greeting, but her throat was parched by fear. The three Paiutes were hard, unfriendly looking men, all armed with old flintlocks and knives.

"Do they have my son?" she finally managed to ask.

Miguel nodded.

"Have you actually *seen* him?"

Again, the almost imperceptible dip of the chin.

"Is he . . . is he all right in the head?"

"Yes, he is good. Not sick anymore."

Libby heaved a sigh of immense relief.

One of the Paiutes spoke in a rough, guttural voice to Miguel who answered back in tongue. Libby waited, feeling the eyes of the other pair boring into her brain.

"What did the Paiute ask you?"

"He wanted to know why you keep your hand in your pocket," Miguel answered. "He thinks you hold a gun."

"Well," she said, "maybe I do. So why didn't you bring Matthew to me?"

"They want you to enter their camp. I do not think this is a good thing to do."

"I have no choice."

The Indian who had first questioned Miguel did so

again and this time he sounded angry. Miguel nervously wiped his mouth with the back of his hand. Each time he tried to speak, he was shouted down.

Finally, Miguel turned to Libby, eyes round with fear, and said, "These are *very* bad Indians. We should try to run away."

"And leave . . ."

Before she could finish, the Indian that Miguel had been speaking to drew his big knife and leaned forward, plunging its long, sharp blade into Miguel's chest. Miguel gasped, and then toppled to the ground. Everything happened so fast that it seemed like a nightmare to Libby. She realized that the other two Indians were forcing their mustangs into her mare. When one of them reached out to grab her mare's bridle, Libby instinctively drew her pistol and fired. The range was so close that there was no chance of missing and she kept firing until all three of her attackers were down and their mustangs were galloping away in terror.

"Miguel!" she cried.

He was dead.

"Oh, Miguel! I'm sorry!"

The rolling drum of hoofbeats caused Libby to spin around and raise her pistol.

"Don't shoot!" Palo yelled. "Dammit, Libby! Now they're all going to come after us! Climb on that mare!"

"I can't leave Matthew now!"

"Come on!" he shouted, leaping from the stallion's back.

Libby tried to argue, tried to explain why she could not abandon her son after such great sorrow and heartache. But Palo wasn't listening. "Get on your damned horse!" he bellowed, almost throwing her back into the saddle.

Palo knelt and searched Miguel's pockets. He found the pistol that he had given the half-breed and also a leather pouch filled with gold nuggets.

"He won't be needing them anymore," Palo said as

he stuffed both the weapon and the pouch into his coat pocket and remounted his stallion. "Let's go!"

So they ran, abandoning Matthew Pike, four dead men, and one braying mule who hurried along in their wake.

CHAPTER

FIFTEEN

Matthew Pike had no idea what all the gunfire and commotion was about. Since being clubbed with the butt of a rifle back in Shoshone Canyon, he had not been able to reason well or to think things to a logical conclusion. This renegade band of Paiute Indians and mixed-blood thieves had almost killed him. They would have killed him except for the intervention of their leader. Kaw was fierce looking and of questionable heritage and sanity. He alone had made the decision to spare Matthew's life. Kaw spoke passable English and liked to brag of stealing young women and fast horses and then trading them for gold down in Mexico. Kaw made it clear that Matthew would be valuable trade goods as well, though for what purpose Matthew could not imagine.

Quite likely, Matthew thought, it would have been far better had he just been put out of his state of misery and confusion. Since regaining consciousness, Matthew's head ached and he suffered almost constant dizziness and nausea. And even when he felt steady, he had great difficulty concentrating. Try as he might, he was unable to piece together more than a few wispy fragments of even his most recent past. He knew he had a living mother, a father, and perhaps a sister. He had a vague picture of a wagon and horses. But beyond those dim recollections, everything in Matthew's past was murky. Confounding the mystery of his past was the reason behind Kaw's decision to keep him alive.

There was one other captive white, a tall, slender girl in her midteens who was understood by everyone to be Kaw's woman. Her name was Jenny. Once, when she had tried to confide something about her own past, the poor girl had become so upset that she never attempted to speak of such things again. All that Matthew knew for certain was that Jenny had two calico dresses, both white with flowers, both dirty and tattered. Jenny was hard-used and grim, but Matthew had noticed that her long, dark brown hair had the sheen of polished copper under the bright, midday sun. And once he had noticed Jenny's unguarded expression as she had succumbed to the beauty of a spectacular sunset and he realized she possessed a warm and secretly wonderful smile.

During the first few days after being clubbed, Jenny had been given the task of tending to Matthew when he had been near death. Now, as the rest of the band prepared to avenge the deaths of their three companions, Jenny hovered protectively near. It was obvious to them both that their captors somehow blamed Matthew for the sudden and violent deaths of the men whose bodies had just been dumped in the middle of Kaw's outlaw camp.

"Where is Kaw?" Matthew whispered after one of the outlaws pointed at him and began to shout in anger.

"He rode off somewhere early this morning," Jenny said under her breath. "I don't know when he will be back."

"I'm in bad trouble," Matthew said, his mouth dry with fear. "Why, Jenny?"

Jenny pointed toward Miguel's body. "Don't you recognize him?"

"Sure, he's the one that came earlier."

"Yes, but he was also a leader among the Shoshone when we visited them near the Humboldt. I think he came for you."

This was much too confusing to Matthew. He stared at the bodies and said, "He came for me?"

Jenny nodded with excitement. "And maybe me."

"Why?" Matthew could not understand what a dead Shoshone would want of him.

Jenny started to explain but an outlaw named Tenoke rushed over and grabbed her long hair, then yanked her head back, and glared into her eyes as he drew his knife and placed it to her throat. Jenny didn't struggle but froze instead, even when blood began to trickle down her neck.

Matthew lurched forward but Tenoke hurled Jenny aside and slashed his belly as laughter bubbled from his mouth. Matthew gasped and felt a burning sensation. Tenoke would have killed him right then and there but that Jenny kicked him behind the knees and then jumped on his back, clawing for his eyes. Matthew threw himself at Tenoke as he heard gunshots and lost consciousness.

Darkness had fallen by the time that Matthew regained consciousness. What remained of the outlaw camp was in turmoil. Kaw had returned and was enraged by the fact that Tenoke and all but a handful of his men had ridden away, off to seek revenge.

"I should go after *them*!" Kaw thundered. "I should kill *them* for being so stupid!"

He marched up to Jenny, grabbed her hair just like Tenoke, and studied the blood mark on her neck. "Tenoke did this to you?"

"Yes," she wheezed. "He was going to kill Matthew."

Kaw twisted her head back a little farther. His face, like his body, was square and hard, eyebrows arched down tightly over his long, aquiline nose. His hair was nearly as long as Jenny's, but he wore a red cloth headband, like an Apache. Now, he drew back his lips and seemed amused by the terror in Jenny's eyes as she squirmed helplessly in his iron grasp. "And *you* tried to stop him?"

"I . . . I did!"

"Why!" Kaw thumped his thick chest. "Do you love this boy more than you love this *man*!"

Jenny knew better than to tell the truth. "No! But you said that you could trade gold for Matthew. He's your property!"

Kaw's eyes tightened at the corners and Matthew was sure that the man was going to snap Jenny's neck. But instead, he kissed her mouth hard. Matthew watched as the slender girl went limp in the outlaw's arms. He was filled with an almost insane rage and wanted to jump up and try to take away Kaw's gun and shoot the man. But Matthew knew that he would be killed should he be foolish enough to try.

Kaw ravaged Jenny's lips and then he tossed her aside and faced the remainder of his band. "We can catch Tenoke and the others and settle this with blood," he declared, "or we can turn and go to Mexico where we split our treasures fewer ways. Which shall it be, my loyal friends?"

Some of the six or seven who had remained in the camp did not speak English and so Kaw's words were quickly translated into several tongues, one of them Matthew recognized as being Spanish. What was immediately clear was that Kaw's reasoning made good sense. Matthew had seen the sacks of gold and currency and there was a buckboard wagon laden with precious silver tableware, candelabra, and other plunder that had no doubt been taken from emigrants unfortunate to be caught without the protection of superior numbers.

"But what do we do when Tenoke and the others come back here and we are gone?" one of the outlaws asked. "Then they will want to kill us!"

"Maybe the sheepmen will kill them all first, eh?"

Kaw spat into the fire. "And, if not, then *we* will kill Tenoke and the other fools."

Kaw smiled slyly. "And, if they kill a few of us too, then those that live will become truly rich men, eh!"

Kaw chuckled and the others, after a few initial moments of indecision, nervously joined in with laughter.

"We must go at once!" Kaw commanded. "Load everything into the wagon."

Jenny must have seen the confusion on Matthew's young face for she grabbed and pulled him aside while Kaw was stomping around just outside the firelight. "You should try to run away now!"

"Why?"

"Because Kaw cannot find you in the darkness. He is in a hurry, so he will have to leave you behind. Go!"

"We can run away together!"

"No," she said, pulling him deeper into the shadows. "For me, he would wait until morning, then he would find us both but kill only you. Just . . . just go, Matthew!"

Matthew's head was even harder than his heart. He stared out into the night and the impulse to run and keep running was very strong.

"Hurry!" she hissed. "Kaw returns now!"

"But . . . but, if I'm not here, you will be beaten!"

"Run!"

Jenny actually gave him a hard shove. Matthew staggered, turned, and began to run. There was enough of a moon to guide him through the rocks and trees but he stopped less than a hundred feet from the outlaws' camp. Twisting around, he heard Kaw begin to shriek in fury, then he heard a sharp cry of pain from Jenny. Matthew plunged back into the outlaw camp.

"Where were you!" Kaw bellowed.

Matthew was too frightened to speak so he pretended to fumble with the buttons of his pants. Kaw's lips curled downward with contempt and he turned and marched back to oversee the breaking of his camp.

"You should have gone when you had the chance," Jenny said, wiping blood from her broken lips. "Kaw won't be this distracted again and he'll keep a closer eye on you from now on."

Matthew tore a piece of his shirttail and used it to clean the blood from Jenny's lips. They were the same height but she was a young woman while he felt himself just a boy.

"Someday soon, Jenny," he vowed, "when I'm stronger and thinking better, I'll figure a way to escape Kaw and this bunch."

"There is nothing but wilderness out there," she said in a small, defeated tone of voice. "We'd die even if we could get away. And, if the land didn't kill us, Kaw would."

The first words that came to Matthew were straight from his heart. "Not if I kill him first."

Jenny threw her arms around Matthew and buried her face into his neck as she began to cry. And, as he held her in the shadows, feeling how thin and frail and frightened she was, Matthew felt himself grow almost into a man.

"Don't worry," he whispered. "It won't be so long before this is over."

"I had a family," she sobbed quietly. "Kaw and his men killed them all. He probably killed all of your family too. He's slaughtered so many."

Matthew thought of all the plunder and all the death and misery that surrounded Kaw and his band. He wondered where Tenoke and the ones who had left on the vengeance trail were now. Hopefully, in hell. And who were the sheepmen that Kaw had mentioned?

None of it fit together for Matthew. The only thing that he understood with certainty was that he and Jenny had to find a way to survive. And to do that, they not only needed to escape, but also to murder Kaw and as many of his followers as they could. Otherwise, they would be hunted down and tortured to death.

Matthew hugged Jenny tight and savored every stolen moment of her in his arms. "Don't worry," he breathed, "you've been taking care of me up until now, but soon, I'll be the one taking care of you, Jenny. I swear it."

Kaw's men broke camp by the light of the moon. Kaw ordered two of his best scouts to hang back and watch for any pursuit, although there was little chance of that happening. Everyone was thinking about Tenoke and the other members of the band who had raced off to seek revenge.

"How far is it to Mexico?" Jenny dared to ask the outlaw leader.

"Long ways," Kaw said as he rode beside the wagon. "Two, maybe even three moons. Maybe have fights before then."

"With white soldiers?"

Kaw snorted with disgust. "No, with Indians. Mojave. Pima. Maricopa. Yuma. Cahuilla. Moapa. All bad Indians. Kill you pretty damned quick."

"Then why go that way?"

He looked at her as if she was stupid. "Mexico that way!"

Jenny chose to say no more.

"Maybe," Kaw said after a time, "we go to Tucson before Mexico. Depends. Why you ask?"

"I . . . I was just wondering."

"All this Paiute lands. Way down south, still Paiute." Then, Kaw actually grinned. "Always be Paiute. No water so no damned good for nobody else."

Matthew was sitting beside Jenny on the buckboard's seat. His head, as usual, was pounding only now it was especially hard because of the wagon's motion.

"Maybe," Kaw said, looking hard at him, "you walk!"

"No!" Jenny exclaimed. "Kaw, he's far too weak."

"Then maybe die, eh?" Kaw asked, reining his horse around to the other side of the buckboard and then reaching out to grab Matthew by the collar and drag him off the wagon.

"Stop it!" Jenny shouted, trying to hang on to Matthew.

Kaw exploded with fury. A rawhide quirt tied around his right wrist slashed at Jenny's face and she fell back, whimpering in pain.

Matthew lost his mind. He jumped at Kaw, tearing his gun out of his holster and falling to the ground. With his head spinning and with Kaw trying to trample him with his horse, Matthew fired blindly upward before a hoof struck him in the face and Kaw dismounted to boot him in the ribs.

Kaw dragged Matthew to his feet and threw him into the back of the wagon. "Maybe," he said, "I trade you to the Apache and watch them kill you slow!"

Matthew wished to tell Kaw that he wasn't afraid anymore. That he was sick and tired of being beaten, starved, and humiliated. That, somehow, he would find a way to end Kaw's life even if it cost him his own. But Kaw didn't even give him that small bit of satisfaction. The renegade picked up his gun, pointed it at Matthew's battered face, and then pretended to kill him a moment before remounting his horse and galloping away.

"Matthew, he's going to kill you soon," Jenny said, glancing over her shoulder as she drove the wagon. "So help me God, Kaw is going to kill you and the trade money be damned."

"As *we* are damned," Matthew choked, rolling onto his back and gazing up at the stars. "Jenny?"

"Yes?"

"Can you get me a gun?"

There was a long silence before she said. "Who do you want to use it on, Kaw . . . or yourself?"

"Kaw."

"You'd be killed."

Matthew felt too much pain to argue so he just closed his eyes and rested. He would need all his strength and wits to get his own gun in order to kill Kaw and make their escape.

CHAPTER

SIXTEEN

"They're still coming after us," Palo said, scurrying down from a higher vantage point. "Libby, they're closing ground. I'd say that they're just a couple of miles back. I can see the trail of their dust. They're pushing it damned hard."

An involuntary shiver passed right through Libby's body. "How many are there?"

"Impossible to say. But from the dust they're raising, at least a dozen. Maybe a lot more."

Palo stooped to inspect the right forefoot of his stallion. The animal could not possibly have thrown its thin shoe at a worse time. "No rock bruise yet," he said, "but it's only a matter of time before this animal goes lame."

"What will we do then?"

Palo dropped the hoof and patted the weary stallion. "I'll have no choice but to make a stand somewhere between here and the sheep camp."

"I won't leave you behind," Libby vowed.

"Sure you will," he said with a cold smile. "When this stud pulls up lame, your best hope is to go on alone. I can bring down three or maybe even a few more Indi-

ans and slow them up considerably. You'd have a fair
chance of making it to our sheep camp. You could give
Xabin and Gus warning and help them make a good
fight."

"I won't leave you," Libby repeated.

Palo scowled. "Well why the hell not? I left you a
few days ago, remember?"

"But you came back."

Palo pegged his hat on his saddle horn and ran his
fingers through his long, straight hair. He finished tight-
ening his cinch and uncapped his canteen before taking
a drink. "Wish this were whiskey," he said with a wink
and a boyish grin.

Libby's hatred and resentment of Palo moderated
and she could almost find it in her heart to forgive him.
He could have run away but here he was offering to stay
behind and sell his life in order to save hers. And despite his haggard, unwashed appearance, Libby thought
that Palo had never seemed more roguishly handsome.

"Why are you staring at me like that?" he asked.
"Are you finally falling in love?"

Libby shook her head and marshaled her scattered
wits. This was no time to daydream no matter how upset
she was at having to abandon her son or how tired she
was from these many hard days on the trail. A trail that
had come so close to reaching Matthew, but instead had
ended with heartbreak, frustration, and the sudden
death of poor Miguel.

"Libby? What *are* you thinking?"

"I was thinking about your horse," she lied. "I had
really expected he would be lame by now."

Palo could not hide his disappointment. "In this
hard, rough country, these Thoroughbreds are being
worn down by mustangs. That's what we should have
ridden out here on instead of these purebred horses."

Libby stroked her mare's neck. She knew they
should be hurrying, but the mare was trembling with
exhaustion and every moment of rest was precious.
"Palo," she said, "even if your horse stayed sound, do

you think these animals have enough strength left to reach the sheep camp?"

"Not at the pace we're pushing them right now."

Palo capped his canteen and replaced his hat on his head. He jammed a boot into his stirrup and wearily climbed back into the saddle. "Are you sure you won't go on alone?"

"Very."

"All right, then we need to pick a spot to prepare an ambush. If I drill two or three, that might persuade the others to give up."

When Libby said nothing, Palo added, "That could be our only hope."

"We should keep running."

"At the rate they're closing the gap, I'd say they'll overtake us in an hour, two at the most." Palo twisted around to the east. "The good news is that they'll be staring directly into the setting sun. When I open up with the Sharps, they'll never know what hit 'em."

Libby took no joy in the prospect of more death. Some people called the Paiutes "Digger" Indians and spoke of them as if they were subhumans. But Libby had no doubt that they were also God's children all doing their very best to survive in this unforgiving land.

As if reading her mind, Palo said, "If they catch us alive, we'll be tortured, so don't you be feeling any guilt about an ambush."

"The thought of more men dying makes me ill."

Palo drew the Sharps from its rifle boot and checked to make sure it was ready. "I'll kill as many as I can and then we'll push these Thoroughbreds hard through the night. With luck, the Indians will turn back to their camp. But, even if they don't, they won't have a clear second try at us until tomorrow."

"How much farther to the sheep camp?"

"Another fifty or sixty miles. If these horses were rested, we could ride all night and be there by midmorning."

"But they aren't rested."

"No," Palo said, "they're shot. That's why I've got to whittle down the odds."

Libby had no idea how to lay an ambush. But Palo seemed to know what was required and, as they galloped westward, his eyes touched on every bit of this high desert landscape with its scattered forests of pinion and juniper pine. The sky was beginning to turn salmon and gold when Palo suddenly raised up in his stirrups and shouted, "Up there, Libby!"

She followed as he reined toward a rise thickly studded with pines. Despite her fears, Libby could see that Palo's chosen ambush place afforded a clear, unobstructed view of their backtrail.

"This is the spot I've been waiting for," Palo announced. "After I scatter 'em, we can ride up over the top of this hill and keep moving as long as these horses will hold up to the punishment."

Libby twisted around in her saddle. The field of fire was a good half-mile long but there still was no sign of their pursuers. Maybe, she thought, the Paiutes had already given up the chase. Libby prayed this was the case as they walked their staggering horses deeper into the trees.

A sharp and unexpected noise sent Palo's hand flashing for his six-gun. His Colt appeared faster than Libby could bat an eye just as a startled pair of deer burst into view. They were twin blurs as they vanished up the steep, rocky hillside leaving nothing behind but the soft sigh of the desert wind.

"Damned deer," Palo muttered. He holstered his gun, dismounted, and yanked his rifle free. "Libby, walk the horses on over the hill and keep going. I'll catch up on foot."

But Libby shook her head. "I'm staying."

"Don't be stubborn! What can you do?"

She patted her coat. "I have a gun. Two guns counting the pepperbox. And I can use them, if I must."

He relaxed. "I know that."

"Well then?"

He paused for a moment, then caught her by surprise. "You said you'd kill me if I ever touched you again. Did you really mean it?"

Her whole body stiffened. "I did."

Palo reached out and dragged Libby from her mare, then crushed her with his arms and lips. He was so powerful that she couldn't even struggle. The best she could manage was to stiffen with resistance.

Her unresponsiveness unnerved and angered him. "You must be feeling something!"

"Yes, revulsion and . . . and disgust."

Palo's cheeks colored and it took him a moment to regain his composure. "Are you still going to kill me?"

"Maybe later," she said, wanting to inflict her own punishment.

Palo looked stung. He turned on his heel and began to move about in search of a good firing position. Each time he came to a likely spot, Palo sighted his Sharps rifle down the backtrail and pretended to squeeze off a shot.

"Perfect," he finally announced. "But I still think you ought to take the horses and go. This won't be pretty."

"I know."

He thumbed back his hat and admired the intensifying colors of what promised to be a brilliant red sunset. "A sunset like this one is called a 'blood sky,' " Palo told her as he began to neatly arrange ten paperwrapped cartridges on a clean, flat rock. "It's usually considered a very good omen."

"There is nothing good that comes out of killing."

He chose not to respond but instead to make his deadly preparations. Libby had watched him expertly handle the big breechloader while hunting for deer. She had never seen anyone to equal Palo with a rifle and knew that he could fire and reload four or even five times a minute. Noting his air of confidence and even anticipation, Libby expected that more than a few Paiutes were about to witness their last sunset.

"Why can't we just ride on?" she asked. "Maybe we could lose them in the darkness and avoid all this bloodshed."

"Not a chance. Besides, they expect us to keep running. That's why they're closing so fast and not showing any signs of wariness."

"But . . ."

Palo glanced up. "I already gave you the chance to leave, but it's too late now. They'd spot your movement in the trees and I'd lose the all-important advantage of surprise."

"Then I'll stay right here," she said, turning her back on the trail below, "but I don't have to watch."

"Take my hat and scatter my rifle's smoke," he ordered. "That might give me an extra shot or two before they spot us."

Palo removed his hat and, when Libby didn't respond, he said, "Are you afraid to even watch?"

"I've already seen enough death."

"Sshhh! Here they come."

The lead Indian materialized from behind a hump of stone followed by another, then another as they rode single file. Libby counted eleven.

Palo's favorite Sharps had a set of double triggers. After the rifle was cocked by pulling back the hammer, squeezing the rear trigger set the front "hair" trigger. Now, as the Paiutes grew closer, Libby heard the cock of the hammer and then the ominous click of the back trigger. She watched as Palo pressed his cheek against the smooth stock of the rifle and took careful aim.

"Don't move a muscle," he whispered. "I'm going to let them get very, very close before I open fire. That way, they'll have to retreat a long way before leaving my killing range."

Libby's breath came faster as the Indians advanced at a fast trot up between the hills. The riders wore white men's clothes and appeared quite large astride their tough little mustangs. Most rode bareback and they all carried rifles. Suddenly, the lead rider's horse stumbled just as Palo fired.

The Sharps' blast was deafening. It's roar swept down the slope and blanketed the shallow canyon. Like a poisonous wind, it sent Paiutes and ponies into frenzied confusion. Because of the stumbling mustang, Palo's first slug sailed over the leader's head.

"Damn!" Palo cried in frustration. He reloaded and fired again. This time, his bullet struck and unseated a rider. The Indians leaped from their horses and scattered into the rocks and trees.

"Let's get out of here," he said, looking disgusted with himself.

Libby was more than happy to leave. She mounted her horse and then gave the mare her head as it followed the stallion up through the pines. The mare stumbled and almost fell trying to cross a patch of loose and dangerous shale, but they kept pushing higher until they reached the crest of the hill.

Palo jumped from his puffing horse and dragged out the Sharps rifle but light was so poor he could not find a target.

"Maybe they'll go back now," he said, jamming the rifle into its boot and climbing back on his horse. "I hope so."

"Me too," Libby said as they hurried on down the other side of the hill, wanting to put as many miles between themselves and the Indians as possible.

They rode all night and there was no sign of their pursuers the next morning. "They may have given it up," Palo said, "but we're not going to bet our lives on it."

"If they come, would they attack our sheep camp?"

"Why stick around and find out?"

"You'd leave your father and brother to face all this trouble?"

"They're men and free to make their own choices. Trouble is, they're too damn stubborn to listen to reason or change their minds. They're like a couple of old locomotives on a one-way track and it don't matter that they'll come to dead end or run over a cliff."

"That's a pretty callous attitude."

"You may think so," he told her, "but I know 'em better'n you and that's the way they think and act. What about you, Libby?"

"If I left now, I'd never see Matthew again."

Palo shook his head. "If he survives long enough, he'll have his chance at escape. He knows you're bound for California and he could come find you and Fay."

"Not very likely."

"So you're staying out here?"

"I am."

"Then stay and fight the damned Indians," he said roughly. "It's a free country . . . even for the stubborn or just plain stupid."

Libby wanted to respond but she knew it would not do any good so she just sealed her lips and kept riding.

It was late afternoon when they finally returned to the sheep camp. Fay was overjoyed and could not let go of Libby. "Mama, I was afraid I'd lose you too," she repeated over and over.

"Matthew is still alive," Libby told her daughter. "But we couldn't rescue him this time."

"What about Miguel?" Xabin asked, looking to Palo.

"He was double-crossed and killed," Palo said, glancing at Libby. "We had a shootout and were lucky to get away. They came after us but I turned 'em back under an ambush."

"Are you sure?" Augustin asked.

"No," Palo said, "I'm not. They might still be coming. They might have gone back to their camp for reinforcements. There's just no way of saying for sure."

"Then we'd better be extra careful," Augustin said. "And the sooner we get the walls of that cabin up, the safer we'll be."

"You could still leave this country and find one

better," Palo said, looking from one man to the next. "We've sort of muddied the waters here and maybe . . ."

"No," Xabin said. "We'll stay."

"Sorry to hear that 'cause I'm leaving as soon as my horse gets rested and I can tack some new shoes on his feet."

Libby took her daughter by the hand and they walked off toward the flock. Lata and Emo chose to come and join them, keeping a sharp eye out for trouble.

"Mama," Fay asked, "what are we going to do?"

"We're going to stick together from now on."

"Even if we go looking for Matthew?"

"Even then."

"Are more Indians coming?"

"I don't know but we have to expect the worst."

"Did you see Matthew?"

"No," she admitted, "but he was in the Paiute camp. We were bargaining for him but . . . well, at the last minute, everything went bad."

"He'll find us someday," Fay said.

"I expect you're right." Libby tried to force optimism into her voice. "We just have to be patient."

"Gus says that I can have some lambs of my own to raise in the spring."

"He did?"

"Uh-huh." Fay brightened. "He's real nice to me. So is Xabin, but for some reason, he tries to act gruff."

"I've noticed."

"Look," Fay pointed. "See how big the cabin will be?"

Fay had been so absorbed with worry and disappointment that she hadn't noticed all the progress that had already been made on the cabin. The exterior log walls were almost waist-high already.

"My, it's going to be huge!" she said, marveling at its size and how expertly the logs had been notched at

the corners and trimmed so that the gaps between them
could easily be filled.

"It will have three separate rooms, Mama. Gus
says, if we want, one of 'em is going to be ours. Gus said
he'll sleep in the sheep wagon. Xabin has his own room
too and the big one is for the kitchen and everyone to
eat and visit. We've all been working real hard. I saw a
porcupine in a tree and the tracks of a bobcat down by
the stream."

"Do you like it here?"

"Yes," Fay gushed. "I like it ever so much better
than the farm we left. There are so many wild animals.
Gus is going to help me build a squirrel trap and . . ."

"What would you do with a squirrel?"

Fay shrugged. "I don't know. Just talk to him and
then tell him not to be so careful. Maybe, if he was just a
baby, I could feed him and make him a pet."

"I see."

Fay ran over to the sheepdogs and their tails began
to wag. "So, Mama! Lata and Emo even let me pet
them now. They wouldn't do that for the longest time."

Libby went over to join her daughter. The two
dogs, still wary of strangers, moved away. "They still
avoid me."

"It just takes time," Fay assured her. "You have to
keep working on 'em for a while before they take to you.
They aren't like most dogs and they don't get much
attention."

"I know."

"Gus says that we can all fish and swim in the
stream. We'd have to dam it up someplace and make a
little pool. He says that they'll dig a well too. We could
have a garden and he says this whole meadow will be
filled with wildflowers when the weather turns warmer.
Can't you just imagine how beautiful it will be!"

"Yes," Libby said, "I think I can."

"Come into the cabin and I'll show you which room
we'll have," Fay said. "Gus marked it off by digging his
heel across the ground. He says we've got to hurry up

and get the walls up, then the roof. After that, we can build the rooms and then maybe even add a porch to sit upon and watch the sunsets every evening."

"My," Libby said, "he sure has been painting you a pretty picture of life up here."

"Gus also told me some things would be hard."

"For instance?"

"I'd miss other kids my own age something terrible. He said we'd both probably miss church, and a school, and places to buy things. He said there would be long, long spells between when we could get away to visit a town. And he said there weren't even any towns to visit for a hundred miles or more."

"He was telling you the truth," Libby said. "You'd have to give up a lot to stay here."

"It'd be worth it until we get Matthew back," Fay said. "Then we could go on to California, couldn't we?"

"Yes, of course."

"Unless we decided to stay," Fay added. "But we don't have to decide that now."

"No," Libby said, "we certainly don't."

Fay smiled. "Gus said we could also trap a raccoon. He said a little raccoon makes a fine pet. I saw a big coon just the day after I saw that porcupine. I didn't know that they got so big! The dogs were pestering him some or I wouldn't have seen him at all."

Fay's excitement was a tonic to Libby and it lifted her earlier despair. "What are these little notches for?" she asked, noting a line of them along the top logs.

"Those are rifle ports," Fay said, frowning. "And they're going to dig a cellar and then add a wood floor someday. Gus says that they'll get glass windows and a door too. Maybe we can even find those things in some wagon that gets left behind down on the Humboldt. Or buy them for almost nothing from an emigrant whose animals need a lighter load."

"It sounds like Augustin has a lot of very big plans."

"He does," Fay said, looking up at her mother. "And *you* are in all of them."

"Is that right?"

"He likes you, Mama. I mean, he likes you *a lot*!"

Libby felt her cheeks warm a moment before remembering the things she had recently seen and done with Palo.

CHAPTER

SEVENTEEN

Augustin laid his ax down, wiped the perspiration from his brow and trudged over to see his father, who was watching his flock. Xabin had been dispirited and unwell the last week and Augustin thought he knew what ailed the old man.

"Father?"

Xabin turned to his son. "Something is wrong?"

"No," Augustin said. "I was just taking a rest."

"You work too hard, Palo too little. That is the way of it," Xabin said bitterly. "Look at him! Palo is worthless!"

Palo had finished shoeing the stallion and now he was brushing the animal and chatting with little Fay. Their easy laughter seemed to gall the old man.

"Father," Augustin said, "Palo is *not* worthless as you will see if we are attacked by the Paiutes. He is a better man than either of us in a fight."

But Xabin scoffed. "I don't know about that anymore. He went off with the half-breed Miguel to get the boy. And what happened? He lets Miguel get killed, doesn't save the boy, and brings trouble upon us."

"Yes but . . ."

"Let me finish," Xabin said angrily. "And now, your brother, my own son, refuses to help us with the cabin. And since I am feeling unwell, it has all fallen upon you."

"When the logs are to be lifted and placed, or when other heavy work is to be done, Palo always is there to help me."

But Xabin shook his silver mane. "He is worthless."

"Father, you must not say that again. And I want you to ask Palo to stay."

"Ha!"

"I mean it," Augustin said, heat rising in his voice. "You have always been too hard on Palo. Now, he is about to leave for the Comstock Lode. We *need* him!"

"No!"

Augustin knew better than to lose his temper. Getting mad at Xabin only made things worse. "Listen," he said, "I've been thinking and maybe this is not a good place for us to make a sheep ranch."

"What!" Now he really had the old man's full attention.

"I fear the altitude is hard on you. You have trouble breathing."

"Who says that!"

"I hear you struggle in the night when you think no one is listening."

Xabin made two fists and drummed them both against his chest. "I am as strong as an ox! This country pleases me."

"Then why are you feeling poorly?"

"I . . . I have been constipated!" Xabin glared at him. "Now, are you satisfied!"

"No," Augustin said. "You know what medicine to take for that. If it is not the altitude, then I think you feel bad because Palo is leaving."

"You are crazy."

Augustin ignored the insult because he refused to be sidetracked. "If you will not speak with Palo and ask him to please stay here with us and the flock, then I think we should return to the Humboldt River and maybe push on into Utah. Or return to California."

"Never!"

"Well then," Augustin said, "you leave me no choice but to think about joining Palo and going to the Comstock Lode."

Xabin's face turned red. "You'd leave *me*?"

"I would not want to, but when a man becomes too proud to ask his son to stay and help, well, then . . ."

Xabin swore under his breath. He got up from the stump he had been sitting on and marched out among his sheep to stand alone, a man hobbled by his own pride. Augustin wanted to go out to his father's side and plead, but he knew that was the wrong thing to do. Xabin needed to make peace with Palo and to humble himself a little for all the hurtful things that he'd said to his youngest son.

"Augustin, what is going on between you men?" Libby asked, coming over to join him.

"Father has an important decision to make."

"Regarding the Indians?"

"No, he needs to ask Palo to stay with us."

"It wouldn't change anything," Libby said. "No one could talk Palo out of seeking fame and fortune on the Comstock Lode."

"I agree," Augustin said, "but no matter what the outcome, Father needs to try—that is what is most important."

Augustin turned and walked back to the tree he had just felled and began to notch the ends. Libby began to pull away some of the branches he'd already trimmed.

"Augustin," Libby said, "you must have more influence than you thought."

"What . . . ?"

"Your father is speaking to Palo."

Augustin lowered his ax and nodded with approval. "I hope Xabin is not going to become angry."

They both watched the men talk. The distance was too great to hear words, but what Libby and Augustin could see was encouraging. And when Palo laid a hand on the old man's shoulder and it was not brushed away in anger, Augustin felt his throat constrict with emotion.

"So," Libby said, "you're not just a shepherd and a cabin builder, but you're also a peacemaker."

"Sometimes," Augustin said with a smile as he swung his ax, wondering who would come to him first to announce the new family truce.

It was Palo. "Guess what!" the young Basque exclaimed a short time later.

Augustin looked up from his work. "What?"

"The old man asked me to *please* stay."

"He actually used the word 'please'?"

"Not exactly. But he said that he regretted saying other things and that he wished I'd stay."

Augustin tried not to grin. "And you said?"

"I said I would stay until the cabin was built and the Paiutes either came to fight or it became obvious they decided not to retaliate."

"I was hoping," Augustin said with a frown, "that you might stay considerably longer. We've seen boomtowns in California. Sooner or later, they all go bust and so do the men who flock to them seeking fortunes."

"The Comstock Lode isn't some Sierra tent city," Palo assured him. "The ore is deep and it is rich. I've heard that there are canyons of gold and silver underneath Virginia City, Gold Hill, and Silver City."

"So that means that big mining corporations will spend fortunes to dig tunnels and send down shafts. Ordinary people like you and me will just pick up the leavings and risk their lives deep underground. Palo, it's not what you think."

"I'm not thinking of going underground," Palo insisted. "I mean to find me an opportunity aboveground and make my fortune with clean hands."

"That's easy talk," Augustin said. "You know nothing about mining."

"But I *can* learn! I'm smart, bold, cunning, and I do have certain talents with cards, guns, and women."

Augustin shook his head. "Those kinds of talents will get you shot or hanged."

Palo didn't get angry. He just smiled. "Well, Gus, I'd rather be a shooting star than a campfire ember. You've always known that. Give me some credit and a chance. I'll come back here in less than one year with enough money to buy our whole outfit. You just wait and see if I don't."

"We sure could use you for the lambing season."

"No," Palo said. "You and father can handle that. Libby and even Fay can help. It will be all right. Mainly, I want to make sure that the cabin is up."

"Thanks for that, at least."

Palo didn't take note of the discouragement in his brother's voice. "Father isn't looking so good. What do you think is wrong with him?"

"I don't know," Augustin said. "Maybe the altitude is hard on him."

"He should see a doctor," Palo said grabbing their second ax and beginning to lop off some of the smaller branches.

Augustin sent his blade deep into the log to start a corner notch. "That will never happen."

"Well, anyway," Palo said, "I will stay until the cabin is finished. It should not take very long."

"No," Augustin said. "But we need to divide it into rooms and dig a cellar and . . ."

"Whoa!" Palo cried, dropping his ax. "Why do you need a root cellar under the floor?"

Augustin had put more than a little thought to this question. "It's not so much for roots or food, but it could prove a lifesaver in case of an Indian attack."

"Why?"

"Well, Indians might burn down the cabin but, if we had a deep cellar with an escape tunnel, we could survive."

"One month," Palo finally agreed. "We will work

like dogs for one whole month and then I am heading for Virginia City."

"Agreed," Augustin said, deciding that he probably had won a small victory and that he could always press for more time later.

"And in case you are thinking about tricking me, I am going to make daily notices on a stick. Thirty notches and I'm Comstock bound. Do you understand?"

"Sure."

"Good, then," Palo said, looking well satisfied as he spit into his palms, snatched up the ax, and began to really make the wood chips fly.

For the next week, Augustin and Palo worked from dawn to dusk and made excellent progress on the cabin. They blocked out windows and tiny gunports in every room and framed in the doorway. They pushed the walls up over six feet using everyone's muscle, and having rigged a pulley atop a tripod arrangement, used ropes and horsepower to lift the uppermost logs into place and to assist them with the roof.

Xabin continued to have trouble at night and seemed to have very little energy. He and the dogs kept a constant lookout for approaching trouble and they began to sleep inside the log corral at night so that they could not be ambushed by a marksman from the distant pines.

Despite the anxiety they all felt about the threat of being attacked by the Paiutes, Libby sensed that these were both happy and productive days. Xabin's apology to Palo brought peace and the end of a constant bitterness and tension. It was clear that Xabin's heart still heavily favored Augustin, but his angry and accusing words had been replaced by an air of acceptance. Libby did not know how long this would last, but she was grateful for the good spirits and camaraderie that now existed. Since there was no sign of the Paiutes, everyone began to hope that there would not be any retaliation.

Each week the Indians from Shoshone Canyon appeared to collect another pair of sheep. When they learned that Miguel had been murdered by Kaw's treacherous band, they became very upset and one of the men, Lakia, argued that the Shoshone men should find and kill all of Kaw's renegade band.

"They are no good," Lakia said. "Bad men kill everyone."

"Then why did you trade my son to them!" Libby demanded in anger.

"Kaw trade many horses and a rifle. No kill son. We need horses and rifle to hunt."

The answer brought cold fury to Libby's heart but she knew better than to push the issue. Lakia, Miguel, and the others were a people caught in a time of change that bore them an ill wind from the east. Their old ways were being destroyed just as surely as their livelihoods.

"Lakia," Xabin said, "I would rather your people stayed hidden close by and helped us to fight Kaw's band if they attack our sheep and camp."

"Cost you two more sheep each week."

"What!"

"If we guard this place, we cannot hunt."

Xabin ground his teeth but, in the end, he managed to nod and growl. "All right. But only for a week or two."

Lakia grinned. "You smart man."

Palo burst out laughing and even Xabin had to grin. "Lakia, you and your friends are not so dumb yourselves."

The Shoshone drove four wethers back to Shoshone Canyon, promising to return the next day with armed men and watch for Kaw and his warriors, should they dare to attack.

"I feel much better now," Libby said, hugging her daughter. "With Lakia and the Shoshone agreeing to help protect us, we haven't nearly as much to fear."

"Sure," Xabin snapped, "you feel better. But what about me? I can't breed and raise sheep fast enough to

feed and fatten every damned Indian in this country!
The Shoshone are going to bankrupt me."

"Nonsense," Libby said. "You've got thousands of
sheep and you'll have hundreds more lambs this
spring."

The old Basque glared, bushy eyebrows knitting
down to a point over his big nose. Palo winked at Libby,
then at Fay. It was all they could do to keep from laughing and sending the old man into a vitriolic frenzy.

That night, a storm rolled in and it began to rain
shortly after midnight. It was a cold, pelting rain and
everyone quickly moved into the sheep wagon. They
were very cramped but soon grew warm and dozed off
listening to the sharp crack and powerful roll of thunder. Every time lightning flashed across the sky, the inside of the wagon glowed like a kerosene lamp, and the
storm was so violent that even the earth beneath them
shivered as if in fear.

"At first light," Xabin said, "we'd better be out with
the flock and the dogs. We can't afford to have them
scatter."

No one said anything and they dozed fitfully. Libby
awoke in the faint light of dawn to see Augustin quietly
push open the door and fill its space. She followed him
outside. The storm had apparently passed just before
dawn and the sky was clearing. Broken black clouds like
stepping stones flowed across a lake of gold and Libby
knew it was going to be a cold, blustery day.

"Where is Xabin?" she asked.

"He got up in the night and went out to be with the
flock and his dogs," Augustin said, peering into the
semidarkness. "He's always done that. Can't stay away
from the sheep if he's worried about losing them in a
bad storm."

They quietly distanced themselves from the sheep
wagon and Augustin called to his father and the dogs.
But there was no answer. The flock was on its feet and
they looked nervous enough to run. There was an omi-

nous tension in the air that had a lot more to it than foul weather.

"Libby," Augustin whispered, "go back to the wagon and get Palo. And tell him to bring my rifle."

"What . . ."

"Hurry! The dogs should have . . ."

Whatever Augustin was about to say died on his lips when he heard a dog's whimper. "Hurry, Libby!"

Augustin had strapped on his six-gun and now he was running toward the sound of the dog. When Emo raised his head, Augustin hurried to the dog's side and that was when he saw the arrow protruding from its shoulder.

"Oh, sweet Jesus!" he whispered, head snapping up. "Father!"

His shout broke the morning silence and it was immediately followed by a volley of rifle fire and the whirring sound of arrows. Augustin threw himself on the wet grass and drew his gun. He fired at shadows along the edge of the forest and was greeted in return by the winking of muzzle flashes.

Augustin felt a bullet tug at his coat sleeve. He heard Emo whine even louder and that's when he knew that he would die if he did not retreat. Scooping up the wounded dog and ignoring its sharp yip of pain, Augustin began to run, trying to weave back and forth as the Paiutes attempted to bring him down in a scattered volley.

"To the cabin!" Augustin yelled, still running with the wounded dog cradled in his arms.

Palo scooped up Fay while already carrying two rifles and a pistol as he sprinted toward the half-completed log cabin. Somehow, everyone reached the sanctuary of its thick walls although there was always a chance that a bullet would find its way between the cracks.

"Where's Xabin!" Palo shouted, jamming his rifle through the gunport and firing a moment later before ducking and starting to reload.

"I don't know!" Augustin said. "He must still be out there somewhere."

Palo finished reloading. "Here," he said, shoving the weapon at Libby so hard he punched her backward. "You know what to do."

"Where are you going!" Augustin yelled.

"I'm going to find Father!"

Before anyone could reply, Palo sprang out of the half-finished cabin and ran like crazy toward the trees. They watched with their hearts in their mouths until he finally threw himself into the forest. They heard a quick burst of rifle fire and Augustin figured that he might just have lost both his father and his brother.

For the next quarter of an hour, they exchanged gunfire with the Indians. Bullets and an occasional arrow kept digging into the logs and Fay proved that she knew how to reload a Colt almost as good as a man. Twice the Indians attempted to make a charge at the cabin, but both times were driven back with their wounded. And then, even as the sun lifted fully off the eastern horizon, the battle fell silent.

Libby pressed close to Augustin. "Do you think that they killed Palo and just decided that was revenge enough?"

"I don't know," Augustin said. "But I'm pretty sure that they killed Xabin and Lata."

Now that she was not reloading pistols, Fay had both arms wrapped around the wounded sheepdog. Libby edged close to her and said, "Maybe he isn't hurt so bad."

Fay looked up and her face was washed with tears. "He's brave and he's lost a lot of blood, Mama. And poor, poor Lata!"

The child began to cry. Augustin dared not try to comfort her because he knew that the Indians could resume their attack at any moment. But he did take heart a little when Libby said, "It's not such a bad wound, darling. We'll take care of Emo and he'll heal just fine."

"But what about Xabin, Palo, and Lata!"

"I don't know," Libby said. "We'll just have to wait and see."

The morning wore on and the sun finally sailed overhead driving away the wet chilliness of shadows. The sunshine felt wonderful. About eleven o'clock, they heard another rapid burst of fire and it caused Augustin to take heart.

"That was a Colt speaking," he said. "Palo may still be alive."

"I never doubted that for a minute," Libby said, surprised by her own words. She added, "If I were one of Kaw's men and knew a man like Palo was out there somewhere hunting me with a six-gun, I'd be scared witless."

Libby had hardly finished speaking when five quick pistol shots erupted from the woods. Two rifle shots answered and then there was silence.

At about two o'clock in the afternoon, they heard more gunfire but it was from a great distance. Libby had already made several trips to the nearby sheep wagon for bandages, medicines, and supplies. Emo, looking comfortable cradled in Fay's protective arms, occasionally beat his tail on the cabin floor to show his gratitude.

Augustin was caught in a sea of indecision. Had he been alone, he would already have run for the trees and tried to find and help Palo. But he dared not leave Libby and Fay unprotected. Maybe, he thought, Palo was dead and the Indians were trying to lull him out of the cabin and into a trap. He *had* to sit tight and be patient, dammit!

It was about four o'clock in the longest day of Augustin's life when Palo and their neighbors, the Shoshone appeared at the north end of the valley.

"Thank heavens, Palo is alive!" Libby exclaimed.

"Yes," Augustin barely managed to whisper, "but that's our father draped over that bay horse."

Augustin could say nothing more and when he

choked with sorrow, Libby hugged him tightly. "I'm so sorry," she whispered, feeling her own eyes sting with tears, "your father was a good man at heart."

The next morning they buried Xabin and his beloved sheepdog Lata side by side not far from their new cabin. Palo wept uncontrollably and even the normally stoic Shoshone seemed to grieve. Augustin used his ax, hammer, and nails to make a cross. He carved Xabin's name and made another little cross and put Lata's name on that as well. Libby read a few psalms from their Bible and then Augustin went back to work felling logs.

"This place is cursed," Palo said to Libby. "Something is wrong when you finish your grave before your home."

"You knew him all your life," Libby said, "while I knew him only a few weeks so what I have to say might not be of value. But I can tell you this, Palo, it is good that you and your father made peace before he died."

Palo's usual glibness was missing. His eyes were bloodshot and he looked very old as he nodded and started to turn away.

"Palo, won't you please stay?"

"I can't. And, if I tried, it would be the end of whatever is left of my family." His eyes were drinking her in. "Don't you understand?"

"Yes," she said, stepping far enough away so that Fay could not hear these words that were passing between them. "I suppose that I do."

"I'll be leaving as soon as the cabin is finished, Libby. If you come with me, Augustin will follow. You're the key now."

She started to protest or at least argue but she knew deep down that this was true. Augustin was steady and strong, but he was not a man who could live entirely alone.

"And what," she said brazenly, "if he finds out what we did together?"

A stricken look came into Palo's eyes. "Don't *ever*

let him know, Libby. Whatever else you do, keep that secret."

"The last few mornings, I have been feeling very sick."

"Of course you have! Our lives have been in constant danger!"

"Palo, I've had two children and both times I knew this morning sickness."

Palo's jaw sagged. He rocked back on his heels, then groaned a moment before he staggered off toward the trees. Libby sank to her knees and wept.

"Mama," Fay said, hurrying over to her, "don't feel so bad. Mr. Arostegi was old and sick. And Lata, well, they're together in heaven now."

Libby hugged her daughter. Swamped by shame and dread, she wondered how she could ever find the strength to make her terrible confession to this child and then to Augustin.

They finished the cabin in early March when the sage began to bloom, the new pale grass began to emerge and the weather turned balmy. It should have been a happy time but the death of Xabin cast a pall over all of them. Palo especially had not been himself since his father had died and Libby alone knew the reason why. He no longer had any joy in him and was studiously avoiding her.

One day Augustin came over and said, "I didn't expect that Palo would take our father's death so hard."

"He'll recover in time," Libby said, realizing even as she spoke how hollow and insincere her words sounded.

"I expect so," Augustin said, "but maybe you could talk to him and give him some advice."

"Why me?"

"I've tried, but he won't listen. Besides, you've lost your husband and your son is missing and look how well you're doing. You don't get down in the dumps like that. Libby, maybe you could . . ."

"No," she said, much too abruptly.

Disappointment flashed across Augustin's dark eyes. Excusing himself, he turned and walked away leaving Libby to feel even worse. How could she possibly tell Augustin that Palo was not only grieving for the loss of his father, but also wrestling with his unwanted and unexpected fatherhood?

Time and again during the past few weeks Libby had resolved to approach Palo and tell him that she would figure out something and that he needn't worry about their unborn child. But then she'd think that he *was* at least equally responsible and that the child she carried deserved to have or at least know the identity of its real father. Adding that to her morning sickness, Libby felt trapped in a web of confusion and shame. She hadn't even been able to tell Fay her dark secret because of an overwhelming sense of dread. Libby had always tried to instill a Christian morality in her children and now she felt like a Jezebel, wicked, immoral, and above all a terrible hypocrite.

"I'm leaving," Palo told her when they were alone together one cool, cloudy morning while Augustin and Fay were out inspecting the flock. "I'm going away this morning."

"Just like that?" she asked, though this was in keeping with his impulsive nature.

He snapped his fingers and nodded. "Just like that."

"Have you told Augustin?"

"I told him a couple of days ago I was about ready to leave. I'll wave on my way out of this valley."

"That's not much of a farewell."

"I don't like farewells," he said, folding his arms across his chest and studying her closely. "Did you tell your daughter about our accident yet?"

Libby took a deep breath and managed to shake her head.

"You'd better tell her pretty soon. You're starting to bulge."

"I know. I've just been waiting for the right words."

"Don't wait much longer." Palo shifted uneasily. "The stallion is fit again. He'll get me to the Comstock Lode and then race and win me a stake. But, if you had some money you could loan me, I'd . . ."

"No!" Libby was shocked at her own venomous reaction. She lowered her voice. "You used me and now you're leaving me with your child and you have the gall to ask for money!"

"Take it easy," he said, throwing up his hands and retreating. "I mean to hit it big on the Comstock and then come back for you and Fay. This is no place for you to live. I'll buy a mansion in Virginia City and make a home for us."

Libby wasn't in a mood to show kindness or flattery. "Palo, you're all talk."

"No, dammit! I *will* find a way to get rich and I *will* come for you and Fay." His eyes dropped to her belly. "That's my kid you're carrying and I mean to do right."

Libby forced herself to calm down. She could tell by the resoluteness in his jawline and the steel in his voice that Palo actually believed what he was saying. Pride pushed hard at Libby to proclaim that she did not need any help and that she would prefer never to see his face again. What mattered now was rescuing Matthew and bringing a healthy child into the world. Instead, she just stood frozen like a dumb, hurt beast.

"Well," he said, flashing his old smile and shrugging his shoulders, "at least Augustin gave me some money and agreed that I now own half the flock. Maybe I'll sell 'em and send someone along for 'em later. I dunno yet. But I *am* going to make it big on the Comstock Lode and I will come back for you and Fay."

"At which point you expect we'd just abandon Augustin?"

His cheeks flushed. "Augustin is a man! If he wants to live way out here in this wilderness, then that's his decision and there's nothing that either of us can do to change it. But you and Fay don't belong here. I'm going to make things right and give you my name, Libby. I swear that I will."

"I don't want *anything* more from you!"

His eyes went dead. "It's my child too, Libby. I mean to give him what he deserves."

"And what if 'him' turns out to be a her?"

Palo ground his teeth for a moment, then grated, "It don't matter. I enjoy Fay almost as much as I would a boy."

"Well," Libby said with biting sarcasm, "that's wonderful news. But I don't need you and I don't want you so do us both a favor. Forget about making things right and don't ever come back."

"I'll be back," he vowed as he turned to leave in anger, "and, if Augustin sends you away, you know where to find me."

"In hell!" she cried, rushing into the cabin.

CHAPTER

EIGHTEEN

Palo followed the Humboldt to where the river drained into an immense sink ringed with salt and alkali deposits that slowly evaporated and seeped into the desert's sandy floor. About fifty miles to the west, Palo could see the faint outline of the snowcapped Sierra Nevadas and knew he had reached the eastern perimeter of the forty-mile desert. Palo gave the stallion all the very foul-tasting water that it would tolerate, then filled his canteens, and pushed into the desert hoping to cross it in a single moonlit night.

As he rode along, Palo was again reminded that he was really crossing a vast basin, or sink, crusted over by hundreds of square miles of salt and alkali deposits. This was an extremely barren and inhospitable land. Along both sides of a rutted track Palo followed lay strewn the abandoned wreckage of hundreds of wagons and carts along with the desiccated carcasses and bleached skeletons of livestock. All too frequently there were human graves marked by a pile of stones or a crude wooden cross. Scattered among the wreckage were yokes, chains, harnesses, tools, bedding, clothing, cooking utensils, and every imaginable type of furniture, some pieces of which would have brought hefty prices back in St. Louis or in distant San Francisco. Palo even saw guns and rifles, but they were broken old single-shots or flintlocks.

Despite their grim surroundings, the Thoroughbred was rested and eager to travel and only once did it give Palo a moment's trouble when a little dust devil came whirling across the flat to send Palo's hat spinning. Because Palo had first seen the horse among the Shoshone people near their canyon, he called the animal "Sho" and when it began to give him fits because of the dust devil, Palo loosened his reins and shouted, "Let's see how fast you can really run!"

The stallion accepted the challenge with a vengeance. Laying its ears flat, it sailed like the wind across the flats, slinging clods of salt and alkali into its wake. Palo leaned far over the animal's neck and grinned with delight. On and on they ran into the moonlight and Sho was as powerful and tireless as a locomotive.

"Yeee-oowwww!" he howled at the melon moon as the wind and the dust of salt and alkali combined to send tears streaming down his cheeks. Finally, he pulled the Thoroughbred down to a walk saying, "Sho, you're no sprinter but I'll match you against any horse around for distance!"

The tall animal nickered, shaking its head at the inky heavens.

Palo could see why, during the past summer, Xabin had detoured far north of this terrible stretch of desert with their flock. It was now obvious to him that they would have lost everything if they'd been foolish enough to attempt this crossing.

Twenty or twenty-five miles into the desert Palo and Sho encountered deep sand which had taken a heavy toll as evidenced by the number of abandoned wagons lining the track like an unbroken chain. Everywhere he looked, Palo saw the signs of epic but futile attempts of men and women to extract their mired wagons. Most of the efforts had obviously ended in failure. In bitterness or anger, some of the emigrants had even torched their badly mired wagons rather than leave them intact.

A few times, Palo came upon fresher animal carcasses indicating that some, like Elias Pike, had attempted a late summer or autumn crossing. And while that might have seemed like a wise idea, Palo suspected that the feed had been so poor on both sides of these badlands that the animals entering it had been too weak to pull wagons through the heavy sand.

The sun peered like an angry eye over the eastern mountains and the day grew hot and bright. Palo's stomach rebelled when he tried to drink the awful water in his canteen and he had a raging thirst when he finally crossed the desert at midmorning, reaching the cold and sparkling Carson River. Sho actually burst into a gallop when he saw the river and did not stop running until he was standing in it up to his sweat- and salt-caked underbelly. Palo toppled like a drunk from his saddle and tumbled into the water. He emerged feeling like a man reborn. Both he and Sho drank until they could drink no more and then they forded the Carson and came to rest on the grassy west bank.

Palo unsaddled then hobbled the Thoroughbred and watched it hungrily feed upon the tasty spring grass. He retrieved some dried rabbit meat and biscuits from his saddlebags and used his saddle for a pillow as he stretched out and watched the Carson in the keen morning light. Wispy clouds flowed over the desert he'd just crossed and dust devils began to play tag across the salt flats, some towering hundreds of feet toward a serene field of clouds. A huge trout burst through the river's surface and Palo caught an instant of flashing silver and salmon before the fish disappeared again.

Palo found himself missing those he had left behind in the wilderness valley. He felt small and vulnerable surrounded by so much sky, empty land, and silence. Pushing up on his elbows, he gazed back eastward toward hazy purple mountains where his woman and his unborn child waited.

Never mind what Libby had said about not wanting him to return. He'd come back, by God. And he'd show her that he wasn't just talk and that he'd make his mark on the Comstock Lode. He and Sho would dance their way back across this horrible desert next autumn or winter and they'd bring presents for his new baby, and for Fay and Libby and even Augustin. He'd repay them every cent he'd ever borrowed—with interest—and they'd enjoy French champagne. He'd magnanimously offer to buy the whole damned sheep outfit just so he could liberate them from the wilderness.

Palo closed his eyes as a broad smile split his cracked lips. Now *that* was a dream to follow. And then Libby would see what a fool she'd been. She'd probably beg him to make love to her again and then to be married on the Comstock. And he'd probably do it, if for no other reason than to give his child legitimacy in the eyes of the world. Yes, Palo thought, I'm going to show them all a thing or two and I'm going to start by racing Sho.

Palo fell asleep wrapped with exhaustion but also with his grand dreams of success and vindication. He did not awaken until late afternoon. Rested and lonesome, he and Sho pushed up the Carson Valley until finally he came to a little settlement called Ragtown.

The first and most impressive of Ragtown's wooden buildings was the Blue Bottle Saloon. Palo could hardly tie Sho to the hitch rail and get inside fast enough. "Whiskey!" he called to a sleepy looking bartender. "Your finest!"

The man was middle-aged with hound-dog watery eyes and a poor excuse for a smile. He placed a full bottle of whiskey on a bare plank bartop and uncorked it with a popping sound. "Old Beaver," he said without enthusiasm, "is the finest whiskey money can buy in Nevada."

"I've been in Nevada," Palo said, almost giddy to be back inside a saloon with something more interesting to look at and talk about than sheep and the weather. "And it doesn't have any good whiskey."

"Try this and you just might change your mind."

Palo didn't bother with a glass. He tilted the bottle upward and let the fiery liquor singe his gullet and boil the lining off his gut.

"Ahhh!" he exclaimed, smacking, then fluttering his lips like a horse. "Now I would have to say that, compared with Humboldt River water, this is just a mite tame!"

He finally got a smile out of the bartender. "You just made the forty-mile crossing, huh?"

"I did."

"Are you from Salt Lake?"

"Nope."

When Palo didn't elaborate, the bartender offered him a cigar. "Pass any emigrant wagons comin' across yet?"

"Nope."

"See any Indians?"

"Yep. There's plenty of Paiute and Shoshone out there."

The bartender poured himself a shot and tossed it down neat. "Murderin' Diggers," he muttered.

Palo took another long drink from the bottle before he bit the tip off the cigar, rolled it around between his cheek and his tongue and leaned forward to have it lit by the bartender.

"Mister, you're the first pilgrim that's been across that desert in weeks. I'm tellin' you, we're all about to go broke here in Ragtown waiting for the wagon trains to start arrivin' this spring."

"Well," Palo said, struggling to generate a shade of sympathy, "they ought to start comin' in another month or two."

"I surely hope so. We not only make a fair amount of money off the goods and the whiskey, but also repairin' their wagons and trading for their poor and damn near dead mules and horses. Some of 'em arrive in such bad shape we butcher 'em and then trade 'em to the local Indians. Washo's, mostly."

"For what?"

"Mustangs and whatever odds and ends they scavenge off the trail that's been left behind. Some pretty nice things come through here that way."

"I expect some were more *stolen* than scavenged."

"Folks in Ragtown don't ask where the Indians and the other traders get their goods. We just buy and sell for a profit. That's all we do."

Palo's eyes happened to chance upon a sign up high behind the makeshift bar and he grinned as he read the list of prices. "Horse or mule meat ten cents a pound?"

"That's what the Indians like best and we sell a lot of it to 'em."

"You get twenty-five cents a pound for beef? That's ridiculous!"

"They're half starved by the time they get here and are happy to pay it."

Palo shook his head. "What do you suppose they'd give for mutton?"

"About the same. Why do you ask?"

"No reason," Palo said with a dismissive wave of his hand as he continued down the list. "Bacon a dollar a pound! I can't believe your prices."

"It costs plenty to fatten a Nevada hog."

Palo took another swig on the bottle. "How much is this bottle of Old Beaver?"

"It's costing you two dollars."

"You're a thief and a highwayman," Palo said good naturedly as he dug a couple of crumpled greenbacks out of his pocket. "Say, does anyone in Ragtown own a racehorse?"

The bartender's eyes narrowed. "I never saw a place that didn't have at least one fast horse that was a local favorite. Do you ride a fast horse?"

"My stud used to be fast," Palo said with just the proper hint of regret in his voice, "but he's just crossed the desert and he's still in shaky condition. Might be he needs to rest up a few weeks before I try and race him.

He lost the last two races and back then he was in far better shape."

"Well," the bartender said, "our local ain't much to brag about either. He mostly loses. We generally require he gets a head start to make things interesting."

"I see."

The bartender came around the edge of the bar and shuffled to the front door. "Is that your tall, skinny black?"

"Yep," Palo admitted. "Pretty sorry looking critter, isn't he?"

The bartender went outside. He walked all around the stallion and studied it closely. "He's a Kentucky racehorse, ain't he?"

"I don't know," Palo said. "I got him off the Shoshone. They used him to pack game."

The bartender snorted with disbelief. "The hell you say! This damn sure ain't no common packhorse."

"You can see that he's about to bow a tendon."

The bartender appeared skeptical as he studied the horse. "Which leg?"

"Take your pick 'cause all of 'em are bad," Palo answered. "Right front is the worst, of course."

The bartender ran his hand up and down that leg. "Not even a shinsplint. Nothing wrong with this animal's legs, Mister. And he sure ain't no mustang. If you got him from the Indians, then they must have stole him from a rich Kentucky horse breeder trying to make it to California."

"Maybe so," Palo said, pressing the case against his own horse. "But, as you can see, he's in terrible condition. Hasn't got much strength left."

"He does appear a little on the lean side," the bartender had to admit as he lifted a freshly shod forefoot. "And someone did an awful damn poor job of shoeing him."

Palo bit back a defensive response. "So where can I find the fastest horse in Ragtown?"

"Down yonder at the blacksmith's shop. Barney

Hager owns a dun horse that can run a little, when he isn't off his feed . . . which I think he is right now."

"Figures," Palo said cryptically.

Palo untied Sho and swung into the saddle still clenching his bottle of Old Beaver. "Well," he drawled, "maybe we should stop by and see that dun and we could have a little excitement since you haven't any customers."

"That'd be good," the bartender eagerly agreed. "Everyone here likes a horse race, even a slow one. Why, folks around here are desperate enough to bet on horned toads and turtles."

"It'd have to be a real short race before I'd risk killin' this sorry animal."

"Of course," the bartender said, nodding as if he understood. "But I do think that Barney's dun really is a shade off his feed."

"Well then, that'd make it an even race," Palo said, rolling his eyes like glass marbles in a jar after he turned his back on the man.

Barney Hager was one of those big, dull-witted looking fellows who was actually as sly as a coyote. He chewed a stem of straw and wore baggy bib coveralls and a straw hat but, when Palo saw the dun, he knew that he'd be in a tough horse race. The dun was tall and lean with one white eye and the other black so he looked sort of goofy. But the animal had long, straight legs, a deep chest, and a correctness about his conformation that just shouted speed. And for another thing, every dun and buckskin that Palo had ever seen had a stubborn streak that made them fierce competitors.

"He's off his feed right now," Hager commiserated. "You can tell by how peaked he's looking. I doubt that he'd be much of a match for that handsome Thoroughbred stallion you're riding."

Palo made his own careful examination. When he finished going over the dun, he said, "This horse's eyes are clear. His muzzle is cool and dry. And he's in better flesh than my black. I think he's plenty fit and that it'd be unfair to run him against my poor animal that just crossed the forty-mile."

"Naw," Hager said, "I just run Charley for the excitement of it. Win or lose, the folks in Ragtown seem to enjoy a little sport."

"You sound like a real regular guy, Mr. Hager."

"Barney." He chewed for a moment, then smiled harmlessly. "Stranger, how much you have to bet . . . if I was willing to put my Charley against your handsome, purebred racehorse? And how much lead would you give me over a mile track?"

"None." Palo rolled a cigarette, lit it, and exhaled slowly. "*I'd* be the one expecting a head start. And I'd want an especially short race since my horse is so tired after the crossing."

"Couldn't do that," Barney said, losing his smile. "Have to be a long race. My Charley, he starts off slower than an old woman in the wintertime. Have to be a long race or I wouldn't even consider a match."

"How long?"

Barney toed the earth and chewed a minute before he said, "At least a couple of miles."

Palo made a face. "My horse just traveled fifty miles today and I haven't got the time to stick around and rest him up for a race."

"No hurry," the bartender said. "I could rent you a room."

"Nope," Palo said. "I've got gold fever and I need to reach Virginia City as soon as possible. That's why I've already pushed this stud to his limits."

"If he was at his limit," Barney drawled, "you and I wouldn't be talking right now."

"Let's race today," Palo said. "Two miles, you give me two-to-one odds and a hundred-yard head start."

"Even money and three miles," Barney countered. "No head start."

"And no kid jockey," Palo said, figuring the blacksmith had to weigh well over two hundred pounds. "You ride the dun, I'll ride my stud. Deal?"

Barney and the bartender exchanged long, meaningful glances and then both men finally nodded their heads.

"How much money you got to bet?" Barney asked suspiciously.

Palo didn't have a lot of money but said, "Two hundred dollars."

"Fair enough. Two hundred. We'll race in one hour."

"I'll want to survey the track first."

"Suit yourself, but after poor-mouthing your stud so bad, I'd have expected you'd want to rest him and save his strength."

"Point the course out to me," Palo ordered, no longer bothering with false cordiality.

The two men led him out to the edge of town. "You see that old busted-down wagon laying on its side way out yonder? We'll race out around it and come running back into town. The crossing and starting lines will both be the same."

"That'd be a good two miles each way!"

"Naw!" Barney scoffed.

"Sure it is!"

"It's a long mile," the bartender said, head dipping up and down like that of a duck.

"It's our usual racecourse," Barney added, folding his big arms across his chest to indicate that there was nothing more to discuss.

Palo made a big show of displeasure but he finally conceded to the distance knowing it would suit his Thoroughbred very well.

"Let's see the color of your money, stranger," Barney ordered.

"Let's see the color of *your* money," Palo replied.

"Oh the hell with that," the blacksmith growled, maybe not having the two hundred himself. "Whoever loses can settle the debt with his horse, saddle, and that rifle and pistol you're packing—if he's a little light on cash."

"You're a very presumptuous man," Palo replied, "but I accept your terms."

Palo slowly rode out to the busted wagon. He'd been right. The distance was at almost two miles but that was good because the Thoroughbred was no sprinter. There were several patches of loose sand and a couple of potholes that Palo made mental notes to avoid. He reined Sho around the wagon and trotted him back to Ragtown nice and easy and was greeted by a sizable crowd of folks all eager to take his money.

"I'm not about to hand over my money to be held by one of you strangers," he informed them. "So I'm not too sure how to handle this."

The dilemma caused some real concern until Barney said, "I'll hold Ragtown's money in my saddlebags the same way that you're holding your money. But we need to see it before we go any farther."

Palo knew that this was reasonable and so he made a big show of dragging out a bundle of bills, which he flashed for just an instant and then crammed back into his own saddlebags.

"Hell," the bartender groused, "you might just have a wad of singles!"

"If that was the case, I'd expect you rough boys would catch and hang me. Right?"

The ten or twelve men that had gathered to match Palo's bets shouted that this was true and that he would be hanged if he couldn't pay his losses.

"Where's the starting line?" Palo asked, eager to change the subject and get the race under way.

"Right here," Barney said, dragging his heel across the dirt.

There wasn't much more to say. Palo checked his cinch and walked the stud up to the line. He was amazed at the transformation that Sho undertook. One minute the horse was acting like a tired plug, the next it was snorting and dancing alongside the equally excited dun. Palo swung into the saddle.

"I guess both these horses have raced a time or two," Barney said, tugging his straw hat down tight.

"I guess," Palo said, leaning forward with anticipation.

The bartender unholstered his six-gun, raised it overhead, and shouted, "Are the racers ready!"

"Sure," Palo said, leaning forward, careful to keep his heels out of the Thoroughbred's flanks.

"Shoot, dammit!" Barney shouted.

When the gun went off, the dun shot into the lead like it had been whipped with a thornbush. Sho groaned from deep in his gut and started slinging clods as he slowly built up speed trying to catch Ragtown's favorite. The people were crowing like randy roosters. Halfway to the wagon, Sho had finally settled into his sweeping stride and was running full out and closing on the dun. Barney glanced back and his jaw dropped. He applied the whip but the Thoroughbred was rolling now and overtook the dun about seventy yards from the wagon. The dun was a fighter, though, and when the two tall horses drew neck and neck, it showed its great heart and found even more speed.

"Come on!" Barney shouted, applying the whip.

Palo didn't dare whip Sho. To have done so would have been an unnecessary insult. The black Thoroughbred tried to take a hunk out of the dun's shoulder, which caused him to lose stride and a little ground. Encouraged, Barney whipped the dun even harder. Sho regained his stride and swept past the dun and then right on by the wagon.

"Whoa!" Palo cried, sawing on Sho's reins.

But the Thoroughbred wasn't about to slow down and the dun had no intention of that either. Both Palo and Barney were shouting and fighting to control their runaways as the two headstrong animals kept running for about another mile.

"Dammit!" Barney raged as they finally drew to a

halt. "What happened! My horse never did that before!"

"He was probably never getting beat before."

"Well, he wasn't beat today, either!"

"Sure he was," Palo argued. "I reached the wagon first and I was still ahead all the way out here. You were eating my dust."

"Damned if we had a proper race," Barney said, twisting around and looking back at Ragtown. "Neither one of us crossed the finish line so we'll just have to do her over . . . maybe."

Palo saw things in a much different light. Sho *had* outrun the Ragtown racer and that was good enough to win the stakes.

"Give me those saddlebags full of money."

"The hell you say!"

Palo's gun flicked up and his barrel came to rest on Barney's broad chest. "You'll go to hell in about two seconds unless you pay me what I'm due."

Barney turned white with rage but when Palo cocked back the hammer of his six-gun, the blacksmith untied his money-stuffed saddlebags and threw them in the dirt.

"Get down and hand 'em to me!" Palo ordered.

Barney started to argue but something in Palo's eyes changed his mind so he climbed off the dun and handed the saddlebags up to Palo. "They're going to catch and then lynch you and I'll be laughing louder than any of 'em," Barney snarled, his face red with suppressed anger.

"Maybe," Palo said, looping the saddlebags over his saddle-horn. "They can damn sure try, but I'll be relaying the fastest pair of horses in Nevada."

And with that, Palo tore the dun's reins away from Barney and galloped off toward the Sierras. He could hear the blacksmith's cursing over the hard drumming of hoofbeats. Palo didn't know how much stamina these two fine racers had left, but he expected to find out soon.

CHAPTER

NINETEEN

Palo hadn't worried about being overtaken by the men of Ragtown. Not with two racehorses to relay southwest along the Carson until he finally arrived at the base of the Comstock Lode and started riding up Gold Hill Canyon.

Everywhere Palo looked he saw the bustling activity that always accompanied optimism and gold rush prosperity. Palo had witnessed the same energy in the early years of California's gold rush and he knew that this boom had to inevitably lead to bust. Palo didn't care. A wise man got in early, made his fortune, and then sold his mining stocks and claims during the time of the bonanza and just before what the Mexicans called *borrasca*.

Timing was everything. Mere unsubstantiated rumors could send a mine stock either soaring or into a steep nosedive. Palo had been just a kid during the California gold rush when Xabin had controlled him and Augustin with an iron fist. It had been, for Palo, a time of frustration for he had watched miners become rich overnight. Now, it was his turn to have a chance at fortune and there was no one that could stop him.

"Hey, handsome!" a saucy looking blond woman called from the second-story balcony of a hotel. "Come on up and little Lola will put a *real* smile on that pretty face!"

Palo laughed and yelled up to her, "Sorry, but I'm bound for Virginia City!"

"Honey, there ain't nothing better'n Lola up there."

"Nothing but money!"

The woman blew him a kiss and called to a pair of horsemen Palo had just passed riding down the canyon. Palo twisted around in the saddle and saw both men rein in sharply at the hotel, dismount, and start to count their money.

Palo drank in the sights, sounds, and smells of the Comstock Lode. The canyon was steep, narrow, and dotted with mine tailings and claims. Before the rich mother veins of gold and silver had been discovered only a few years before, Gold Canyon had probably been crowded with thirsty cottonwood trees along the banks of its seasonal stream. And the canyonsides were dotted with stumps telling Palo that forests of pinion and juniper pines had once graced those steep slopes but had all been chopped down for firewood or mine timbering.

The contrast between the Comstock and the Sierra mining camps could hardly have been greater. Over on the western slopes of the Sierras the rivers were big and thundering, the forests thick and green. Here, there was little except rock, sage, and a great azure canopy of sky. And where the California streams had been filled with placer miners, Palo saw that all these mines were underground and marked by their immense yellowish-brown tailings. Only a handful of prospectors panned the muddy canyon stream while thousands up on the slopes were busy burrowing shafts and tunnels. To Palo, it looked sort of like a giant prairie dog colony hard at work.

"Hey, Mister!" a liveryman shouted. "Why don't

you board them two fine animals right here at my stable! You take 'em up to Virginia City, they'll get stolen for certain."

Palo reined in his exhausted horses. "How much would you charge?"

The young proprietor snapped his suspenders and grinned hopefully. "Just two dollars a day . . . grain is extra."

"For each horse?"

"Why sure!" The grin faded. "Stranger, hay and grain are like gold in these parts."

"Whew!" Palo wheezed, urging his weary horses on past the livery. "That's robbery."

"It'll cost you twice as much up in Virginia City," the young liveryman called at him. "You wait and see if it don't! And then you come on back."

"I'll keep you in mind."

Gold Hill Canyon was lined with saloons and all manner of businesses. Just like along the forty-mile desert, this winding canyon road was littered with debris, especially broken whiskey bottles, rusting cans, and junk mining machinery. It was all that Palo could do to keep from getting run over because huge, lumbering ore wagons choked the road as they moved ponderously up and down from the mines to the stamping and processing mills located on the Carson River. The sound of screeching wagon brakes sounded like a thousand tormented banshees and were enough to set any man's nerves to jangling. Crowding up behind Palo were cursing teamsters with clackity ore wagons making a fast return trip to the mines. Some of the biggest freight wagons were pulled by straining horse, mule, and oxen teams dragging immense pieces of mining machinery whose workings were a mystery to all but the mining engineers.

"Hey, stranger, do you want to sell one of those fine horses?" asked a tall, well-dressed man in his thirties with a sweeping handlebar mustache and a Southern drawl. "I'm bound for Tennessee to fight for the

Confederacy and I'll need horses fast enough to outrun the Indians that I come across."

Palo knew a prosperous gentleman when he saw one and he could not help but compare his shabby appearance and vow to soon model himself after this dashing fellow. He reined the stallion to a halt and said, "Are you really going to war?"

"I sure am! Going to join the Confederate Army and whip the Northerners. There's an entire company forming in Virginia City. We're drilling and training right now."

The Southern patriot smiled. "Sir, are you interested in the preservation of states' rights and Southern independence?"

"I'm afraid not," Palo said, almost wishing he were.

"How unfortunate that few men can see much past the end of a pick or a shovel," the Southerner lamented. "However, I am interested in buying one of your horses. Preferably, that black stallion. He looks very much like the Thoroughbreds my father used to raise before the Yankees plundered our horse farm."

"I'm afraid that this stallion is not for sale at any price," Palo told the man. "I mean to win some prize money on him."

"If he's as fast as he looks and, if you play the game intelligently, you should do very well. And what of the dun?"

"He's even faster at a half mile or less."

The man knew horses and quickly gave the weary dun a thorough going-over. "He is a fine animal. Name your price."

Palo had grown attached to the dun. He especially liked its heart and the fact that it never acted up on cool mornings or shied at the strange sights and sounds that now surrounded them in this canyon.

"I'm sorry," he said, lifting his reins and preparing to ride on. "But I think I'll just keep both horses."

"Would an offer of one hundred dollars change your mind?" the Southerner asked.

"No."

"Then one-fifty and that's three times what he's worth anywhere else."

Palo scowled. "What does it *really* cost to board a horse up here?"

"Three dollars a day in Virginia City. So you see," the man said, "in less than two months, your board bill will equal the animal's entire value."

"Then he's sold," Palo said, also realizing it would be healthy to have sold the dun in case anyone from Ragtown found him on the Comstock and went to see the sheriff. "And you've got yourself a superior animal."

"I know that," the Southern gentleman said as he stroked the dun's neck. "But I would give you two hundred for your black stallion. And, as with the dun, I'll expect a bill of sale. My name is Benjamin Chapel."

"Palo is mine but I'm still not interested in parting with this stallion."

The Southerner nodded with understanding. "Just be careful where you board that fine animal. Horse thieves are thicker than fleas up on the Comstock. Why, I'd judge that there are men watching us right now thinking about how they'd like to steal both your horses."

"All they'd get for their trouble is an early grave," Palo vowed. "Any suggestions on what I should do to protect my property?"

"Of course. Sell both horses to me, pocket the money and eliminate both a considerable worry and expense."

Palo had to smile at the man's persistence. "Any advice other than that?"

"Mickey's Livery up on B Street in Virginia City employs armed guards. They advertise box stalls to rent for those willing to pay five dollars a day."

"Five dollars!" Palo was shocked. He would not have expected to pay nearly that much for his *own* hotel room.

"That's right." Chapel took the dun's lead rope. "Changing your mind about selling that stallion?"

"No," Palo said. "I'll just need to win a few quick races."

"And then everyone will know his speed and you won't find any bettors."

"You sure are full of bad news."

"I arrived here with three Thoroughbreds," Chapel said, eyes assuming a faraway look. "You might say they were part of my inheritance. But they all were stolen, one by one. To be honest, Palo, I bet that you don't have that stallion more than a week."

Palo's normal confidence was starting to erode. "Even if I do pay Mickey five dollars a night?"

"That's right. *Especially* after you win a race."

Palo gazed up the steep, heavily trafficked canyon road. "How much farther is it to Virginia City?"

"Less than three miles. You pass directly through Gold Hill, then hump it over The Divide and there she is in all her corrupted splendor and glory."

"Three miles, huh?" Palo was a man who had always prided himself on being willing to change course when it seemed the right thing to do under unexpected circumstances. "All right, Mr. Chapel. If you have two hundred and fifty dollars—cash—I'll throw in my saddle, blanket, and bridle."

"Very well," the Southerner agreed, dragging out a very thick wallet. "Palo, you've made a very wise decision. But I do need a couple of bills of sale."

"Not a problem," Palo said, dismounting. "Do you have paper and something to write with?"

"No, but they're available at the desk of this excellent hotel," Chapel said, gesturing to a prosperous looking hotel and saloon.

Palo dismounted and tied both animals at the hitch rail in front of the building. "Then let's take care of business. I'm in a hurry to see Virginia City."

They walked into the hotel and the Southerner marched right up to the registration desk. "Mr. Lorringer," he said to the hotel desk clerk, "we require writing materials and your presence as a witness to the sale of Palo's two horses."

"Yes sir, Mr. Chapel," the desk clerk said. "I'll get paper and pen for you right now."

There was a saloon in one corner of the hotel and Palo licked his lips. "I'm so thirsty I couldn't work up a spit if my life depended on it."

"Then I should buy you a drink! You appear to have ridden a long, hard trail."

Palo scrubbed his unshaven cheeks. He knew that he looked even rougher than usual and felt downright slovenly in the company of this elegant fellow.

"What about the paper and writing. . . ."

"Mr. Lorringer will bring them to our table momentarily. In the meantime, we can avail ourselves of some excellent spirits."

"That sounds fine to me," Palo said, following the man into the saloon. "But only one drink and then I'm on my way."

"Of course! Bartender," he called, "two of your best whiskeys!"

"Make them doubles," Palo added.

"Two doubles it is, one for each horse!"

Palo glanced impatiently back into the hotel lobby. It was empty. Lorringer must have had to go to one of the rooms for the writing materials.

"And so," Chapel said, "what brings you to the Comstock Lode?"

"Fortune, same as everyone."

"Very difficult. Very, very difficult indeed."

"Beats going to war," Palo said, adding quickly, "but a man has to stand up for his family."

Chapel nodded and drummed his fingers on the tabletop. "Do you have a family?"

"Not much of one," Palo said as the drinks were delivered to their table. "I just lost my father to the Indians. I have a brother, Augustin, and half interest in a large flock of sheep."

"How quaint," Chapel said, eyes tight around the corners. "I thought I detected their strong . . . bouquet."

Palo flushed, feeling extremely self-conscious. "I'm going to get new clothes when I reach Virginia City. A fine suit . . . one like you're wearing. And a handsome new hat and shoes. The works."

"There are some excellent tailors in Virginia City," Chapel confided. "Remind me to recommend one the next time we chance to meet as you're passing through Silver City."

Palo had been about to say something but now he leaned back in his chair and eyed Chapel closely. "I thought you were off to fight in the war between the states."

"Oh, certainly I am!" Chapel drained his glass. "We're leaving any day now. There's no time to waste."

"Then why would we meet again?"

Chapel shrugged. "I was thinking that you might happen to come by in a day or two."

"Why would I do that?"

"I have no idea," Chapel said, his voice losing its cordiality as he glanced toward the adjoining hotel lobby.

Palo followed the man's hasty glance. Lorringer was still missing. "What the devil do you suppose could be keeping Mr. Lorringer so long?"

"Beats me. How about another whiskey? Bartender! Two more of the same."

Palo, however, was on his feet. "I'd best find out."

"Yes," Chapel said, hurrying after him.

Lorringer appeared looking a little out of sorts. "I'm sorry for taking so long, but I had to go out back to my own place and get paper and pen."

"That's all right," Chapel said, acting nervous as he pushed the writing materials in Palo's direction saying, "Now, I want to make sure that we have an accurate description of both horses, especially the stallion. He has two stocking feet, right?"

"Only one."

"Are you sure?" Chapel asked. "I could swear he had two."

"He's *my* horse and I ought to know," Palo said with his pen poised over the blank sheet of paper.

"But the stallion does have a small blaze, doesn't he?" Chapel asked.

"Just a star on his forehead," Palo said, wishing the Southerner would shut up for a moment and allow him to concentrate on the wording of this legal document.

Chapel marched over to the hotel's front door to look for himself. "I swear, that whiskey must be stronger than I thought! And I was sure . . . what the hell!"

Palo dropped the pen and swung about to see Chapel's jaw sag as the man stared out the front door of the hotel. "What's wrong?"

"They're gone!" Chapel exclaimed, jumping outside.

Palo sprinted out onto the boardwalk. Both horses *were* gone! Palo ran into the street and was almost run over by a freight wagon. He looked both ways but saw neither horse. He spun completely around searching for someone who must have witnessed the theft of his two valuable racehorses. Everyone who'd been sitting in the chairs lined before the hotel only minutes ago had disappeared.

"Hey, you drunk or something!" a mule skinner yelled, cracking his whip right in Palo's face. "Get the hell off the street before someone runs you over!"

Palo dodged between two more wagons and their cursing drivers and jumped to the safety of the boardwalk.

"Damn," Chapel swore with half-hearted sympathy, "I *am* sorry! I surely wanted to buy those horses."

Right then and there it struck Palo like a fist between the eyes that this entire sale business had been a clever ruse to separate him from his two exceptional horses while they were stolen.

Chapel clucked his tongue and started to go back inside.

"Hold it!" Palo shouted, unbuttoning his coat to expose his six-gun.

Chapel slowly turned and his eyes dropped to Palo's side arm, then lifted his face. "Kid," he said, "I am sorry about your misfortune but those things happen on the Comstock every day."

"Not to me, they don't."

"Tell you what," Chapel said, forcing a smile. "You walk up the street and I'll walk back down the street. There's always a slight chance that one or the other of us will find those horses and the thieving rascals that took them."

Chapel started to leave but Palo's voice froze him in place. "Chapel, *you're* the thief and neither one of us is going anywhere until someone brings my horses back!"

Chapel sighed and turned to confront Palo. "I'm going to forgive you for saying that," he replied. "You're obviously upset and with good reason. I offer my sincere condolences. Remember, I was prepared to pay you well for those horses."

"No you weren't. You set me up to steal them."

Chapel's tolerant smile died and his lips twisted with derision. "I think," he said, "that you had better start walking. It's a strenuous hike but you will have cooled down and still be alive by the time you reach Virginia City."

"You are a liar and a horse thief!" Palo recklessly shouted as traffic in the street came to a halt and men stared with anticipation.

Chapel unbuttoned his fine suit coat and pushed it back to reveal a pearl-handled Colt resting in a tooled leather holster. "Goat herder," he spat contemptuously, "you have pushed the limits of my patience. Now, git your stinking, filthy self out of my sight."

"Draw," Palo hissed, every nerve in his body tingling.

Chapel wore a big diamond ring on his finger and it flashed as his hand swooped downward toward the butt of his gun. Palo's hands were calloused and dirty but his well-worn and oiled Colt bucked in his fist before Chapel's gun cleared its fancy holster. Palo fired twice and Chapel elevated to his toes, face turning chalky white as his own gun clattered to the boardwalk. Palo shot the man a third time bowling him over into the hotel lobby.

Palo hopped up on the boardwalk and strode over to Chapel's body. "You saw it, Lorringer," he said, eyes flicking up to the desk clerk. "You saw Mr. Chapel draw first. Right?"

Lorringer dipped his chin in quick assent. He was a short, nondescript fellow in a coat, white shirt, and tie. "Yes sir, Mr. Chapel drew first. I saw that."

"So . . . where are my horses?"

"Sir?" Lorringer's face burst sweat from every pore.

Palo glanced over his shoulder. He didn't know what kind of trouble the gunfire might bring running. Perhaps Chapel, if that really was his name, had a lot of friends and there would be more blood spilled. Or maybe there was a sheriff in cahoots with this bunch of thieves, but whatever was going on, Palo meant to get to the bottom of it—starting with Lorringer.

"Where did they take my horses?" Palo repeated, cocking back the hammer of his gun and pointing it at the man, who threw his hands into the air. "Last chance."

"I don't know!" the desk clerk wailed. "I honestly don't know! I just . . ."

"You were in on it, Lorringer!"

"Yes, sir! But I don't know where they took those horses!"

Palo went over to the dead man and removed his wallet. He holstered his gun and discovered that the wallet contained well over a thousand dollars. Palo nodded with satisfaction and pocketed every last dollar.

And then he saw that Chapel's expensive boots were about his size and so removed and replaced them for his own poor, sheep-smelly clodhoppers.

"Fine hat," Palo said, trying it on for size. "Might as well take his gun and pocket watch too, huh, Lorringer?"

The desk clerk nodded vigorously. "He's got no more use for 'em now."

"Mr. Chapel offered me a lot of money for my horses so I'll just take these other things. Any problem with that, Lorringer?"

"No sir!" The desk clerk found the courage to swipe a handkerchief from his coat pocket and mop his perspiring face.

"Pity I ruined his suit with all the blood," Palo said, guessing that the suit would have fit him quite nicely. "Probably cost a lot of money. Do you know the name of his Virginia City tailor?"

"No sir!"

"Well," Palo said, "it doesn't matter. I'll find my own."

Palo backed to the door. "Lorringer," he called. "You tell whoever took my horses that I'll gun them down if I ever come across them up in Virginia City. Is that clear?"

The man jerked his head up and down with understanding. Out of the corner of his eye, Palo caught a sudden movement in the saloon. He spun and fired, bullet shattering a huge back-bar mirror that sent a cascade of glass down on the bartender. Then Palo ducked out of the hotel and headed up the road with both Colts in his fists and eyes tracking everything that moved. Mr. Chapel's expensive boots were such a perfect fit that they felt like bedroom slippers.

Palo guessed that, sooner or later, he would come across his stolen horses. The Comstock Lode wasn't *that* big. In the meantime, he would be plenty happy to save himself a large livery bill and enjoy the fruits of Benjamin Chapel's fatal misfortune.

CHAPTER

TWENTY

Virginia City was even more exciting than Palo had hoped. The huge gold and silver strike below Sun Mountain had quickly emptied California's worked out mining towns of its thousands of restless and unemployed prospectors, merchants, gamblers, prostitutes, freighters, and fortune seekers. Each year since its birth, Virginia City had doubled, then tripled in size. When Palo crossed the Divide, he saw a city that never slept and boasted a population of over ten thousand. Hundreds more were arriving every day from as far away as England and Wales, lured by the highest wages in the world—five dollars a day, thanks to the newly formed Miner's Union.

Palo trudged down C Street in his new boots and hat reveling in an excitement that surpassed anything he'd known in the California gold fields. Huge new buildings were already in place and dozens more were undergoing rapid construction. Everywhere he looked, Palo saw impressive stores, shops, and mansions along with the usual packed and bawdy saloons with names like the Bucket of Blood, the Delta, the Silver Dollar, and the Silver Queen. At most of them, hawkers and

226

shills handed out free drinks and food to anyone that would come inside and gamble. Prostitutes, pimps, and pickpockets joined the miners on the boardwalks to conduct business, and public drunkenness was so prevalent that Palo supposed the only law in Virginia City, save the gun, might be self-appointed vigilantes.

"Hey," Palo called to a pair of glassy-eyed miners sharing a bottle, "what's the finest hotel in Virginia City?"

The two men swayed crookedly over to Palo, eyed him up and down, and then one said, "Mister, you wouldn't be allowed in the front door the way you look and smell."

Palo didn't take offense. Sure, he had a nice new pair of boots, a fancy hat, and a gunbelt, but he was dirty and unshaven. His shirt, coat, and pants were greasy from wool and an absolute disgrace. These men were right, he wouldn't get into a respectable establishment.

"Then I'll start with a bathhouse and a place to get a haircut and shave," he said.

The two miners pointed him toward an establishment just down the street. Palo got his hair cut, then took a bath in the barber's back room for an extra dollar. He soaked the sheep stink out of his pores for nearly an hour, then found a tailor shop and bought himself two complete outfits although Virginia City prices were triple what he would have expected to pay in Sacramento.

"Where is your finest hotel?" he asked the tailor as the man finished hemming up his pants.

"I'd recommend the Silver Dollar. You got the saloon right below with gambling and a fine dining room." The man winked. "You'll find the women that work there are pretty good too."

"I'll keep that in mind . . . if I'm ever desperate enough to pay for it."

Palo left his filthy shepherd's outfit at the tailor's shop and when he stepped out onto the boardwalk, he could tell at once that he had gained some respect. Ladies strolling along no longer averted their eyes but smiled. Gentlemen tipped their hats. Palo tipped his hat in return feeling as if he were in some exclusive fraternity.

That night, Palo dined at the Golden Bar Restaurant, which specialized in shrimp, crabmeat, and oyster stew. The meal was delicious, almost as good as he remembered tasting in San Francisco. He savored French brandy after a dessert of cherries jubilee and then lit a one-dollar cigar. With Benjamin Chapel's money burning a hole in his pockets, Palo was feeling very prosperous indeed. The dining room had class and a piano player that could actually play something besides the usual bawdy saloon songs. There were candles and real linen on the table. The utensils were solid silver and the glassware English crystal. This was, Palo thought, the good life. He found himself pitying Augustin and Libby and wondered if they really had the capacity to enjoy the finer things in life. Augustin, like Xabin, was a simple man. Libby was . . . well, she was educated, smart, tough, and resourceful, but he doubted that she would fit into this kind of sophisticated setting. Palo ordered a second brandy and leaned back in his chair, content to listen to talk of mining stocks, money, and commerce. Matters of importance to worldly men.

By and by, Palo's eye came to rest on a woman blessed with extraordinary beauty. She was, he thought, quite irresistible and obviously bored with her far more elderly companions. The woman was only in her mid-twenties, with an unforgettable heart-shaped face and dark brown hair that cascaded down to the middle of her back. She wore an emerald and diamond necklace and kept turning a wedding ring whose diamond must have cost a small fortune. Palo decided that the man who sat with his arm draped over the back of her chair was not her father but instead her husband. This was confirmed when the man slipped his hand under her long hair and began to stroke her back, thinking no one would notice. The young woman gave him a condescending smile, and was drinking more champagne than anyone else at the crowded table.

Palo smiled and studied her through the lazy blue haze of his cigar smoke. He had a theory that no woman could ignore his gaze for more than a few minutes. It was as if he alone had a certain magnetism that could not be ignored. And sure enough, the woman turned and saw him, then boldly met Palo's eyes.

Their lingering exchange across the big dining room was somehow more intimate than had they shared close physical contact. For a few heartbeats, everyone and everything else between them vanished. Palo smiled and raised his glass to salute her beauty from across the room. Her eyes flashed like her diamonds and Palo knew he'd caught her fancy. Her husband, full of his own self-importance, was oblivious to everything for the next half hour as his young wife and Palo played romantic guessing games.

When the young woman's party paid their bill and exited the hotel, Palo left soon enough to see her being helped into a fine carriage. Just before the woman was seated, his eyes pulled her gaze back to him. The woman tossed her hair and laughed.

"Who are they?" Palo asked a one-armed man loitering by the door begging for spare money.

"That's Mr. Henry Ward and his wife, Mrs. Jasmine Ward. She's a beauty, isn't she?"

"What does he do?"

"He owns the Silverbowl Mining Company. It's one of the biggest new strikes on the Comstock. Three years ago, Ward was a hard-luck miner that didn't have two nickels to his name. I even drank with him a time or two."

The one-armed beggar spat into the dirt. "Ward had all the luck, I'll tell you. He staked out a claim and damned if it wasn't right on top of a vein of pure silver! He don't want to remember me. Won't loan me a cent.

He's got a beautiful wife. Mansion up on A Street. He's got everything but charity in his black heart."

"Where did he find such a woman?"

"Mister, when you strike it rich, beautiful women find *you*. There is a rumor about her, though."

"I'm listening."

The man stuck out his hand, palm turned up. "You appear to be a man who has had considerable good fortune early in life. My name is Mickey, and I wished like hell that I could say the same. Had a mining accident and now I can't find work. Not any that pays enough."

Palo greased Mickey's palm with five dollars. "This story about Mrs. Ward had better be more than a rumor."

"It is," Mickey promised, grinning to show his front teeth were missing. "Mrs. Ward was a high-priced woman of the night over in San Francisco."

Palo was neither shocked nor surprised by this revelation. Jasmine knew and enjoyed men, of that he was very certain. "Keep talking."

"The rumor is that she betrayed another older man and absconded with a pile of his money. Jasmine has expensive tastes."

"Does her husband know about her past?"

"With a face and a figure like hers, why would that fat old geezer even care?" Mickey leaned closer and chuckled obscenely. "I can tell you this for certain. Jasmine wasn't in Virginia City a month before she hooked old Henry and he's been smiling ever since. He built her that mansion up on A Street, but Jasmine can't buy respect from the high society wives. She's a pariah—too rich to consort with whores or dance hall girls, too tainted to have tea with the ladies. That's why you'll generally see her alone."

"How interesting. Which way is A Street?"

"Two streets up the hill." Mickey studied him closely. "Say, mate, are you expectin' an invitation from the Wards or something?"

"In one form or another," Palo said as he walked away puffing on his expensive cigar.

During that first month on the Comstock, Palo used every possible occasion to "accidentally" meet and exchange increasingly warm pleasantries with Jasmine Ward. He learned that she went shopping every day and usually bought a dress or some decoration for the Ward Mansion. Jasmine had a fondness for poker too, but she didn't advertise the fact and played only among a select group of men and women in the secrecy of a house over on B Street.

Palo discovered that the woman was also fond of riding a spirited little dapple-gray mare. Jasmine seemed to enjoy turning the heads of lonely miners wherever she rode and there were plenty of heads to turn. Palo thought it was a little foolish for Jasmine to ride out alone in the hills, but she was an expert horse-woman and probably figured her mare could outrun any danger she encountered on the Comstock.

As for his own two stolen horses, Palo saw nothing of either, although he was constantly on the lookout. Whenever he heard of a horserace, which usually took place down on D Street near the new Virginia and Truckee Railroad depot station, he'd saunter down and see if either of his horses was entered, but they never were. Whoever had stolen them must have decided that it was healthier to take both animals to California.

As for his own interests, Palo became addicted to speculating in mining stocks although they were an expensive and highly risky pastime. The stocks soared or plummeted according to rumors rather than actual profits or production. On the Comstock Lode, rumors sped down C Street faster than a bullet. This was why mines without any history of production at all might suddenly become very valuable. Never mind facts or figures. All that was required was a whispered rumor that such and such a mine had secretly struck a huge vein of ore. Almost instantly, men who had formerly ridiculed the mine's stock now rushed to buy it at *any* price, which only served to create even more of a buying frenzy. Overnight, mines adjacent to the one whose stock was soaring tripled in value.

Palo himself invested heavily in such ventures and several times, he even made thousands of dollars in paper profits. But like everyone else, he was not content to double or even triple his modest investment. No, when a stock and paper profits were soaring every day, a man would be a fool to divest. Palo, caught up in the excitement, would hang on, feeling as rich and heady as his fellow investors, many of whom played the market by telegraph from their San Francisco offices.

But inevitably and for no reason that anyone could fathom, the rumors soured and the stock began to decline. Men who'd bought at the inflated prices invariably decided to hold steady. Never mind that the stock was a little "off" or "soft" that day. It would soon take a turn for the better and *then* they would sell. Palo learned the hard way that things sometimes did get better for a few days . . . just before the final plunge that wiped men out. Unfortunately, Palo did not learn these valuable lessons until he was nearly broke.

It was on the day of one such painful loss that Palo chanced to meet Jasmine Ward as she rode her mare down A Street. He had been so disconsolate about losing all but his last hundred dollars that he didn't even see the beautiful woman until she called, "Good day, sir!"

"Why, Mrs. Ward," he said with his sunniest smile, "what a nice surprise!"

She drew rein. "Yes, isn't it. We seem destined to run into each other quite often. It *is* merely by chance, is it not?"

"Of course!"

They were already playing the game that both knew so well.

Jasmine tossed her dark mane. "Do you prefer to walk everywhere?"

"No," he said, thinking about all the thousands of

miles he'd already followed a bunch of damned sheep. "But I had two of my horses stolen over in Gold Hill just as I was arriving."

"How unfortunate!" Jasmine did not look all that upset.

"Yes," he said with a shrug as if it was of small consequence, "isn't it."

"Would you like to borrow one of our horses tomorrow and go for a ride?" Before Palo could accept this wonderful offer, Jasmine added, "I sometimes feel a little unsafe out in these hills by myself, for not everyone is a gentleman like you."

Palo's spirits took full flight. He completely forgot about his sizable losses on the Comstock. How could any man think of mere money when he beheld the prospect of sharing the company of such a beauty?

"I believe that I would," he said, not wanting to sound too eager.

"Then we'll do that," she said, looking quite pleased. "Tomorrow, say up behind the livery at this hour?"

"I promise that I won't forget," Palo said, not failing to note that they were to meet secretly.

"Of course you won't," she said, dropping pretenses. "It's the chance you've been dreaming about, isn't it?"

Palo was momentarily at a loss for words. Never mind, he thought as she smiled sweetly and rode on past. He would be prepared tomorrow.

And he was. The next day, Palo was filled with confidence when Jasmine appeared leading a spirited bay gelding alongside her own pretty gray mare. She wore a beige riding habit and high, laced boots. Her horse was brushed, and the sidesaddle she rode glistened with leather oil.

"This bay gelding desperately needs exercise but no one feels safe riding him," she explained. "I didn't ask, but I hope you are an accomplished rider."

"I am. I'm the son of a rancher."

"Oh, really? Where is the ranch?"

"Colorado," he lied.

"Why did you leave?"

"My older brother and I had differences of opinion."

"What a shame."

"Not really," Palo assured her as he adjusted the stirrups and took the reins firmly in hand. "The ranch will always be half mine."

She allowed him to help her mount the mare and then she asked, "Is it a *nice* ranch?"

"Yes," he said, expertly swinging onto the bay and knowing that "nice" meant vast and profitable. "We hold about fifteen thousand acres and it is stocked with Longhorn cattle. We also run a few sheep and do some logging. One way or another, we seem to make ends meet."

"I'm sure that you do, Mister . . ."

"Arostegi."

She raised her eyebrows. "Are you by chance Portuguese?"

"Basque," he said proudly.

"I know nothing about your people. Where are they from?"

"Between France and Spain. We're rebels," he boasted. "An untamed breed."

"My," she replied, "how very exciting."

Before he could think of a clever reply, she quirted her mare and went galloping up a dirt road.

"I hope you know where we're going!" Palo shouted, trying to keep the bay's head up so that it did not start bucking.

"I *always* know where I'm going!"

"So do I," he called out as he followed the lovely Jasmine across the face of Sun Mountain.

CHAPTER

TWENTY-ONE

It was springtime and Libby no longer had morning sickness but she could feel the first stirrings of the child she carried in her womb. Time and time again she had attempted to tell both her daughter and Augustin about her condition, but she never seemed to find the right moment. Libby was fairly certain that Fay would be excited and understanding but she had no idea how Augustin would react, especially if he knew that she carried Palo's child.

While fretting about this late one night, Libby decided that Augustin might be convinced that the child had been fathered by her late husband, Elias. It had been, after all, less than a month between his disappearance and the time when she had actually become pregnant by Palo. Women did go past their terms and Libby was quite sure that Augustin would not even think to question the legitimacy of her child. And, to be honest, there was some resemblance between poor Elias and Palo. Both were dark complected and taller than average.

The more that Libby considered this deceit, the more she hated herself but became convinced that it

was one she must employ. After all, it was all for the
sake of her baby, rather than to save her own reputation. And, more than anything, Libby wanted legitimacy
for her newborn. The only real problem was what would
happen when or if Palo ever returned and announced
his fatherhood. Libby didn't even want to think of that.
She hoped never to see Palo again.

At this time of year, a sheepman like Augustin was
oblivious to everything except the newborn lambs. He
arose long before daylight and took Emo out into the
flock and began to tend to the new arrivals. Fay would
invariably follow a short time later and it gave Libby a
good feeling to see her daughter and the Basque sheepman working as a team.

Libby also enjoyed plunging in and helping with the
newborn lambs. Some mornings she felt much better
and more energetic than others and she tired earlier in
the day and had to rest, but she very much enjoyed the
season and was surprised to discover a great deal of
satisfaction in lambing. There was so much to learn.

"To begin with," Augustin told them, "you must
understand that for the first few days, a ewe knows her
lamb only by smell. Gradually, the ewe will begin to
recognize her lamb's voice. Because of this, she and her
lamb must be kept very close together at first."

"And if they are not?" Libby asked.

"The lamb will soon die or the mother might go
about adopting some other ewe's lamb by mistake." Augustin frowned. "It is not uncommon for a ewe to become discouraged after only an hour or two of searching
for her newborn and then give up the hunt. Once she
does that, she will probably refuse her lamb even if it is
later found and returned to her."

"They are not very motherly, are they?" Libby said
with a hint of disapproval.

Augustin shrugged his broad shoulders. "I'm afraid
not. You see, a cow will always know the location of its
calf. Even if you find her alone, she knows and might
have just hidden the calf for a short time. And a mare

will not run away from her colt or filly and you will always see them together. But a ewe . . . well, she has other things besides motherhood on her mind and discourages easily."

"Does that happen very often?"

"At least one time out of twenty," Augustin said. "Most ewes are very good to their lambs for the first few hours."

"Is that all?" Fay asked.

"Yes," Augustin confessed. "When a ewe stands over her newborn lamb, you will both learn to recognize her special sound of affection. It is a low rumble in the throat which she makes without opening her mouth. This rumble is only used by a ewe talking to her lamb, or a ram talking to the ewe when he is . . ."

"Attentive," Libby said, helping the man out of his embarrassment.

"Exactly," Augustin said, smiling with gratitude. "You will hear the ewe rumble to her newborn and then the lamb will bleat in return. This goes on constantly."

A grin formed on his lips.

"What?" Fay asked.

"When there are thousands of newborns and their anxious mothers, the rumbles and the bleats can drive you crazy after just a few days, let alone weeks."

"I can imagine," Libby said, not wanting to even think about the constant din.

"When a lamb is born," Augustin continued, "a good mother will lick it constantly and stand in place rumbling with concern until her baby rises on its shaky legs and begins its first meal. But after that first very important meal, the mother will never again be so good to her lamb. She will allow it to suckle, but often on the move."

"A lamb can suckle that way?" Libby asked with surprise.

"It is hard," Augustin conceded. "The important thing for us is to make sure that the newborn lamb gets a good first feeding. This gives him great strength. It seems to learn who his mother is faster than the mother learns the identity of her own lamb."

"I can see that might be a big problem if we have thousands of newborns," Libby decided out loud.

"Yes, a *big* problem. With only us and one dog . . . well, we will lose many lambs but we can do our best." He smiled at Fay. "And you know that I am counting on you, eh?"

"Don't worry," Fay assured him. "I'll be a big help."

"I know that," Augustin said. "You will *both* be a great help and I promise to find some way to repay you."

"You already have many times over," Libby told him.

"I just wish that my father and my brother were here to help us too," Augustin said, a faraway look stealing into his brown eyes. "We shared many lambings together and worked like a team. It was good but very hard work. It was my father's happiest time of the year."

Fay squeezed his arm. "We'll have a happy time too," she promised. "And I know that we'll be a good team."

Augustin pulled himself back from his dark reverie and cleared his throat. "Yes," he said, brightening. "I'm sure that this is true. And maybe Palo will change his mind and hurry back in time to help."

Libby caught herself thinking that she hoped Palo *didn't* return. It would only complicate her already complicated life and probably ruin everything. Augustin had strong feelings for her and she was beginning to share those feelings. Palo's unexpected return would be a disaster.

In the days and weeks that followed, Libby had no chance to worry about anything. And despite the many hours that Augustin had talked about all the rewards and troubles that went with lambing, she was totally unprepared for the arrival of several thousand newborns. And they *all* looked exactly alike!

"After you've been around them awhile, you'll start to see differences," Augustin promised. "You'll note their individual habits, the way they move, the way they sound."

"I don't think so," Libby replied.

To her, the lambs were as identical as cookie-cutter biscuits. They were all spindly, always hungry, and when they weren't suckling, they were lost and bleating. Augustin and Emo never stopped trying to match up each lost lamb with its proper mother.

"That ewe's lamb died and this lamb's mother won't cooperate," Augustin said, pointing into a band of hundreds before yanking out his knife and advancing toward the sea of wooly confusion.

"What are we going to do?" Libby asked, as she and Fay hurried after him.

"Watch," Augustin said, "if you've both the stomach for it."

Libby and Fay did watch as Augustin quickly skinned the pelt off the dead lamb and tied it on the one with the standoffish mother.

"He looks terrible now!" Fay wailed, wrinkling her nose at the poor lamb with its bloody disguise.

"I promise you that lamb doesn't care about anything but a mother's milk," Augustin grunted as he picked the orphan lamb up and carried it to the distressed ewe. When he put the pair together, the grieving ewe at first tried to knock the impostor away.

"You won't fool her," Libby said.

"Sure I will," Augustin promised, marching back into the flock to rescue another lamb. "Just make sure that those two stick together for the next ten or fifteen minutes!"

And sure enough, the grieving mother *was* fooled.

"I wonder how long that poor lamb will have to wear that awful, bloody pelt," Fay asked, making a face.

"Maybe all spring and summer," Libby said, shaking her head. "Who knows? If I've learned one thing in this sheep camp, it's that woolies and chickens are equally stupid."

"Watch that pair," Augustin said with a wink that same afternoon, "watch 'em and learn a lesson in larceny."

"What do you mean?" Fay asked.

"Just watch those two lambs and you'll see quick enough."

Libby saw one lamb followed closely by another, both heading for an anxious ewe looking for its newborn. Libby was amazed to see both lambs rush forward, butt in, and begin to suckle. The ewe bleated in consternation and confusion. Twisting her head back and forth, she counted *two* lambs and finally remembered that there was only supposed to be one. By the time she regained her wits and sorted out the mystery, the interloper had probably sucked down a pint of her milk and dashed away to follow another lamb searching for its anxious mother.

"He *is* a thief!" Fay laughed, listening to the unhappy protests of the ewe who had been robbed.

Augustin beamed. "Yes, and a good one."

"But why?"

"The thief either had a mother that refused him, or else one that died. Either way, he was forced between a choice of larceny or death by starvation. The weak and timid lambs will chose starvation, but I like the spunk of our little thieves."

"So do I," Libby said, taking a fresh perspective on the matter.

During the height of the lambing season, there were so many lambs being born around the clock that even the three of them with Emo's help couldn't save every newborn. Like a godsend, the Shoshone came to the rescue. They were patient and hardworking people and Augustin quickly became far more generous with both his praise and payment in fresh mutton than Xabin. The Indians also kept away the predators which were attracted by the scent of birth and death. The women cooked and the men took pride in learning alongside Fay and Libby.

"They've won me over as friends," Augustin said one warm afternoon when he noted with approval how the Shoshone were pelting and disguising the orphan lambs and then quickly matching them up with new mothers. Fay was right in there working side by side with them and talking a mile a minute.

Libby had been about to say something when she was seized by a cramp. Grabbing her swollen abdomen, she gasped and must have looked stricken because Augustin dropped a newborn lamb and rushed to her side. "What's wrong!"

"Nothing," she whispered, feeling weak and dizzy. "I guess I've just been out in the sun too long."

"Here," Augustin said, slipping his arm around her waist and starting to lead her to their cabin. He took two, maybe three steps and halted. "Libby, are you . . . pregnant!"

Tears sprang to her eyes. "I need to sit down."

"We *both* better sit down," he said, looking as shaky as she felt as he eased her down beside the stream that ran through their high mountain valley.

Libby had a handkerchief and asked him to wet it in the cool water. When she'd wiped her face and her head stopped spinning, she turned to regard Augustin with what could only be described as dread. "You might as well know," she began, "I'm going to have a baby before long."

Augustin leaned forward, cupped water, and splashed it into his own face. He pulled off his hat and worked its brim over in his big, rough hands. "You've known about this for quite a while?"

"Yes." She took a deep breath and looked away. "You see, my husband always wanted at least three children."

He blinked. "It's . . . it's your husband's child?"

Libby faked surprise and a little bit of indignation. "Why . . . why, of course! What . . ."

He jumped up, face reddening. "I didn't mean anything! Forget that I asked that dumb question. I . . . congratulations, Mrs. Pike!"

And then, completely flustered, Augustin hurried away leaving Libby to feel more shame than relief. She gently rubbed her swelling womb. "It's done," she whispered. "God help me, but the poor man bought the lie."

When Fay heard the news she was thrilled although the event turned sort of bittersweet when they talked about Matthew still lost somewhere out in the wilderness.

"If my brother ever comes back," Fay said quietly, "won't he be the surprised one to discover he's got a new baby sister or brother."

"Yes," Libby agreed. "Which would you prefer?"

Fay gave that some thought. "Well," she finally began, "if Matthew comes back . . ."

"He *will* come back," Fay repeated.

"All right," Fay said, "then I'd want a sister. But if he didn't . . . I'd want another brother."

Libby hugged her daughter tightly. She finally let her go saying, "You'd better hurry off and help Augustin with those lambs."

Fay nodded but she didn't leave until she'd kissed her mother and laid her hand on her stomach. "Thank you, Mama!"

Libby wiped a sleeve across her eyes and managed to nod as her daughter ran off to help tend the lambs.

Later, Libby came to realize that her little girl became a woman that spring and summer despite her young age. Fay had always been bright, optimistic, hardworking, and eager to learn. And, under Augustin's instruction and given the responsibility of lambing, she had really blossomed. And so it was that Libby had no qualms about asking Fay to help her give birth.

Actually, it was far easier than the lambing. It was

Libby's third child and it came without much pain or labor. The infant arrived so quickly after the first contractions that it caught everyone by surprise. Fay did exactly as she'd been instructed and, as a reward, Libby allowed her to cradle and rock her new baby brother.

"What is it?" Augustin shouted anxiously as he paced back and forth outside their room.

"It's a boy," Libby called. "Come inside and see him."

Augustin rushed through the door looking as if he were about to attack a rabid wolf. He was so nervous that Fay laughed and said, "Mama, is it all right if Gus holds him too?"

"Oh, no!" Augustin said, retreating so fast that he almost tripped over his own heels.

"Go ahead, Augustin," Libby told him. "Babies aren't as tough as lambs, but neither are they going to break like an eggshell."

When Augustin raised the infant in his arms, wonder transformed his rugged features. Looking up at Libby, he said, "Do you have a name for him yet?"

"No," she said. "You've been keeping me so busy that I just haven't had time to think of one."

"You will now," Augustin promised. "You just rest easy the rest of the summer while Fay and I take care of everything."

"One more newborn is all you need," Libby said, taking her baby back and holding it close.

"When I get a little more time," Augustin promised, "I'll build him a new cradle so he can be rocked back and forth."

"He'd like that," Libby said, feeling extremely happy.

"Well then," Augustin said, grinning broadly, "I might just get started on it right now!"

"Why don't you wait until evening," Libby suggested. "A mother likes to rock her own baby at first."

"Oh, well sure!" he exclaimed. "I didn't mean to hurry you or . . ."

"Thanks," Libby said. "Thanks for everything."

Augustin tried to respond but could not. His mouth worked, but there were no words. Seeing his dilemma, Fay jumped up, took the sheepman's hand, and led him outside. Libby fed her baby and fell asleep that night listening to the bleating sheep, her daughter and Augustin's low talk, and the happy cooing and suckling of her child.

CHAPTER
TWENTY-TWO

"D arling," she said, yawning and stretching like a cat after their lovemaking. "I really have to get up now and ride back to town."

Palo reached for Jasmine and drew her back down to his side. "Another hour," he pleaded.

"No," she whispered, kissing his bare chest. "I think that Henry is getting suspicious of these daylong rides. He even suggested that one of his guards start to accompany me. I can't risk doing this so often."

Palo pushed himself up in the bed as Jasmine slipped away and began to dress. He admired her long, beautiful legs, her small waist, and perfect breasts. Palo had never had such a magnificent or beguiling creature. Every moment they shared was a treasure and that was why he had spent the last of his money on this worthless claim because its cabin afforded them this precious trysting place. Now, however, it sounded as if it was all coming to an end.

Palo rolled a cigarette. "Can I at least ride back to town with you?"

"You know the answer to that. Someone is bound to see us and get word to my husband." Jasmine offered him a consoling smile. "Honey, I just can't risk ruining everything, even for you."

When Palo said nothing, she added, "The Silverbowl is making Henry a fortune. I'm his wife and only heir. You can understand that, can't you?"

"Divorce him and marry me."

"Let's not go into that again," Jasmine said. "I've explained over and over that Henry controls all the money and is friends with the best lawyers on the Comstock. If I asked for a divorce, I'd be lucky to wind up with a pittance."

"You spend money like water. Surely you could set aside enough to hire your own lawyer and win a handsome settlement."

Jasmine shook her head as she continued to dress and drive Palo to distraction. But when he tried to grab her, Jasmine threw her hands up. "Don't," she warned. "We've had a wonderful time, but I'm afraid that all good things must come to an end."

"But you love me!" Palo shouted, his own words an echo of so many he'd heard in the past from the women he'd jilted.

"Yes, I do," Jasmine said, "but I also love money. Palo, when the time is right, maybe I finally can divorce Henry and marry you. But that time is still a long way off. The Silverbowl is just too rich to walk away from now."

"And what am I supposed to do until you *might* decide to get that divorce?"

Jasmine finished dressing. "I don't know," she told him with studied unconcern. "But, in the meantime, why don't you go back to Colorado and claim your share of that cattle ranch? Sell out and hurry back to me. I'm sure that you would do better the next time in mining stocks."

When he fell to brooding, Jasmine said, "Palo, if you had money . . . real money, I could help you invest it in the Silverbowl at insider's prices."

"Everything comes down to money, doesn't it?" he said without bitterness.

"Listen," she replied, laying her head on his shoulder, "you know I despise Henry. I find him repulsive and disgusting. But he's as rich as a king and I've been scratching for money all my life. I'm never going back to the way it was before."

When she started to leave, Palo's fingers tightened on her arms. "Jasmine, what if . . ."

Palo couldn't finish the thought that had just surfaced like a swamp monster from the darkest recesses of his mind.

She stared into his eyes. "What if what?"

"Never mind."

"Very well." She pulled free and began to smooth her mussed hair. "But I'm afraid that I won't be able to come here for a while. It's just too risky."

"How long is a while?" he asked, feeling desolate.

"Darling, please don't make this any more difficult for me than it already is. We've had a wonderful fling. I really do love you but . . . well, you understand."

Palo jumped out of bed. Without Jasmine Ward, there was nothing left for him on the Comstock. He'd never recovered his horses and he'd spent all of his money trying to maintain the illusion of a wealthy ranching background. So, all at once, everything was turning to smoke. There would be nothing left for him to do but to crawl back to Augustin, hat in hand. His bold promise of returning wealthy and victorious would be ashes on his tongue.

"Jasmine," he blurted, "I love you. And since you also love me, there must be *some* way that we can be together."

She sadly shook her head. "Not unless Henry's heart stops beating or he has an accident and I become his rich, outwardly grieving widow."

Jasmine finished brushing her hair and sat down beside him to pull on her riding boots and ride out of his life.

"He *could* have an accident," Palo heard himself say.

Her eyebrows lifted in question. "What do you mean?"

"I mean that accidents happen a lot on the Comstock."

"Not to rich men like Henry," she reminded him, "and his health is excellent. He is really quite . . . a vigorous man."

Palo expelled a deep breath. "But if something did happen to him. You'd inherit the Silverbowl, right?"

"Yes. I've seen the will. I'm the sole heir. I'd be worth a fortune."

"And you'd marry me?"

She laughed sweetly. "Whom else, my darling?"

Palo began to pace back and forth in the buff. "I've heard that your husband is a heartless sonofabitch who cuts every corner he can when it comes to mine safety."

"We lose a miner almost every month to preventable accidents," Jasmine said, "but what has all this to do with . . ."

"There's blood on his hands, Jasmine! If we owned the Silverbowl, we'd put in more safety measures to cut down on the loss of life. Wouldn't we?"

"Of course. I've already pleaded with Henry to install heavier timbering and . . ."

"Then lives would be saved if your husband had an accident," Palo rushed. "In a way, it would be justice if he died because of indifference to the deaths of his miners."

"Why are you talking like this?"

He wanted to tell her but was afraid. "Never mind."

"No," she insisted. "Are you thinking about *staging* my husband's fatal accident?"

Palo knew that she'd know if he tried to lie. "It would save lives and give us a chance for happiness, Jasmine! We could make love on satin sheets. Travel and live like royalty. We'd be perfect together. We could . . . we could even have children."

"I never want to have children."

"Then we could just have each other," he said quickly. "That's all we'd ever want or need."

He wrapped her up in his arms and kissed Jasmine hard, pushing his tongue into her mouth and stroking her body until she squirmed with desire. Palo began to undress Jasmine again knowing she didn't really want to resist.

Their lovemaking was a whirlwind of passion that carried them high above their shabby little cabin to beautiful places. And when it was over, Jasmine clung to him and whispered, "Tell me how you are going to do it, my darling. And *when!*"

"I don't know," he confessed.

"But you *will* do it, won't you?"

"Yes."

"Have you killed men before?"

He nodded.

"That's what I thought," she said. "I sensed danger in you the first time our eyes met."

"I'm not a murderer, though," he added. "I've always killed in self-defense. This would be a lot different."

"Of course, but my husband's neglect and irresponsibility have caused a lot of miners to die."

"That's right," he said, relieved that she also saw the issue clearly.

"Will you need my help?" she asked.

"I don't know yet. I do need some money. I'm flat busted."

She give him several hundred dollars.

"We'll need to meet again," he said, pocketing the cash.

But Jasmine shook her head. "However you kill Henry, it *must* be made to appear as an accident. Is that perfectly clear?"

"Of course!"

"It's the only way it could work," she said earnestly. "The *only* way."

"I understand, dammit!" Palo yearned for a glass of whiskey. "But, like you said, rich men don't have accidents. Your husband never goes anywhere alone. He's always got a guard or two near him on the street. What am I supposed to do?"

"You're a bright and cunning man, Palo. Think of something."

"Yeah," he vowed. "I will."

Jasmine kissed him once more before she left. Palo listened to the hoofbeats of her mare fade into the distance. He stretched back out on the bed feeling exhilarated but also quite anxious. He focused on the idea that he would actually be saving lives by killing Henry Ward. And besides, Ward already had more than his share of good fortune. Palo figured now it was his turn.

A week, then two passed and Palo still could not think of a way to kill Ward in a manner that would be judged an accident. The man simply was never alone. He was either at his heavily guarded mining office or else surrounded by friends and employees. Palo caught only a few brief, tantalizing glimpses of Jasmine, always when she was with her husband going to dinner or returning from a major social event at the famed Piper's Opera House. On each occasion, she was stunning in her expensive European gowns and diamonds. Just the sight of that woman drove Palo half wild with desire and heightened his mounting desperation.

"What do you know about Henry Ward?" Palo casually asked a man named Tom Barkley who had just been fired from his reporting job with the *Territorial Enterprise.*

"Ward has more than his share of enemies," Barkley confided as they sat drinking at a private table in the Bucket of Blood Saloon. "That's why he always stays in the company of friends or guards."

"What enemies are you talking about?"

"Well, for starters," Barkley said, "the friends and

families of all the miners that have died working for the Silverbowl Mining Company. Don't you think for a minute that Ward hasn't had plenty of death threats. There are at least a half-dozen men that I know of personally that wouldn't hesitate to put a bullet through his guts."

"But they're afraid of being caught?"

"Hell, yes! Nobody wants to dance at the end of a rope."

"Ward would be a tough man to assassinate."

"Someone would have to do him in at night."

Palo poured them both more whiskey. "Do you mean sneak into the Ward Mansion?"

"Sure." Barkley regarded Palo with angry, bloodshot eyes. "Where else?"

"How many men do you suppose he keeps on staff at the mansion?"

"No more than a couple. Ward is cheap. Hell, he might just have a guard dog inside. Anyway, who cares?"

"Just wondering. Making talk is all."

"Stupid talk," Barkley muttered.

Palo wasn't listening. He knew that there were no guard dogs in the mansion because Jasmine had once told him that she was allergic to dog and cat hair.

Barkley poured them both another drink from their now nearly empty bottle and tossed it down before slamming his empty glass to the table. He grabbed Palo's forearm. "I'm a better writer than Dan DeQuill or Mark Twain, ain't I!"

"Sure you are."

"Then why the hell did they fire me and keep them two hacks employed at the paper? I had seniority over both of them!"

"Life isn't fair," Palo dutifully commiserated, thinking that this man was sinking fast and would never remember a word of this conversation in the morning. "Men like Henry Ward get rich, men like us are poor. There's no justice."

"You can say that again!" Barkley choked, eyes wet

and unfocused. "I may say to hell with it and leave Virginia City and the Comstock Lode once and for all."

"A fresh start would be the best thing for you."

"You want to come with me?" Barkley asked. "I've heard there's another big strike down south."

"Naw," Palo said, extracting the man's fingers from his sleeve. "I haven't quite had my fill of it here yet."

"You will soon," Barkley vowed. "This place breaks your spirit."

Palo tossed his drink down and arose unsteadily to his feet.

"Say, where you going?" Barkley asked, dragging an ink-stained hand across his eyes as he struggled to focus.

"To get some sleep."

"Well, dammit, it's your turn to buy the next bottle!"

Palo dug into his pockets and pulled out three crumpled greenbacks. "Here, you drink it yourself," he said, taking a deep breath and heading out for some badly needed fresh air.

The next morning, Palo's hands were shaking and he nicked himself twice as he shaved. He had been drinking too much lately and vowed to cut back, knowing he'd need steady nerves and a clear head if he were to carry off the plan to assassinate Henry Ward that was slowly forming in his mind. It was a plan that required speaking to Jasmine and so he made sure that he was waiting to intercept her customary morning ride.

"You've been avoiding me," he said, stepping out from between a pair of buildings and grabbing her mare's reins.

"Palo, you look terrible," she exclaimed, looking genuinely shocked.

"Thanks," he said cryptically. "It comes with bad whiskey and being ignored."

"I'm sorry," she said without sounding sorry at all, "but we just can't risk being seen together anymore."

"That's about to change," he vowed. "Jasmine, how many guards watch your mansion at night?"

"You're not going to come to kill him in his sleep!"

Palo shrugged. "Why not? He wouldn't suffer."

"Because we agreed that you were supposed to make it look like an *accident*!"

"There is no way that could happen!" he shouted. "The man is always surrounded."

Jasmine's eyes blazed. "Then just forget it!"

Palo yanked so hard on the reins that the mare reared, almost unseating Jasmine and spilling her into the street. Palo didn't care. He was shaking with anger and it was all that he could do not to tear Jasmine off the horse and give her beautiful face the back of his hand.

"Damn you!" she spat, hanging on to her saddle for dear life. "Have you completely lost your mind!"

"We have an understanding!"

"To do what?" she shrilly demanded. "To be stupid enough to be arrested, tried, and convicted of murder!"

When Palo had no immediate answer, Jasmine's voice turned icy with scorn. "Palo, I don't trust you anymore. I've come to believe that you've lied to me all along about your big cattle ranch."

"I have a part interest in a flock of damned sheep," he spat.

"Sheep?" Her lip curled and he felt lashed by her contempt.

"Palo, we're finished."

"No, we're not!" Palo savagely yanked the mare's bit, causing the animal to toss its head and begin backing up. "I spent a lot of time and money on you and you're not dumping me!"

A derringer materialized in Jasmine's gloved fist. Palo released the mare and jumped back, more angry than afraid. "Are you going to kill me?"

"I could," she said, glancing up the street toward a group of men who had stopped to watch them. "There are witnesses. I could put a bullet through your heart claiming you grabbed my horse and tried to rob me."

"Then pull the gawddamn trigger!"

"Get away from me," she hissed. "You're half drunk and crazy. You look terrible and you're dirty. We *are* finished."

"We'll see about that," he said, raising his hands and retreating so that there could be no doubt among witnesses that he posed no immediate danger. "I'm looking forward to telling your husband about all those wonderful afternoons we shared at the cabin."

She couldn't disguise the fact that the blood drained from her lovely face. "Henry wouldn't believe a nobody like you."

"Oh, wouldn't he?" Palo planted his boots wide apart and placed his hands on his hips. "Does Henry know about your sordid San Francisco past? If he does, he'll believe me. If he doesn't, you can bet that I'll tell him—and I can find men who once paid you for pleasure."

"What do you want?" she raggedly breathed.

"To marry you and become rich. What else?"

Jasmine's hand was shaking as she lowered the derringer. "There's only one guard at the front of the house and one in the back. The one in the back is always asleep by midnight, but my husband doesn't know it."

"How do *you* know it?" Palo asked with a stab of jealousy. "Or have you kept the one in the front awake yourself?"

"Don't bother to insult me with your suspicious little thoughts," Jasmine snapped. "Henry and I do not sleep in the same room. His is in the upstairs bedroom, northwest corner of the house."

"All right," Palo said. "His body will be discovered and tomorrow morning you'll be a very rich widow. After a few weeks of mourning, we'll be married and this lovers' spat we've just had will be no more than a fading memory. Correct?"

"Don't let him suffer."

"He'll never awaken," Palo promised, "and he'll be unmarked."

"What about the guards?"

"I'll slip right past them."

"The back door is never locked," Jasmine offered, touching her heels to the mare's flanks.

"We'll need to meet afterward . . . at the cabin."

"Too dangerous. I'll be in mourning and tied up with Henry's funeral arrangements."

"We'll meet at the cabin exactly one week from this hour," he informed her. "I don't care if you come to me dressed in black and riding in a hearse. Just be there."

Their eyes locked and hers broke contact first as she dipped her chin in agreement.

Palo was almost giddy with his victory. His head was clear again and he felt wonderful. "And, Mrs. Ward," he said grandly, "bring money! Lot's of money. You see, it's high time that I start getting used to living very well."

Jasmine quirted her mare hard and almost ran him down as she galloped up toward Sun Mountain.

That night, Palo waited until the last light was extinguished in the Ward Mansion. He moved swiftly around behind the house, right hand close to his gun, left hand clutching a hunting knife. He reached the back door and it was unlocked. When he entered the mansion, Palo saw that he was inside the kitchen and he could hear someone nearby snoring. Palo tiptoed toward the sound and discovered a guard asleep in the pantry, head resting on a sack of potatoes. Palo left him undisturbed.

It was easy locating the stairway and Palo crept silently up to the second-story landing. There was no evidence of the other guard and Palo hoped the man was camped out on the front porch, or asleep in the parlor. Either way, he would not be a problem if everything went according to plan.

He eased down the hallway until he came to Henry Ward's bedroom on the northwest corner of the house. The door was unlocked and Palo gently turned the knob and pushed the door open. Ward, dressed in his pajamas, lay snoring on a huge bed. Palo swallowed dryly as he studied the interior of the man's room, noting the heavy baroque furniture and all the rich trappings of wealth. Moonlight streamed in the upstairs window and it was easy to see that the room was cluttered with books and clothes, many of which were tossed about the floor. Piled on a bedside table were Henry's wallet and jewelry. A diamond ring sparkled in the moonlight and Palo could not resist trying it on for size. It was too big but Palo realized that such a ring could send him straight to the gallows. Returning the ring to its place on the table, Palo emptied Ward's thick wallet, cramming a stack of hundred dollar bills into his coat pockets.

Taking a very deep breath, Palo crept quietly over to the sleeping figure. He stared down at the round, corpulent face with its double chins and the great, sagging jowls. Dressed in his tailored suits, Henry Ward was authoritative and impressive. Dressed in pajamas with his mouth hanging open and his fat face slack in repose, Ward reminded Palo of a pig. Why, Palo asked himself as he reached for one of the pillows on the bed, should a swine like this live so well?

The answer was that he shouldn't. Palo raised the pillow. He would smother Ward in his sleep so that it would appear that the rich mine owner had died of sudden heart failure, possibly brought on by his obesity and rich living. A local physician would undoubtedly consider the cause of death to be an accident of nature, so to speak, and that would be far more palatable than murder. No investigation. No questions. Just a big funeral. Jasmine would approve. She might be angry at him now, but she would be glad in a few weeks. Very glad.

Palo hung poised over Ward's bloated face. He had

never murdered a man before and so he had to remind himself that this act was one of justice and retribution for all the poor miners who had died in the Silverbowl Mine because of Ward's greed. And of all the lives that would be saved.

"Lord," Palo breathed raggedly as he squashed the pillow down over the rich man's face, "forgive me."

Henry bucked like a bronc. He was old and soft but Palo was amazed at how savagely the man fought for his life. Pinned under the blankets, Ward still managed to get his arms up and flail at Palo's face, fingernails scratching deeply into flesh. Palo leaped up onto Henry's chest, pinning him deep into the soft mattress. He strained down on the pillow trying to ignore Ward's muffled screams. It took a good three minutes before the man finally shuddered and went limp.

Palo was out of breath when he rolled off Ward. The pillow slipped aside and Palo shivered to see Ward's eyes bulging and frozen with horror, his mouth locked open in a silent, primal scream. It took several moments before Palo could force himself to check the man's pulse. There was none whatsoever. Palo heaved a deep sigh of relief and his eyes swept around the room, hoping to find a bottle, for he most desperately needed a quick drink.

"Well, are you sure he is dead?" a soft voice from the hallway inquired.

Palo spun around to see Jasmine with a gun in her fist. "My poor sheepman and lover, is poor Henry really dead?"

"Yes." Palo's eyes locked on the six-gun and he broke out in a cold, clammy sweat. "Jasmine, what . . . ?"

Palo never finished asking the question because her answer was to pull the trigger. He saw the muzzle flash and felt the impact of a bullet punching him in the chest. Palo cursed, hand stabbing toward his own Colt but another bullet knocked him a step backward and he choked. From far, far away, he heard the sound of rolling thunder but the very last thing Palo heard before he tumbled into a black and bottomless abyss was the sound of Jasmine Ward's high, mocking laughter.

——————— CHAPTER ———————
TWENTY-THREE

Matthew Pike had survived the searing Mojave Desert, unlike some of Kaw's horses who had died of thirst and exhaustion during the long trek southward toward Mexico. And now, only a few miles below sun-blistered Fort Yuma, they were camped beside the broad Colorado River waiting for Mexican outlaws and horse traders.

Kaw and his men had already traded two horses for enough tequila to keep them happy during their wait and the cool river water was a blessing. There was enough grass along the California side to fatten their thin horses and the fishing and hunting were good. Besides that, they were close enough to the old southern emigrant trail leading from Tucson into California to be assured that there would be wagons to attack and plunder. But, even beside the river, the desert heat was punishing. In the daytime, temperatures soared so that Kaw and his men could only find relief by lying up to their necks in the shallow water watching the big river roll past. At night, the land still cooked and temperatures stayed near one hundred.

Every few days a paddle wheel steamer would come

thrashing up the river, no doubt bound for Fort Yuma
or some little mining settlement. The paddle wheeler
would belch black smoke and its blades would churn
rainbows across the river. Kaw and his men, drunk and
full of hell, would scramble for their guns. Shots and
curses would be exchanged and Matthew would see the
boatmen frantically heaving more wood into their fur-
nace in order to generate speed while their captain
would angle toward the far side of the river. It was their
main excitement while they waited for the Mexican bandits who would soon arrive to dicker and then buy their
emigrant plunder.

"Maybe the United States Army at Fort Yuma will
hear of Kaw and send troops to attack," Jenny said one
blistering afternoon when they had a few minutes alone
together.

"Kaw is expecting the Mexicans soon," Matthew
replied.

"He will sell me to them," Jenny said with a catch
in her voice.

"What gives you that idea?"

"The way he is looking and acting."

Matthew considered this for only a minute before
he said, "I won't let that happen, Jenny. We'll just have
to escape to Fort Yuma."

"Tonight?"

Matthew felt his heart begin to pound. He knew
that if he and Jenny were caught, they would be tortured to death in ways too horrible to imagine.

"Soon," he promised.

"Tonight!"

"Shhh!" he whispered, afraid that they would be
overheard. "Jenny, I don't even have a gun."

"If I get one, will you take me away tonight?"

There was such earnestness in Jenny's eyes that
Matthew didn't have the heart to say no. "All right," he
vowed.

But late that same afternoon, the Mexican bandits
finally appeared. By the way Kaw and his band acted,

Matthew was sure that there was little trust between these two bands of hardened killers and outlaws.

Matthew stayed apart from Kaw and the leader of the bandits as the two men began a long session of haggling over horses and the other prizes that Kaw had brought south to sell. Their bargaining was in Spanish and Matthew did not understand much of what was said, only that passions were high and the tequila was flowing. Jenny sat behind Kaw and it was clear that she was part of the negotiations, for the Mexican outlaws kept looking at her with smiles and occasional bursts of coarse laughter. Their manners and appearance caused Matthew's skin to crawl and, as evening passed into night and the talking became more heated and animated, Matthew became even more convinced that he and Jenny needed to escape before tomorrow's sunrise.

About midnight, Jenny was dragged over to the circle and Kaw kissed and fondled her for several minutes to the delight of everyone. They roared even louder when Jenny slapped Kaw's face and then was knocked flat by a bruising backhand. Matthew almost lost control as Jenny slunk out of the firelight on her way down to the river. The leader of the Mexicans, a large man with a huge sombrero, gold teeth, and a flowing mustache, seemed especially amused and the negotiations continued as Kaw and his men again displayed what they had plundered from the emigrants making the Humboldt River crossing between Utah and California.

Later that night when everyone had finally passed out or fallen asleep, Jenny found Matthew and slipped him a gun. "I got one for myself," she said. "And I won't be taken alive."

Matthew felt the same way. He led Jenny upriver but the brush soon became so impenetrable that they had to go into the water. In some places, deep and swift channels cut in close to the bank forcing them back on the riverbank to fight their way through the choking and spiny creosote, mesquite, and tall palo verde. All the while, Matthew worried about Kaw and the outlaws that would certainly come hunting after daybreak and they'd have a ready-made trail to follow.

Dawn arrived all too soon. Flocks of egrets, mallards, and other waterfowl took wing, their noisy protests advertising Matthew and Jenny's exact position.

"How far do you think it is to Fort Yuma?" Matthew gasped, as they struggled along the riverbank.

"I don't know."

They were both drenched with sweat and covered with leaves and dirt. Matthew twisted around and studied the path they'd just broken through and said, "They're not going to have any trouble overtaking us, Jenny. We'd better reach help soon or we're finished."

A short time later, they came to another feeder lagoon, one of many they had already waded across. But here the water was obviously much too deep and wide to wade to the other side.

"We can either swim, or try and hike around this thing," Matthew said, noting how the lagoon disappeared under a stand of overhanging palo verde.

"I can swim," Jenny said, glancing nervously back over her shoulder. "We'd lose at least a half hour going around."

"Give me your gun," he told her. "I'll try to dog paddle with one arm and keep our powder dry."

"Maybe we should go around after all," Jenny said, looking worried.

But Matthew shook his head. He had the feeling that Kaw and the outlaws had already discovered their absence and were coming. If that were true, then every minute counted. "Let's go!"

Jenny gave him her six-gun and waded into the lagoon, skirts floating up around her waist. A few more steps and she was swimming. Matthew stuck his thumb through both trigger guards and raised his arm overhead. He waded up to his neck in water that was as warm as a bath. When the water reached his chin, Matthew launched himself forward, kicking hard and pawing with his free hand.

"Snake!" Jenny screamed.

Matthew saw the huge viper from somewhere along the riverbank. It was undulating through the water toward him and he was seized by such panic that he reversed directions, swimming for his life.

Jenny began to chuck rocks at the viper and Matthew didn't waste any time looking back. It seemed to take forever to reach the shore again. He finally scrambled up the muddy bank, dropping both guns. He scooped one of them up but the snake had disappeared.

"I think I might have hit and sunk him!" Jenny called. "But . . . but maybe not."

Matthew surveyed the now muddy water, doubting that a rock had killed the huge rattler. His chest was heaving and he'd be damned if he'd go back into the lagoon and give that snake another chance at him.

"I'm walking around!" he called across the lagoon.

Jenny nodded, her face strained. Matthew picked up the fallen gun and with a weapon in each hand, began to skirt the lagoon. He knew that this was snaky ground and all his attention was riveted on the footing just ahead.

"Matt!" Jenny cried.

His first thought was that she had seen another snake that he'd missed and was about to strike him from behind. But even as Matthew twisted around, he heard the popping of quirts and sage and knew that Kaw and the Mexicans were whipping their horses through the thick underbrush.

Matthew hesitated for only a moment before he again raised the two Colts high overhead, hurried back out into the lagoon, and frantically began his one-armed dog paddling. He swam with his eyes fixed on Jenny and expecting to be struck by either the viper or a hail of outlaw bullets. But somehow, he made it safely to the other side.

"Hurry!" Jenny pleaded, dragging him into the cover of brush. They could both hear Kaw and the Mexicans yelling back and forth and the odds seemed impossibly long that they would ever reach Fort Yuma.

"That little island!" Matthew said, dragging Jenny deeper into the water. "If we could reach it and hide in those tules, they might not find us."

Jenny's face was badly scratched and tight with fear but she didn't hesitate. As she plunged forward into the swift but narrow channel she started swimming hard for the slender finger of island resting just seventy or eighty feet from shore. Matthew raised the pistols overhead and went after her.

Somehow, they made it to the island and slipped into the marsh grass and tules, gasping and lathered with mud. Moments later, Kaw and several of his men appeared along with at least a half dozen of the Mexicans bandits. They were swearing and punishing their horses in a rage and were no doubt still feeling the effects of the tequila. Pointing to footprints on both sides of the lagoon, they drove their horses into the warm water and swam across.

"Where is that damned snake now when you need him," Matthew wailed.

Their pursuers disappeared into the brush, howling and whipping their horses. Jenny gripped Matthew's arm and said, "What if they come back?"

"Pretty soon they *will* come back."

"Then where can we go?"

Matthew didn't have an answer. If it had still been dark, the answer would have been to float downriver past Kaw's camp and stay in the water until they reached a settlement or some kind of safe haven. But now . . . now he just didn't know. All he could think about was reaching Fort Yuma, which was located just upriver.

"Listen!" Jenny cried. "Did you hear it?"

Matthew's body contracted with fear. "Another rattlesnake!"

"No, gunshots. The outlaws back at camp must be taking potshots at another paddle wheeler!"

Now Matthew understood the reason for Jenny's excitement. If a paddle wheeler was coming, it could be their salvation. All that was required was to somehow swim out and be rescued!

They kept low in the tules, heads twisting back and forth wondering which would appear first, Kaw, the Mexicans, or the paddle wheeler.

Matthew and Jenny saw the rising black smoke from the paddle wheeler several minutes before the besieged vessel actually appeared from downriver. The paddle wheeler was under a full head of steam and her crew was exchanging shots with the outlaws that had remained in Kaw's camp. When she came swinging around a bend and burst into view, Matthew could see that she was really churning the water. He judged that the vessel would pass about fifty yards from their island where the current was deepest, and the surface water hid powerful currents that could pull even the strongest swimmer to the bottom.

"I think you'd better make a break for it," Matthew said as the steamer moved closer. "The current will sweep you downriver so there's no time to lose."

"Then let's go!" she said, tugging on his shirt.

"Go *now*," he said, seeing Kaw and the outlaws reemerge from the brush. "I'll be along in a minute or two."

"I won't leave you!"

"You have to," Matthew insisted. "If they see us both, they'll swim their horses over here and pick us both off with their rifles before we can be rescued. I've got to keep them on shore."

Jenny started to protest, but Matthew gave her a rough shove toward the water. She threw him a last glance, and then she slid into the water like a crocodile and began to pull for the middle of the channel. Matthew wondered what the odds were of her being dragged under and either beaten to death or drowned by the huge paddle wheels.

One of the outlaws spotted Jenny in the water. He

began to shout and point. Kaw and his men did what
Matthew had expected; they spurred and whipped their
horses toward the island from which Jenny would be an
easy target.

Matthew had twelve rounds in the two six-guns. He
prayed that the powder was dry and that he would have
no misfires as he took a slow and deliberate aim on
Kaw. His first shot exploded out of the tules, white
smoke rolling across the muddy water. Kaw cried out
and grabbed his side. He tried to saw on his reins and
retreat. Matthew raised his aim a hair and drilled Kaw
through the chest. The outlaws panicked. Caught swimming in the middle of the narrow channel, they were
helpless as Matthew began to methodically empty saddles. Several rounds whistled past his face and Matthew
rolled over twice and continued to fire, seeing men dive
from the mounts and take their chances in the river.
When his guns were empty, Matthew shoved them into
his pants pockets, then retreated across the island. He
slid into the center of the river and swam for his life.

The men on board the paddle wheeler had all witnessed the deadly ambush and it didn't take much
guesswork to understand the desperate plight of the two
swimmers. The sailors opened fire on the remaining
horsemen. One crewman grabbed a pair of life buoys
and stood poised on deck, yelling something over the
din of the thrashing paddles.

Jenny was not as strong a swimmer as Matthew and
he caught up with her as she began to fade. "Hang on!"
he yelled as the vessel thrashed ever closer.

Suddenly, the paddle wheels stopped churning. The
river fell silent and the paddle wheeler's momentum
carried it forward against the current for a few yards as
the sailor tossed the lines and their attached buoys to
Matthew and Jenny. Moments later, they were dragged
on board and the captain shouted for full power.

A few of the surviving outlaws who had managed to
get back to shore opened fire but their shots were

harmless. Minutes later, everyone on board the paddle wheeler was crowding around Matthew and Jenny.

"You've got some explaining to do, young'uns!" the captain shouted. "Who the blazes were those murderin' sonsabitches!"

Matthew held Jenny in his arms. Although the air was hot, the sun bright and blazing over the water, they were both shivering.

"They were killers," Matthew told the captain. "And, if you hadn't showed up, we'd be dead."

"Fort Yuma is just up ahead," the captain announced. "The United States Army will want to mop up on the rest of that bunch. Say, are you brother and sister?"

"No," Jenny said, hugging Matthew tightly. "Someday soon we're going to be married."

"Married?"

She nodded.

The captain smiled and stuffed an old corncob pipe in his mouth. "How old are you two?"

"A lot older than we look," Matthew told the man without batting an eye.

"Yeah," the captain said, glancing back downriver at all the riderless horses, "I expect that's true enough. Come on into my quarters and let's find you both some dry clothes and maybe a touch of whiskey to take away your chills."

That sounded just fine. And, as the paddle wheeler turned a bend and its steam whistle blasted a greeting to Fort Yuma, Matthew held Jenny's hand very tight and finally started thinking about sharing a future together.

CHAPTER

TWENTY-FOUR

Eight years later, Summer of 1868

Matthew had a special way with livestock, especially mules and horses; he'd enjoyed and cultivated the gift as long as he could remember, that being the age of fourteen. After a successful five years as a supplier of well-broken cavalry mounts down in the Arizona Territory, he and Jenny had drifted north because the Central Pacific Railroad was rumored to be in need of good stockmen. As it turned out, the rumors were true and so Matthew hired on with the railroad in Sacramento. While fighting its way over the Sierra Nevadas, Matthew had earned the admiration and respect of Mr. Strobridge and Mr. Crocker, winning for himself the title of Superintendent of Livestock.

Once they had finally beaten the Sierras, the mostly Chinese crews began to slam down steel with amazing speed eastward across the vast Humboldt Sink. Jenny and the other wives who would not consider being left behind were paid by the railroad to cook and clean for its officials. The work wasn't hard, though the women found living in tents especially unpleasant when blustery winds scoured the desert creating immense dust storms. But they were a tight-knit group and everyone seemed to understand that they were making history and locked into an epic race against the Union Pacific Railroad with its mostly Irish crews.

"When this railroad is finished," Matthew told Jenny late one summer evening when the heat had subsided and they stood enjoying a cooling breeze lifting off the lazy Humboldt River, "we ought to think about taking the money we've been saving and settle down."

"I'm not sure that 'settling down' is in your blood," Jenny replied. 'You're always searching."

"For the perfect horse, or the perfect ranching area?"

"Both . . . and for your past." Jenny squeezed his hand. "Is the reason we haven't had children yet because you can't rediscover your past?"

Matthew gazed out at the sage-covered hills, wondering.

Jenny was persistent. "Matthew, is that why we've finally come back to this country? To search out your family?"

"Maybe."

"I hope so. I've even wondered if Pike is your real surname."

"It is," he told her. "I forgot most everything after I had my head cracked open by that rifle butt. Everything except my name."

"I don't want you to be disappointed if you don't find your family. If we ever do stumble across them, I expect that it will be in Oregon or California. That's where they and all the other emigrants were heading, just like my family."

He pulled Jenny close, wondering again if he wasn't the lucky one not to be able to remember what Kaw and his band of murderers had done to so many emigrants less than a decade ago. Now, the Shoshone and the Paiute were mostly all on reservations. The killing time had passed in the West and back East the terrible war between the states had finally reached its bloody resolution. "Jenny, the truth is that this Nevada country all seems vaguely familiar. And you know what?"

She craned her head back and gazed up at him. "What?"

"Even though I knew better, I had a taste of that bad Humboldt River water. And I remembered that taste from years before."

"Maybe," she said, teasing now, "if you drink enough of the Humboldt, the taste will flood all the memories back into you."

"Nope." Matthew felt her jab him in the ribs and he chuckled. "That foul river water would just rot out my belly."

He grew serious. "Besides, maybe I'm never supposed to remember my past. Maybe my family was massacred like yours."

"Sometimes," Jenny managed to say, "it really is better not knowing."

Matthew had grown very tall, with broad shoulders and distinctive, chiseled features. He always wore high-heeled riding boots, spurs with jingle-bobs, and a bandanna around his neck. From his days as a captive of Kaw and his band, he retained a slightly detached view when faced toward especially difficult or even dangerous situations. And although he would never have admitted it, Matthew occasionally had powerful cravings for roasted horsemeat. Matthew had one other thing, and that was the reputation he had gained when he'd killed a bunch of outlaws down on the Colorado River. It was a reputation that he never cultivated nor ever spoke of, but it was always reflected in the deference he was accorded by even the roughest teamsters and mule skinners whom he sometimes had to confront.

Jenny stepped around in front of him. "You know what I found eerie since we left the Sierras?"

"No."

"That forty-mile desert with all those broken salt and alkali flats. I'll never forget those piles of bleached bones and the wreckage those poor people were forced to leave behind."

"At least," he said, "we know that they must have made it to the Carson River and then over to California."

"I think that your family did too," Jenny said softly. "I know that mine didn't. But yours did."

Matthew felt her pain and hugged his wife tightly. "We're going to be linking rails with the Union Pacific sometime next spring, Jenny. After we do, we'll both be out of jobs."

"I don't care. I want to settle down and raise a family. It doesn't matter where, Matthew. Really it doesn't. You pick the place and, if you're happy, I'll be happy."

"All right," he said. "We'll find good ranch land to homestead. A place where we can run cattle and horses and build something for the future."

"What about this country?"

Matthew deliberated a good while before he answered. "I was thinking yesterday that I wished I could remember when I first saw you with Kaw."

"I don't *want* you to remember."

"But," Matthew continued, "I do recall that we crossed east over some fine country. I remember mountains and huge, empty valleys where you could build a fine ranch. And I still recollect many friendly Shoshone and Paiutes. None of which were like Kaw and his bunch of half-breed killers."

"But what if . . ."

Jenny couldn't finish but Matthew felt her tremble and he understood her deep-seated fears. Kaw and his band had left permanent scars on them both.

"If it isn't safe, we won't go," he promised. "They'll be building more railroads in the West. I expect we could . . ."

"No," she said, interrupting his thought. "I need to settle down and raise a family."

"That's fine with me," he agreed. "Fact of the matter is, I am looking forward to putting down roots and raising some young sprouts."

"We've saved almost eight hundred dollars, Matt. We'll have well over a thousand before the rails join. That ought to be enough to start up ranching and mustanging."

"And a family," he reminded her.

"Yes," she told him with a smile, "that most of all."

When the stars began to fill the heavens, they strolled back to the construction camp with its hundreds of white canvas tents and with the big construction train resting at the end of the line. They were formally greeted by clusters of Chinese sitting around their own little sagebrush campfires drinking their ever present tea.

"Will they all return to the Orient after this work is done?" Jenny asked.

"Most of them, I expect. Others talk about settling in San Francisco. Don't forget, Jenny, there were a lot of Chinese already here during the forty-niner gold rush and I expect that there are quite a few working right now on the Comstock Lode."

"Crocker's Pets," Jenny said with a shake of her head. "That's what they were first called when Mr. Crocker hired them out of desperation because everyone else had rushed off to strike it rich on the Comstock Lode. Well, they've sure earned more than their fair share of respect."

"Yep," he said, "they sure have."

Matthew left Jenny at their tent and took a few minutes to check on the hostlers watching the livestock holding pens where they kept the dozens of teams needed to pull the wagons up and down the line delivering rails and supplies not only to the track layers, but to the forward parties of graders and bridge builders. In addition, the railroad kept about twenty good saddle horses and cattle, the latter to butcher for the Americans who worked alongside the Chinese.

"There's some sheep being brought down from the

mountains," one of the hostlers informed him as he was about to call it a night. "A whole band of them camped less than a mile upriver."

"Who says?" Matthew asked doubtfully.

"One of the surveyors came in a couple hours ago. He passed the band and talked to their owners. Said that they were hoping to sell us some mutton. Be a real nice change from beef, Mr. Pike. Real nice."

"I expect that's true enough."

The hostler, a strapping young Irish lad named Tommy O'Brien, grinned and said, "Beef, rabbit stew, and boiled potatoes is about all we ever get to eat on this job. Maybe we'll have some nice lamb chops, huh?"

"It's up to Mr. Crocker and Mr. Strobridge," Matthew said. "They do the buying, we're just the caretakers."

"Yeah, I know, but those sheep can get fat in this country. We wouldn't have to keep a carload of hay around like we do for the horses and cattle. You being superintendent of livestock, maybe you ought to point out that money-saving fact to Mr. Crocker and Mr. Strobridge."

"I will."

"In Ireland, we mostly ate pork and mutton," O'Brien told him. "Tastes better than tough, stringy beef."

Some impishness inside of Matthew made him ask, "Tommy, have you ever enjoyed roasted horsemeat?"

O'Brien screwed up his face. "Horsemeat?"

"That's right," Matthew said, enjoying himself. "It's got a flavor all it's own."

"Jaysus, Mr. Pike! I would never eat a *horse*!"

Matthew chuckled and started back to Jenny and their tent.

"I sure do *hunger* for some mutton!" O'Brien called.

Matthew had to admit that a change in their diet would be most welcome. He would speak to his bosses

in the morning about buying some sheep and he was
quite sure they would appreciate the opportunity.

Matthew awoke early the next morning and went
out to oversee the hitching up of the wagon teams.
Some of the mule skinners and teamsters had a ten-
dency to get unnecessarily rough and Matthew would
not tolerate that. He also had the responsibility of making sure that no sick or injured animals were forced to
work until they were sound.

There were no problems this morning and it was
almost nine o'clock when Matthew finally managed to
have a word with Mr. Harvey Strobridge, a tall New
Englander whose impatience had cost him an eye while
when he'd rushed forward to check on a sputtering
charge of black powder up in the Sierras. With a big
black patch over the empty socket, the Chinese secretly
referred to him as their "One Eye Bossy Man."

"Hell, go ahead and buy the sheep!" Strobridge
swore after Matthew had posed the question and
pointed out the cost advantages. "Crocker loves nothing
better than to eat and he damned sure won't object.
Besides, he'll be tied up all day with that surveyor that
rode in last night. Seems we've got another big bridge to
construct over a deep arroyo that wasn't supposed to
exist."

Matthew knew that this would cause delays and
that Mr. Crocker would be in a foul mood because
bridges, even short ones, were exceedingly expensive
and time-consuming. "How many sheep do you suppose
I ought to buy?"

"If we don't have to feed 'em hay or grain, buy as
many as you can," Strobridge urged before he marched
away, shouting obscenities and orders at his scrambling
American and Chinese track layers.

Matthew saddled a good horse and headed out
alone to meet the flock of sheep and see if he could cut
a deal for the railroad. He didn't know anything about
woolies and, the more he thought about it, he wasn't

sure that he *wanted* to learn anything about them. He'd seen plenty of big flocks grazing in lonely patches of the Arizona Territory but had never watched the tending of any small band such as he expected to buy. And what about dogs? Did a man need sheepdogs, or could he just herd sheep like he could horses or cattle?

The longer Matthew considered the uncertainties of tending sheep, the fewer he believed he would purchase this day. He was all the way down to a couple of dozen when he finally saw the shepherd's camp and then the family that was tending them alongside the Humboldt River. At a distance, the first thing that he noticed was that there were two women, a man, and three smaller children. And damned if every last one of them wasn't sitting astride the handsomest black horses he'd ever seen. They were *tall* horses, horses unlike anything he'd seen since . . .

Matthew's heart began to pound. He touched spurs to his own mount and sent it racing forward. The older woman was in her forties, tall, and good-looking. When their eyes met, a sob exploded from Matthew's throat. The woman shouted his name and the younger woman shrieked with joy.

"Fay!" he bellowed, flying across the sage. "Mother!"

After that, things were a little crazy for a while with everyone talking and laughing and yes, even crying. Matthew had jumped down from his horse and let it wander away while he hugged his mother and his sister. Then he swept up armfuls of his squirming and laughing half-brothers and -sisters. And finally, he took Augustin Arostegi's heavily calloused hand and pumped it vigorously.

"Thank you," Matthew choked, "for giving me back my family."

The Basque sheep rancher's eyes glistened and he tried to speak but was too overcome with emotion. Libby had to keep biting her lip in order to remind herself that this wasn't just a happy dream. She'd never really given up hope of finding her son, but it had been so long. And now, here he was, taller than his late father and ever so strong and handsome.

"Where did you get all these horses?" Matthew finally asked. "They're beautiful!"

"Then you don't remember?" Fay said.

"It's coming back," he told her. "But it's going to take time."

"We have time," Libby told her son. "And we've a ranch to build."

"I've a wife," he blurted. "She's back at the construction site. You'll love Jenny."

Libby buried her face against Matthew's chest. So many lost . . . but not this precious son. So many things to explain. She released her son and hugged Augustin and the old dilemma rushed back into her thoughts. Should she finally tell him that a son had been fathered by Palo?

"Once I had a brother," Augustin was telling Matthew. "Palo was taller and far more handsome than me. He was a little wild, but a very good man. Unfortunately, Palo died somewhere on the Comstock. You remind me a little of him, Matthew."

Libby heard the pride in her husband's voice and knew that he had just given her son a high compliment. Augustin had dearly loved his brother despite all Palo's faults and many weaknesses.

No, she decided once again, *in kindness, you must never tell dear Augustin the truth about his brother.* Besides, Matthew's return had just swept away the heartaches of the past and all that Libby cared about now was healing and forgiveness.

ABOUT THE AUTHOR

GARY MCCARTHY grew up in California and spent his boyhood around horses and horsemen. His education took him to Nevada, where he spent many years living and working. A prolific novelist of the American West, Mr. McCarthy has written several historical novels in the Rivers West series including *The Colorado, The Russian River, The American River,* and *The Gila River,* winner of the prestigious Spur Award. He makes his home in Ojai, California, with his wife and family.

The exciting frontier series continues!

 # RIVERS WEST

Native Americans, hunters and trappers, pioneer families—all who braved the emerging American frontier drew their very lives and fortunes from the great rivers. From the earliest days of the settlement movement to the dawn of the twentieth century, here, in all their awesome splendor, are the RIVERS WEST.

NARRATIVES *of* AMERICA

by Allan W. Eckert

Allan W. Eckert's Narratives of America *are true sagas of the brave men and courageous women who won our land. Every character and event in this sweeping series is drawn from actual history and woven into the vast and powerful epic that was America's westward expansion. Allan Eckert has made America's heritage an authentic, exciting, and powerful reading experience.*

"Reading Eckert is like listening to a master storyteller: he presents his material in vivid detail, using the novelist's technique to enhance dramatic events." —*Publishers Weekly*

Also by Allan W. Eckert

- -